Praise for *Beyond Tomorrow's Sun*

"a fully original sci-fi mythology…vividly rendered and suspenseful…tonally similar to the HUNGER GAMES and DIVERGENT series…enjoyably akin to works like the ENDER'S GAME novels and VALERIAN comic series…"
Launchpad Prose Competition, 2022

"a well-written science fiction story that doesn't lose sight of the humanity of its characters…[with] mirrors of The Great Depression…[and] hints of the classic western…the world-building in this novel is excellent."
ScreenCraft 2023 Cinematic Book Competition

"Refreshing sci-fi…Comparable to Marko Kloos's Terms of Enlistment, Kyle Noland's S.E.T. The Earth on Fire."
BookLife Editor's Choice, January 2025

"…the kind of book that makes you pause. Makes you think. Reminds you why science fiction matters…Beyond Tomorrow's Sun deserves a place on your shelf."
Coffee.Book.Couch

"…this book was worth every minute. Highly recommend…."
Criminal Venture Books

"…combines quiet resilience and just enough wonder to keep you thinking past the last page…"
Carola Schmidt, award-winning author of *Chubby's Tale*

Also by Ronald McGuire
Beyond Tomorrow's Sun

Collections:
Nightmares & Lullabies
Pax Liminalis

BEYOND THE RIVERS OF TIME

Ronald McGuire

Beach Book Press

Published in the United States by Beach Book Press, Norwell, MA
First Beach Book Press Paperback Edition: 2025

10 9 8 7 6 5 4 3 2 1

Library of Congress Control Number: 2025907245
Paperback ISBN: 978-1-965621-04-2
eBook ISBN: 978-1-965621-05-9

For Shawn, as always.

And once again, with gratitude and appreciation
for everyone who helped make this book possible.

A human being is a part of the whole
called by us universe;
a part limited in time and space. He
experiences himself, his thoughts, and his
feelings as something separate from the
rest - a kind of optical delusion of
consciousness.

Albert Einstein

1

A Discovery

Humanity's first attempt at interstellar travel should have been a glorious event. Instead, it became a horrifying experience. The human-made wormhole expanded to a size greater than anyone had anticipated. The ship, dubbed the *Katie* by her crew of two, became another twisting thread of light within the swirling yellow and black vortex, no longer recognizable as a ship, except for the portion that had yet to cross the event horizon. The ship melted into the churning cauldron of the wormhole, and at the very moment the last recognizable portion of the ship's stern reached the event horizon, the wormhole simultaneously collapsed and erupted into a colossal explosion, sending shockwaves, physical and psychological, through the assembled fleet. There were no secondary explosions, no emergency beacons from the *Katie*, nothing more than a hint of debris. To the people aboard the ships assembled around Deimos to witness the launch, it seemed no one could survive such a cataclysm.

The ship, its occupants, and the wormhole, were gone, as if they'd never existed.

People across the Sol Federation concluded the spectacular explosion they'd witnessed was the end of the journey, not the beginning. An epic mission failure. Many believed the crew, young Captain Bimmy and his wife, Becca Kiel, had died as a result of the explosion, their remains scattered across the vastness of interstellar space.

A few, including President Peter Jay of the Deimos Colony, whose people had built the ship, held out hope the couple had survived the journey but, for reasons unknown, could not return.

As time passed and the one-year anniversary of the launch approached, even the most optimistic began to lose hope.

Until a young astrophysicist on Deimos made a startling discovery.

"President Jay, Fleet Admiral Wilson is here."

"Thank you, Thomas, send her in, and let Dex Farber know we're ready for him."

"He's here, sir. He's been waiting most of the morning," Thomas replied.

"Of course he has; send him in."

Fleet Admiral Amanda Wilson entered the President's office and shook his hand, followed closely by Dex Farber, who remained waiting near the doorway.

"Amanda, good to see you again. Thank you for coming."

"Of course, Peter. I assume it's urgent if it can't wait until the service on Phobos."

"I won't be attending the memorial," the President said, as Dex Farber fidgeted behind the admiral. "Dex, have a seat." He pointed to a chair at the end of his conference table. "Admiral, if you please." Dex took his place at the end of the table, the admiral sat across from the President.

"Peter, I know Gorman is angry, but no one blames Deimos, or you, for what happened."

"Chairman Gorman's complaints aside, blame does not concern me. I'm not attending, no one from Deimos is attending. We refuse to memorialize friends we believe are alive. I have focused all our available resources on a rescue mission."

"How? We both know what it takes to build a Gateway device, and unless you've been...wait," the admiral leaned in, scrutinizing the President. "Peter, don't tell me you've got sufficient Promethium to build a second device. If you've been holding out..."

"That's precisely the case. Test flights of the *Hyperion* begin in four months, by your calendar."

The admiral's face flushed red with anger. She sat back in her chair and glared her disapproval at the President, who responded with relaxed silence.

Dex cleared his throat, drawing their attention.

"And who might this be," the admiral asked, without taking her eyes off the President.

"Dex Farber," the President said, "meet Fleet Admiral Wilson. I'd like you to tell her what you discovered."

"Yes sir," Dex replied.

"I'm sure you'll find this quite compelling."

The admiral turned and scrutinized Dex. "How old are you?"

Dex straightened his posture, crossed his hands on the table, and looked Admiral Wilson directly in the eye. "Admiral, I'll be nineteen in three months. I may not look the part, but I know what I'm talking about. I'm as good an astrophysicist as you'll find anywhere."

"Dex helped Becca plot the *Katie's* course to Luyten b. You should hear him out."

The admiral sat back in her seat and waited. The President smiled, looked down at his watch, then back at Dex.

Dex took a moment to gather his thoughts. "Admiral, the *Katie* wasn't destroyed. They couldn't jump back because the ship was damaged, but it wasn't destroyed. The missile didn't hit its target, not directly, and the energy signature…"

"What missile? How do you know this?"

"Grace Cheng, this was her doing. I've watched the recording of the launch, many, many times, more than I can count."

"Mister Farber, explain. These are bold claims, and a serious accusation. We all watched the launch, I saw the explosion with my own eyes, I didn't see a missile."

"Our eyes," Dex said, "human eyes, aren't as good as you think, we miss details all the time. But the camera, the optics, the digital pickup, the tech doesn't miss a thing, if you know how to compile the data, to analyze the raw footage…"

"Show me."

"We have to go to the astrophysics lab to see the multidimensional overlay I created."

The admiral pointed at the door. "Let's not waste time, lead the way."

The President tapped an icon on a recessed panel in the conference table, "Thomas, have Captain Roberts and Major Mulzac meet us in astrophysics immediately."

The launch of the *Katie* had been recorded from multiple angles, but the events unfolded quickly. The tiny speck drifting near the stern of the ship went unnoticed, overshadowed by the hole in the fabric of space-time torn open by the Gateway device attached to the ship.

Dex played his composite recording for his audience. The ship once again generated the wormhole, slipped forward into the vortex, and exploded as the wormhole collapsed. As the images played out, Dex pointed at a section of space behind and below the ship. "Did you see it?" he asked.

"Run it again, the last 20 seconds" the admiral ordered, "enhance the lower right quadrant to maximum and reduce speed to ten percent real-time."

In the next pass, a brief flash of propellant revealed an object moving toward the ship, the moment the last of the ship crossed the event horizon, followed by an explosion as the wormhole closed.

Dex paused the playback, and Captain Sally Roberts pointed at the screen. "That is the messenger beacon we sent into Jupiter orbit," she said, "to Grace Cheng's forces, at Captain Bimmy's request. They gave it an EM-resistant coating to hide it and strapped a missile to it."

"Why go to the trouble, why not fire a missile from a ship?" the admiral asked. "It's exponentially more accurate."

Major Mulzac turned to the admiral. "They know we can see through their ships' camouflage; they wouldn't risk a ship. A loitering munition is hard to spot, minuscule energy signature, easy to trigger, or automate. They knew the timing of the launch. This is Grace Cheng's handiwork, I'm sure of it."

"If the missile was a miss, how do you know the ship was damaged?" the admiral asked.

Dex pointed at the frozen image. "Yes, a miss, but right here, debris hits the ship, causing this yellow flash. There's no propellant in a soliton drive, all its energy is derived from gravitational waves. But to initiate it, to start it up, you need a small amount of energy. To keep the drive isolated from the rest of the ship, we power it up with a lithium-sulfur battery. If you crack open the battery, if it's exposed to space, the sulfur component crystalizes. It looks like gas, but it's actually millions of tiny particles. The missile took out the soliton drive, the yellow color is proof, anything else would be blue or orange or white, not yellow."

"If you're right, then explain to me how they made the transit without the soliton drive."

"They don't need the drive once they enter the wormhole. Momentum, and the nature of an Einstein-Rosen Bridge, make it unnecessary."

"You can't be certain the ship survived the flight, there could be more extensive damage."

"We can." Dex tapped the control panel and the recording was replaced with a simulation of the wormhole, changing the perspective to an oblique view of the event horizon. The simulation ran and the bright explosion froze in place. "They made it to Luyten b, the ship is intact. I checked all the data we have on artificial wormholes from the Hoffman Institute. One thing is certain, these wormholes maintain a constant energy signature, but it's unidirectional, not like heat or light, it's focused in one direction, away from the event horizon." He tapped the controls again and the explosion disappeared. "If the ship blew up, we would have a different signature, a multidirectional signature. I filtered out the energy from the missile detonation, and the result matches what you'd expect, a unidirectional signature. They made it, Admiral. I'd bet my life on it."

The admiral addressed Major Mulzac. "Are you certain Cheng had a hand in this?"

"Our sources tell us she's been bragging about it," the Major said, "although it hasn't gone over well with her people."

"Grace has a minor rebellion on her hands," Captain Roberts said.

"When were you planning to share this information?" the admiral asked.

The President stepped around the control console, positioning himself next to the frozen image of the wormhole, facing the admiral. "Today. With you, in person, no one else, and not over comms. We have to keep these developments quiet. Some of Cheng's pirates accepted the amnesty, but she still has a significant fighting force. And Gorman can be quite persuasive. If he knew we had the last of the Promethium, he'd find a way to get it for the Venusians. I won't allow it, and we're not taking any more chances with Cheng. I've got the bulk of our fleet hunting her as we speak."

The admiral stared at the image of the wormhole she once believed had killed her young protege, Captain Bimmy, and his scientist wife, Becca Kiel. She had given up hope for their survival. Confronted with new and compelling evidence, she began to formulate a plan.

"What do you need from me?" she asked.

"The search for Cheng is draining our resources, we're spread thin," the President said. "We'd like you to commit Federation forces to work with us. We also need experienced crew: a pilot, nav officer, tactical officer, for the *Hyperion*. Then there's supplies, equipment."

"Materiel support is not a problem; the end of the war left a surplus in the supply chain. Personnel will be a challenge. I can commit forces to your Cheng initiative, but I'd have to get approval from the council to assign Federation officers to another interstellar launch…"

The Major turned to the President, his adoptive father, then back to the admiral. "We were thinking outside the Federation ranks, some familiar faces, people we can trust."

The admiral looked between the two men, then at Captain Roberts. She paused to consider their request and wondered whether she was being drawn into a heroic endeavor, or a dangerous conspiracy. There was only one way to know. "Give me a few orbits, I'll see what I can do. I might know just the team for a mission like this."

2

In the Blood

Surviving our crash landing on Luyten b, and the destruction of the *Katie*, was the true beginning of our odyssey. Becca and I were lucky to be alive. The phenomenon we experienced in the forest, after leaving our ship, had given us, through means we had yet to determine, the ability to understand the language of the people who had once inhabited the city we now called home. A city filled with beautiful architecture, advanced technology, a spaceport, complete with multiple ships in pristine condition, and exactly zero occupants, other than the two of us. Based on the design and scale of everything from doors to walkways to windows, the fountains and gardens, and given the beings depicted on the fountain in the main park, it didn't take much to conclude those who had built and lived in the place were, at least in physical form, similar to us.

At the end of our first day, after leaving the spaceport and retracing our steps through the building I had dubbed "the welcome center," we took up residence in a building overlooking the harbor. A large apartment on the top floor, a luxurious home, on par with the finest in Arcadia. We entered several buildings and found three different styles of home, each similar in function but somewhat different in appearance. We chose one most familiar to us, and despite Becca's assertions we didn't need a 'penthouse,' I insisted we choose a residence on the top floor, with a commanding view of both the harbor and the spaceport. It gave us a degree of security, though we hadn't come across anything overtly dangerous in the city. My military experience had taught me that not encountering anything dangerous didn't mean danger didn't exist.

In those early days, we worried about food. I thought I would have to return to our wrecked ship, and perhaps to the forest to hunt, but we soon found not only were lush gardens common throughout the city, the plants were prolific growers as well. The fruits and vegetables, after a few furtive tastes, were edible, safe, and to our surprise, began to regenerate within a day or two of our harvests. With drinkable water and a steady food supply, we set about exploring the city.

As the days turned into weeks, every discovery raised new questions.

Our ability to understand the written language, though bizarre, was a welcome mystery as we surveyed the spaceport and its adjoining construction facilities, where we discovered the complex had multiple levels below ground, a subterranean city unto itself. With each passing day, our knowledge of our new home expanded, and we began to learn of its rich history, culture, and technology, both strange and familiar at the same time.

The art in the galleries and museums had varying styles, but common themes. The three humanoid species represented on the fountain at the harbor-side park were depicted, in dozens of variations; sailing on the lake, swimming at the beach, dancing, dining together, enjoying the sunset or sunrise. Recurring themes of unity, peace, happiness, a sense of common purpose, ran through all of the works we encountered. It reminded me of the Alliance propaganda I grew up with on Earth.

One day we came upon an exhibit detailing, in holographic images and scale models, the construction of the harbor and some of the adjacent buildings, by an army of what appeared to be autonomous machines. But there was nothing in writing to explain the individual components of the exhibit, and we found it odd there was no mention of the city's name, or the planet's. At least, nothing that we recognized as a name. As with the written language, when we looked at an item, its name and meaning would usually come to us, but out of context, with no narrative to tie it all together. At times, no understandable information would come to us, and the purpose of some objects remained elusive, as did the age of the metropolis, though we felt certain it was much older than it appeared.

"I don't understand how everything is immaculate," I said during one of our excursions, "it looks brand new."

"Except the boats in the harbor," Becca reminded me, "most of those are trashed."

"Correct, except the boats," I said, "but the rest of it, putting aside the why of it all, the how of it has me thinking there'd be robots, or androids like the ones we saw on the orbital station, maintenance bots polishing, planting, fixing things. Because stuff breaks, like the boats, whether there are people around or not. We've seen nothing."

"In two months, by my counting, we've covered less than half the city, and haven't fully searched the parts we've seen."

"Two months," I said, "does it feel weird to you a day here is about the same as a day on Earth, but a year is less than three weeks?"

"I don't give it much thought," Becca replied, "the planet is over twice the size of Earth, but it's as close to Luyten's red dwarf star as Mercury is to Sol. Fast orbit, slow rotation, it's nothing more than math to me. At least we don't have to worry about freezing winters, or blazing hot summers."

"It must rain here," I said, "the streets, the cobblestone ones and the paved ones, they all have drainage systems, and the rooftops of the buildings too. Nothing stays perfect forever, exposed metal should rust, plants should grow in random places, roofs should eventually leak. Everything is perfect, nothing is out of place. Then there's the orbital station, there's been no effort to repair it. Whatever happened there, the people who built it abandoned it."

"The fixer bots and the farmer bots could be someplace we haven't been yet. Maybe they come out when nobody's looking."

"That's a possibility we can test."

"How?"

"We break something and don't take our eyes off it until it's repaired."

Becca shook her head in disbelief. "For the sake of argument, because I could debate the wisdom of this idea, let's say we decide to commit this act of vandalism. What would be the target of this experiment?"

"You mean subject…"

"I mean target. You don't break the subject of an experiment."

"Fine, have it your way, I say we target the fountain, in the main park. We can break a little piece off with minimal consequences. It's decorative, non-essential, shouldn't be a problem."

"That's quite an optimistic assessment Bimmy. If you do this, please choose something you can fix, in case the repair doesn't magically happen."

"I can fix anything," I said.

As with many experiments, ours did not go as planned, though we learned more than we expected.

At the center of the park abutting the harbor, we circled the multitiered fountain and wide oval splash-pad, until I found what I needed. I chose a thin curved piece of metal designed to direct the flow of water away from the structure into one of the many circular patterns in the pavement. But the fountain had activated when we approached, and the flowing water made it difficult to grip the metal. My hand slipped across its sharp edge, opening a ten-centimeter slice through my palm and wrist.

Becca took my wrist in a fierce grip, clenching her jaw as she applied strong pressure to the wound, intending to staunch the flow. "You were supposed to break the fountain, not yourself," she snapped.

The wound should have bled profusely. It should have required stitches. Instead, the blood stopped pulsing out of the wound, the wound closed over, and the spilled blood dried up, became a light powder, then vanished all together; from my arm, Becca's hand, and off the ground.

Becca stepped back and stared wide-eyed at my hand, then looked up at me. "I'm calling off this experiment, this is insane. How… I'm glad you're not bleeding out, but our next order of business needs to be figuring this out." She pointed at my wrist, waving her finger and shaking her head, "This is one mystery too many for me today."

"Me too, but…it hurt when it happened, and when you grabbed me, but not as much as I would expect. And how does blood just vanish into thin air? What does it say about the people who built this place? I mean, a wound that heals itself, a mess that cleans up on its own. This has gotta be part of the bigger picture. What are we missing?"

"I need to think."

I knew 'I need to think' was Becca's way of telling me 'please be quiet for a while.' We left the fountain and for several minutes sat in silence on the steps leading down to the still water of the harbor. I stared at my hand and wrist until Becca made a startling announcement.

"I need some of your blood," she said.

"What?"

"And a microscope, a good one. I have an idea, a hypothesis. I want to test it."

"On me?"

"It's a blood sample, recent experience tells me you can spare it."

"That's not the point. Have you ever drawn blood before?"

"No but…."

"With alien tech, no less…"

"Are you scared, Captain Bimmy? The hero of the Federation, afraid of a little needle?"

"I'm not afraid, I…I'm abundantly cautious, as needed."

Becca stood up, looked down at me, extended her hand and smiled, "How hard can it be? Come on, let's go find ourselves a hospital."

I could never resist her smile. I took her hand and rose to my feet. "And you called my experiment a bad idea."

Finding a medical facility became our top priority, but after searching for three days, we'd found nothing. Our search left us perplexed. We didn't find a single hospital, infirmary, not even a first aid kit. The results of our search left me wondering if the same healing process I experienced meant there was never a need for the builders to include medical facilities in their planning. When I considered a return to our wrecked ship, I realized what we needed had been right in front of us all along.

"The spaceport," I said, "we've barely explored the ships. If they're anything like ours, and a lot here is, they'll have some kind of medical facility, even the *Katie* had a basic infirmary, and the ships here are way bigger."

"Good idea, what took you so long?"

"At least I got there."

"Let's go, genius."

We returned to the spaceport and entered the first of the three ships. The ships were many times larger than the *Katie*, leading us to assume an infirmary, if one existed, would be somewhere near midship. This proved accurate, and within an hour we had found what we needed. We couldn't identify all of the equipment, or the supplies, despite being able to read their labels. It's one thing to know the name of a drug or an implement, another thing to understand its function. One thing was abundantly clear, the facility outclassed any on a Federation battle cruiser.

Becca searched a supply closet while I looked through what I recognized as a laboratory. There were two identical devices side-by-side on a narrow bench with stools in front of them. Their names weren't coming to me, but they invoked thoughts of intensity and amplification.

I called out to Becca, "I found you a microscope, I think. No idea how to use it."

"I found these," she said when she entered the lab, presenting two syringes sealed in a kind of vacuum wrap, and a bottle of clear liquid. "I think this is antiseptic, not sure we need it though. Let's get to it."

I took off my shirt to expose my arm and sat down in front of her. I rubbed the inside of my elbow, feeling nervous, "You never answered my question. Have you done this before?"

Becca shook her head and grinned, "No, they don't teach phlebotomy in the astrophysics lab. If you want to draw your own blood, be my guest, I'd like to see you try."

I thought about her university, how she'd been buried alive during its bombardment and destruction by the separatist attack on Earth.

"Becca, I've never told you…I'm…I want you to know I'm sorry, about what happened. You worked hard to get into the university, the war, it…"

"Sorry?" she interrupted, "Why should you be sorry? We survived the war, we're here, together. Any scientist would be thrilled to be here instead of stuck in a lab. As far as I'm concerned, being an interstellar traveler is better than being a college student any day. Besides, I always felt strange being the youngest student on campus." She tied a tourniquet around my bicep and swabbed my arm. "Make a fist, show me those big Bimmy veins."

I made a fist, then smiled and leaned toward her, "Kiss me, in case you stab me to death."

She placed one hand on my cheek, held her lips close to mine, and before kissing me said, "A kiss won't get you out of this, captain."

I laughed, leaned back, and presented my arm, "Try not to break the needle off in there."

"I'll do my best," she said. She took aim and jabbed the needle at my vein.

I winced, and through gritted teeth said, "Hot on the approach, don't you think?"

"Your vein moved, it's like it knows I'm coming."

"Yes, of course, it's the vein's fault. Ouch," I said as Becca took another stab at me with the needle, "maybe I should do this myself."

"Be still and we might get through this with a minimum of punctures."

"Roger that Commander Kiel, being still. Why can't we cut my finger?"

"You saw what happened with your hand. I need the sample from the vein. You're healing faster than I can poke you, you're not going to bleed to death. I need a few milliliters…. got it. I'm in the vein…"

"Lucky me."

Becca took the sample she needed, withdrew the needle, and turned to the device next to her. There was no need to apply pressure to the puncture wound, it closed itself before more than a drop of blood could escape.

"Have you figured out how it works?" I asked.

"It's kind of telling me what to do as I look it over," she said, "I don't know if I'm ever going to get used to this, it's like having an interpreter and instructor whispering inside my head at the same time."

"You seem to be enjoying it. I'd be fine with a basic translator, or a guide book."

"I wouldn't say I'm enjoying it, but I am embracing it. We'd be lost without it; we might as well accept it."

I pulled the tourniquet from my arm, dropped it on the counter, and waved my hand in the air, "We're not exactly found right now. The more we learn, the less we know. I could live without the paradox. You think my blood is going to explain how it all works."

"Possibly," Becca said, as she prepared to examine her prize. "If my theory is correct, we should see thousands of the little beasties in every milliliter."

"Beasties? What do you mean, beasties…"

Becca ignored me and focused on operating the equipment.

"Talk to me. What are you looking for? All this suspense, with no popcorn…"

"Shush, I'm trying to…wait…there, eureka," she said, "I'm right."

"Eureka? Who are you…right about what? What are you…"

Becca leaned back and pointed at a gyrating cluster of tiny objects on the screen, "Nanobots," she said, "intracellular nanoscale robots. You, Captain Bimmy, are a cyborg."

"Cyborg? If I'm a cyborg, then you…"

"I would be Missus Cyborg."

3

Flight of the Hyperion

"Deimos Control, this is Arcturus shuttle one-one-nine requesting clearance," Blake said on final approach to the colony.

"Arcturus shuttle you are cleared to dock 3. Lieutenant Blake, please observe speed regulations, we don't want a repeat…"

"Roger, Deimos Control, slow and steady, Arcturus shuttle out."

"Something tells me you pulled one of your high-speed maneuvers inside the dock."

"Come on, Rachel, it's me we're talking about," Blake said, "these colonials can't keep up. It's no big deal."

"Oh, the colonials, I see," Breuger said, "it's got nothing to do with being inside a giant space dock, no, it's all about you and your 'amazing' piloting skills."

"Don't encourage her," Jones said, "we can't pull rank anymore."

Blake ignored the jabs and continued to maneuver the shuttle into the dock. "Isn't this great? The three of us, gettin' along, flyin' through space, havin' fun… Life has been downright boring since the war ended. Not that I enjoyed the war, far from it, but being the admiral's shuttle pilot is boring. She's a stickler for regulations, cramps my style."

"It explains why she's an admiral and you're still a shuttle pilot," Jones said.

"Nah, that's not it. I'm not interested in all the responsibility. Leadership takes the joy outta havin' access to all these awesome toys."

Breuger and Blake laughed but Rachel didn't join them. The docking clamps locked on and the pressurized gantry made its way out to the shuttle's airlock.

"Arcturus shuttle, Deimos control, you are cleared to disembark on gangway Alpha 2. Welcome to Deimos. Nice job Lieutenant, thanks for not…"

"Roger Deimos control, disembarking on gangway Alpha 2, Arcturus shuttle out," Blake said, cutting off the comm.

"You have to tell us what you did," Jones said.

"Some other time," Blake replied. "Look, we've got a greeting party."

Breuger looked down at the two people standing on the transfer hub, a woman and a man.

"I don't recognize her, but that's Major Mulzac," he said, "I should have known he came up with this."

"Care to bet?" Blake asked. "Before you take the action, I should warn yah, I've got friends in high places."

The trio began the slow passage from the zero gravity dock, through the interconnected tubes of the hub, on their way to the transfer platform.

"Admiral Wilson described this as a civilian effort," Jones said, "strictly off the books, no Federation involvement."

"That's correct," Blake said, "but Deimos asked for reinforcements, and she handpicked us to join the crew. When she told me about it, I was like, heck yeah, sign me up."

"Hold up," Breuger said, bringing them to a stop, "if you're joining a civilian mission…"

"You resigned your commission," Jones finished for him.

"Yup, sure did. Wouldn't miss this for anything…"

"All kidding aside," Breuger said, "you're the best pilot in the Federation, you've got a future in Space Force. You need to rethink your priorities."

Blake stopped smiling, placed her hand on the wall of the docking tube, and turned around to face her former shipmate. "My priorities are in perfect order, Eric. Sometimes you have to put aside what you think you were meant to do in favor of what you know you have to do."

"We're not even sure what the mission is," Breuger said.

"Why did you answer the admiral's call?" Blake asked.

Breuger and Jones looked at each other, then turned back to Blake.

"Admiral Wilson personally asked us to join this mission, a secret mission out of Deimos, which is basically Bimmy's home-away, and she wouldn't name the ship," Jones said. "It doesn't take a genius to connect this to the Luyten project. It's a recovery mission."

"Not a recovery mission, a rescue mission," Blake said, "Wilson is convinced they made it to Luyten b, and we're going there to find them and bring them home."

"I've never seen you like this," Jones said. "Serious, determined, focused. A minute ago, you were the same Blake as always."

"You taught me an important lesson on Phobos."

"Times were different, I didn't mean…"

"It's okay. You told me my sense of humor was out of line. You were right. I had to learn to find an off switch. To read the room, as the admiral likes to say."

"I'm sorry," Jones began, "we were dealing with a lot."

"The fate of the entire human race, I get it. You don't have to apologize, but I've got some advice, if you'll hear it."

"Of course."

"You're too serious, you need to find the on switch now and again."

Jones gave Breuger a pleading look.

"Don't look at me," he said, "I want no part of this conversation. I was there, remember?"

Jones looked back at Blake and after a pause said, "I never thought of myself as lacking in humor."

"That's not what I'm saying. You need to lighten up when the opportunity presents itself, because life can turn in a second. You gotta grab the good parts while you can."

"Why resign, why go on this mission?" Jones asked, "Eric is right, you've got a future in Space Force."

"Captain Bimmy saved my life. Now he needs me, he needs us. That's why I'm here. I assume that's why the both of you are here."

"He'll tell you himself he's no hero," Breuger said. "You didn't serve on the Mercury mission. He put us in constant danger, it's one of the reasons we left Space Force."

"Then why did you answer the admiral's call?"

"Because," Jones said, "he risked his mission, his crew, his life, to save me. Like it or not, we owe him."

"That's the spirit," Blake said, smiling again, "let's go, don't want to keep the major waitin'."

***

As Blake, Breuger, and Jones were disembarking, President Jay and Dex Farber waited in a briefing room in Deimos Control. While the President found long stretches of silence comfortable, Dex did not. He peppered the President with questions and comments about President Jay's eldest son, Major Mulzac.

"I read his book."

"We're very proud of his work."

"He really hates pirates."

"They murdered his family, he was a little boy, left alone to…"

"Yeah, but you adopted him. He never would've been a Marine, never would've become *the Major*…"

"Possibly, but I think he'd rather have his family back."

"He has a family now. He's got you, two kid brothers, an awesome mom. I was wondering, since he's a major, how did he serve under a captain?"

"It's a difference in the branches, nothing more. He's a Colonial Marine, Captain Bimmy served in the Federation, simple."

"Did he like it, serving on the Ajax?"

"We've never discussed it in those terms. I know he has the utmost respect for Captain Bimmy, they're close friends."

"He helped him steal a starship."

"They didn't steal the *Katie*, that was a cover story…"

"I heard the cover story was the real story. All the same, why would he…"

"Dex, why all the curiosity about my son? You'll have plenty of time to get to know him during the mission."

"Well, sir, it's…I mean he's…I worry I won't measure up. I know what I bring to the table, but I've never been anywhere but Mars. What if I screw this up?"

"The mission is bigger than one person. You'll be surrounded by the best crew we can muster. That includes you. You'll do fine. The mission is in good hands."

"I wasn't talking entirely about the mission…"

"Then what are we talking about? You've lost me."

Before Dex could reply, the metal door slid away into the wall, and the Major entered, followed by Captain Roberts and the three newest members of her crew.

President Jay rose from his seat, "Welcome back to Deimos. Please, have a seat and we'll…"

"With Respect, Mister President," Jones said, "we know why we're here. When do we leave?"

***

With construction and flight testing of the *Hyperion* complete, and no sign of the *Katie*, President Jay gave final authorization to launch the rescue mission to Luyten b.

He and his wife, Letitia Jay, watched the launch from the observation deck of the orbiting shipyard, as they had the launch of the *Katie*. They listened to the comm traffic, anticipation growing as the ship moved to its launch coordinates.

Like the previous launch, the whirling vortex of the wormhole appeared and the ship moved forward. The Gateway framework folded back, and the ship elongated over the event horizon.

The white hull of the *Hyperion* began to meld with the swirling colors and frothy textures of the vortex. The remaining portion of the ship crossed the event horizon, then vanished into the collapsing wormhole. To the relief of those present, this time, there was no explosion.

***

Major Mulzac joined Captain Roberts on the bridge, and she gave the order to proceed. The Gateway framework expanded forward from the ship's bow, followed by the tell-tale amber glow of the device powering up.

The rift in space-time opened, revealing the swirling abyss of color and light, a dark circular patch at its center, speckled with the sparkling white light of the stars at their destination, 13 light years away.

"I hope this never gets old," the Major said, though his words went unnoticed by the crew. With preparations complete, they sat awestruck by the spectacle their ship had created.

Automated systems took over the ship's movement, the soliton drive engaged, and the ship soon captured, focused, and tuned the energy of a gravity wave and rode it forward into the unknown.

"Not much different from our test runs around Sol," the captain said, reassuring her crew, and herself. "Stand ready, this jump will only be a few seconds longer than our shake-down flights, but we don't know what we'll find when we get there."

No sooner had she spoken the words than the ship slipped entirely into the wormhole. There was no sense of motion aboard, only pulse after pulse of light streaking over and around the ship, filling the forward view screen and portals. For Breuger, it was nauseating to watch, and he returned his attention to his duty console. As the captain had assured them, it was over in seconds. The movement and color and light ceased, and was replaced with the vastness of space, and its innumerable stars.

But the arrival of the *Hyperion* over Luyten b coincided with the approach of an enormous derelict orbital station, drifting through its orbit surrounded by debris, quickly filling the ship's forward view, blocking out the stars and the planet beyond it. With the two vessels on a collision course, alarms began blaring, filling the bridge with their clamoring.

"Evasive, make for high orbit," Captain Roberts shouted. "Comms, hail that ship," she ordered, "Breuger, scan for weapons and life signs."

"It's not a ship," the Major said, "it's a station. Bigger than any I've ever seen. Must be eight, ten kilometers in diameter. To build such a thing…the technology…the cost….why? Is it armed?"

"No life signs, no weapons, nothing our scans can identify," Breuger reported.

"No response on comms," Jones added.

"Kill those alarms. Breuger, sensor sweep, maximum range," the captain said, "scan for other ships, any signals."

"Yes ma'am," Breuger said, "scanning, maximum range."

"Dex," the captain said, "you put us right on the doorstep. Let's not do that again. Get me the lay of the system. Be quick about it."

"Yes, Captain."

"Breuger, report."

"Nothing yet…."

"Keep at it. Jones, scan the quadrant for signals, full spectrum. I want to know if anybody else is out here."

The crew bent to their respective duties, occasionally casting furtive glances toward the captain while she and Major Mulzac followed the progress of the space station toward Luyten b.

"Look at the debris field. Forward quadrant. The station is damaged. Can we get a closer look?" the Major asked.

"Breuger, give me magnification, port it to the aft view screen."

"Yes, captain."

Dex, seated near the back of the bridge, turned and scrutinized the station.

"It looks rough. How's that thing still in orbit?" he asked.

"That's a good question. Save it for later," the captain said.

"The symbols," Dex said, "the blue ones especially. There's something familiar about them."

"You can spend all the time you want trying to decipher it when the mission is over," the Major said.

"Are we gonna board it?" Dex asked.

"If it's no threat to us," the captain said, "we'll leave it be."

"Look," Dex said, pointing at the planet now in view on the screen, "it's beautiful…"

As the ship reached higher orbit, the planet's lone continent swung into view below the station. A white glow formed beneath the derelict's lower hull. Together, the three of them turned to look at the scene on the larger forward screen.

"Distress signal from the surface. It's weak," Jones called out, "but definitely one of ours."

"Transfer coordinates to the lander," the captain ordered. "Tell our pilot I want her to put it down as close to the marker as possible."

"Can I come with you?" Dex asked.

"No," Captain Roberts and the Major said in unison.

The Major saw Dex's pained expression. "Mission profile Dex. Get in, get out. Once we have a proper risk assessment, we can talk about sending you down on a future mission."

"We need you here, safe, to guide us home," the captain added.

"No response from the surface," Jones said.

"Keep trying. Breuger, I want constant visual on the site. When the lander is away, we move to geosynchronous orbit. We're not taking our eyes off the continent. Continuous scanning, no more surprises."

"Roger that captain," Breuger replied.

"Send the word. Mission's a go."

Jones tapped her console, "Blake, mission is a go, prep the lander, you drop in twenty minutes."

"Finally, some action," Blake replied. "Ready to drop in twenty.

***

When the captain saw the first images of the *Katie,* her optimism faded. Only the bridge lifeboat remained, a few scorched sections of hull visible, the rest enveloped in vegetation.

Major Mulzac and Michael Jay boarded the lander. Once she finished her preflight checks, Blake piloted the small craft from the ship and burned a path through the atmosphere, setting down in an open field near the crash site.

Blake peered through the portal at the world outside, at the green foliage and blue sky. "It's amazing," she said. "Atmospheric readings are as close to Earth as you can get, maybe better."

"We take no chances," the Major said, "helmets on, weapons charged, full alert mode."

"Roger that," Michael replied.

"Weapons? No one told me to bring a weapon."

"Somebody's gotta look non-threatening, might as well be you," Michael said.

"Very funny, try not to shoot me if you hear any scary noises."

"Knock it off, both of you. Gear up," the Major said, "we've got four hours, tops, then we're bouncing back to the *Hyperion.* If we don't find 'em on this trip, we'll get one more shot."

"What happens if we don't find them at all?" Blake asked.

"We go back, report what we've learned, try again on a follow-up mission."

The team donned helmets, collected their gear, and stepped into the soft light of the new world.

Blake ran her gloved hand over the ferns dancing in the breeze. "I wish I could feel these for real, and smell the air. My family left Earth about the time I learned to walk; I can't remember what it was like."

"Now's not the time, stay focused."

"Yes sir, will do."

Michael looked at the screen on the forearm of his pressure suit. He turned left, then right, until the blinking locater icon on the panel turned to a steady glow. "This way," he said, "hundred meters."

Following Michael, the party made its way through the forest, searching the ground and peering into the dense undergrowth for any signs of the crew, or possible danger, until they reached the remains of the *Katie.*

Michael and Blake cut away the vines growing into and over the open airlock, then examined the interior. Michael entered and tapped the control panel. "Not enough power," he said, then began manually opening the inner door.

"You see anything not human in there, feel free to kill it," the Major said.

"Roger that, weapons hot."

Michael went directly to the bridge. He plugged a portable power supply into the main console and the message indicator flickered to life. He played Captain Bimmy's last holo-message, his helmet cam relaying it to the rest of the team, and to the crew aboard the Hyperion via the lander's uplink.

"This is Captain Charles Bimmy. Commander Kiel left the ship to reconnoiter and something went wrong. I'm going out to look for her. I'll be on a heading of one seven zero degrees, if my compass can be trusted. If you're watching this, assume this planet is hostile. Bimmy, out."

Michael shut off the distress signal and searched the remainder of the ship, then rejoined his team.

"They weren't here long," he said, "there's plenty of food and water. You saw the message, they left the ship, never made it back. There's lots of metal oxidation, parts of the hull are practically crumbling. Power is minimal. If we were any later, we wouldn't have picked up the distress signal." Michael had served under Captain Bimmy during the war, and knew him well. "Whatever happened, it got to Bimmy, he looked panicked, scared. It's not like him."

"Can't argue with that assessment," the Major replied.

"Isn't staying with the ship S-O-P?" Blake asked.

"There's nothing standard about crashing on an alien planet."

"And don't forget the Bimmy factor," Michael said.

"Never heard of it…"

Michael activated his suit's scanner and began a slow turn, searching the forest. "Yeah, but you've lived it," he said, "Captain Bimmy has a history of getting creative with standard operating procedures."

"Can't argue with that either. Which means," the Major said, "if they're alive, and I'm betting they are, they could be anywhere."

"I'm picking up a significant energy reading, less than four kilometers due east."

"Sounds like a good place to start looking," Blake said, "which way is east?"

The Major waved his hand toward the bow of the ruined *Katie*, "And you call yourself a pilot," he said, "east is that way."

The trio came to a stream and followed its course, arriving at a white-sand beach on the shore of a long, narrow, clear blue lake. A collection of towers and blocks, a city, stood guard over the opposite shore.

"Holy smoke… a city," Blake said, "why didn't we see this…"

"The energy readings are consistent with a shielding system, a huge one, big enough to hide an entire city, at least from an orbital perspective," Michael said.

The Major smiled as he spotted a small boat approaching across the lake, carrying two people, "Forget the city, I told you they were alive."

The Major estimated the point where the boat would come ashore and began to walk toward it. Blake and Michael followed.

When the boat neared the shore, Blake waved excitedly. She grasped the locking mechanism on the helmet of her pressure suit, unsnapped it, and lifted the helmet away, smiling, "Bimmy, you made it! We found you!"

4

Blake

While I struggled with the idea of being something other than human, Becca grew increasingly more comfortable with the prospect of millions of tiny robots taking up residence inside us.

"I feel like you're a little too happy about this," I told her on our way out of the spaceport, "we might want to think through the implications."

"Like what?" she said. "We're self-healing, we can read an alien language, we're fully adapted to an alien environment…"

"We're the aliens, and we're not ourselves anymore, these things could have an ulterior motive."

"Robots don't have motive, they have function, and in this case a very specific form."

"Forget motive then, what about purpose? That's not the same as function."

"True, but I know I'm still me and I believe you're still you, and thus far we've experienced a net benefit from…"

"From an infestation of nanobots…"

"From the symbiotic relationship…"

"If it's symbiotic, what do the nanobots get out of it?"

"Maybe it's the wrong word, but parasitic sounds gross."

We walked into the welcome center and halfway through the central hall, on our way to the airlock doors leading out to the park, she stopped and looked around.

"What is it?"

"I don't know what the bots get from us, if anything," she said, "but I might have an idea about their purpose." She stared at the doors lining one side of the expansive hall and started walking.

"Are you going to tell me…"

"We've never opened one of these. I've got a theory but I want to see what's behind these doors before I tell you what it is."

"Your last idea turned me into a lab rat."

She smiled over her shoulder and kept walking.

I expected the room to be an office, or storage, or some other utilitarian space. I could not have been more wrong. When we entered, overhead lights switched on, revealing a large glass room-within-the-room. Two tubes connected the enclosure to ports next to a glossy black panel on the right wall. Four transparent reclining chairs sat in a row within the glass room. On the left side of the room, opposite the control panel, two benches lined the wall. One corner was occupied by a tall cabinet.

I opened the cabinet and found it was stocked with bottled beverages and what appeared to be packaged food, based on the images on the wrappers. I could read the labels, but they made no sense.

Becca laughed when she saw the contents. "Not what I was expecting, but okay. I don't know what a 'gugah gugah' is, but based on the picture I'm going with candy bar."

"I'd say protein bar." When I picked up one of the bars it crumbled into dust. "An extremely old protein bar. Does this support your theory?"

"Were you hungry when you woke up in the forest?"

"Yeah, but I was more worried about finding you than finding food."

"You were thirsty too," she said.

"And?"

"This does support my hypothesis."

Becca examined the surface of the panel, tracing the tubes leading from the wall to the glass enclosure. When she waved her hand over the lower edge of the panel, two icons appeared, one of them a bright, steady light, another pulsing slowly. As we read the labels, the door to the enclosure closed.

"This is promising," she said to herself, "Supply and exhaust. It's all making sense."

"I'm lost, when are you gonna fill me in?"

She tapped the 'Supply' icon. "Patience," she said.

A rumbling sound and gentle vibration emanated from the wall as a hidden mechanism activated. A light mist began to fill the glass chamber.

"What's with the fog?"

"It's not fog," Becca said, "it's nanites, billions and billions of them."

The mechanical mist grew into a cloud, then filled the chamber, until the 'exhaust' label began to pulse. Becca tapped the screen and the process reversed, the chamber became clear again, and the door to the enclosure opened.

"What are you thinking?" I asked.

"Let's go," she said, "I want another look at the fountain."

We left the building, pausing in the airlock to read the message we'd found when we arrived: 'People of the Triad, Go Forth in Harmony.'

At the fountain, Becca raised her arm toward the structure's top, at the metallic sphere with three rods of unequal length protruding from it.

"That iconography is repeated on the three ships at the spaceport, what do you think it means?"

"If the sphere represents Luyten's Star, the three rods might represent three planets, three advanced species, in which case this entire place is central to their existence. Otherwise, why build a city like this?"

"What if it's not Luyten's Star? Maybe it represents this planet, and the arrangement of the rods represents a planetary alignment?"

"Three worlds…three species…all of them space-faring…they arrive at the spaceport, move through controlled airspace, through massive airlocks, have some sort of…procedure…then 'go forth in harmony.' Whatever that means. I don't know what to make of it."

"Remember when I asked you about the difference between inside and outside?"

"Sure, but we came in through…"

"Exactly, we can breathe either atmosphere, whatever is out here, and whatever is in there," she said, pointing over her shoulder. "We can breathe alien atmosphere, read an alien language, operate alien technology. There's a connection between these capabilities and the nanobots."

"How deep do you think it goes?"

"Think about it from the perspective of someone boarding a ship and traveling here from their home world, like us traveling to Deimos, except in our case we know the air inside Deimos is breathable, because we all come from the same home world. But here, if there are three different home worlds, it's unlikely they'd have the same atmosphere. Similar perhaps, but not identical."

"Why aren't there three airlocks?"

"I don't know, add it to the mystery list. I want to go back to the Katie."

"Why? It's not likely to have power anymore."

"The scans we took from orbit, there's a pile of atmospheric readings for two of the other planets. I never got to review it. If I can transfer the data to a tablet, I think we may find some answers. I might have enough data to plot the alignment, figure out when it happens, how often, if it's approaching. Could be useful."

Becca walked down the steps to one of the small boats at rest in its notch in the lowest terrace of the harbor wall. She stood next to the skiff we arrived in and the blue light at the stern began to pulse.

"We're taking a boat ride," she said, smiling.

"Aye, Aye, captain," I said, forcing myself to smile back at her.

A loud boom overhead shattered the quiet of the bright clear day. I recognized the sound of reentry; I'd heard it often enough in Arcadia. We looked skyward and saw a ship descending toward the forest on the far side of the lake.

"Is that one of ours?" Becca asked.

"It could be...but the lander doesn't look like Space Force inventory. Looks to me like somebody sent a rescue mission, maybe Deimos?"

"How?" Becca replied. "We crashed the only ship capable of interstellar travel."

"They could have built another one."

"In nine weeks? Not possible."

"Nothing is impossible," I said, "especially when Deimos is involved. We don't know how much time has passed there compared to here. Our transit might have taken longer than we realized."

"Who's to say it isn't an alien ship?"

"We're the aliens. I think the locals would use the spaceport."

Becca took a seat in the boat and I followed. The boat lowered into the water, backed out of the notch, and turned around to head out of the harbor.

We passed across the placid surface of the lake, the distant white-sand beach growing ever closer. The relaxing motion of the boat and the gentle breeze did nothing to quell my misgivings about our discovery. And I worried about the safety of the crew, whoever they were. I hoped they'd see the message I left behind at our wrecked ship. I found myself wishing the boat would go faster. I tried to calm my nerves, to relax and slow my breathing. We were close to the beach, entering shallow water, when three figures emerged from the forest. I recognized their pressure suits. I knew they were from Deimos, but I couldn't make out their faces from where we were.

They walked along the shore, toward the spot where we would land, and one of them began waving. Then, to my horror, I saw Blake remove her helmet.

I stood up in the bow and shouted, "Blake, put it back on, put it on…"

I lost my balance. The boat started rolling as I tried to regain my footing, until I plunged head-first into the shallow water, scraping my head on the rocky bottom.

"Bimmy," Becca yelled, "what are you doing?"

"She's gonna die," I said, sputtering water.

"She won't, we didn't…get back in the boat…"

"You can't be certain," I said and pushed my way to shore, moving faster than the boat. I dragged my soaking body ashore and ran toward Blake.

Reggie's confused look was clear behind his visor. He opened his arms to embrace me, but I shoved him out of my way. Behind him Micheal stepped aside, out of my path. Blake dropped her helmet when I gripped the locking ring around the neck opening of her suit. "What are you doing?" I shouted. "Didn't you see my message? This planet is hostile, what were you thinking?"

"What…what…," she stuttered.

I stared at her, my heart pounding, waiting for the inevitable to happen, hoping she would survive, but overwhelmed by the fear Blake, my friend, would soon die before my eyes. She saw the wound on my forehead heal, the blood dissipating into thin air.

"Bimmy," she said, "you're not wearing a suit, you're breathing the air, I thought…what's happened to your head…what the…"

"We're not human anymore," I said, grinding the words between my teeth.

"Bimmy," I heard Reggie say, "take it easy, we'll…"

Blake began to struggle against me, slapping at my arms, trying to break free, "Let go of me! Let go!" she shouted.

I refused to let go. She began to gasp for air, her face grew taut, her lips pulled back. When she couldn't breathe anymore, I could see in her eyes she understood.

"I'm sorry," I said, "I'm sorry."

Her strength left her. The light faded from her eyes, and she collapsed into my arms. I lowered her to the sand as gently as I could and leaned over her, watching her face twist and contort, her flesh desiccating, pulling away from her skull. I was witnessing what had happened to Becca and me.

I thought then, even if she lived, she would be like us, and I still didn't understand what it meant, beyond the fact we were no longer what we once had been. My heart ached as her body decayed before my eyes, broken down by the molecular machines we now understood were endemic in the atmosphere.

Sadness overwhelmed me, I felt I was going to cry, until Becca laid a gentle hand on my shoulder, "It's going to be all right," she said, "give it time."

"It's not all right," I said, "none of this is all right."

I could hardly breathe, I felt a part of me breaking apart and falling away, dissolving into nothing, as I watched Blake's body undergo the transformation from human to…whatever we were. Becca stepped away from me, then looked at Reggie and Michael, both of them trying to make sense of the gruesome scene playing out before them.

"Come with me," Becca said, turning toward the stream, back toward the *Katie.*

"What the hell are you talking about," the Major said, "Blake is dead. How can you be…"

"She's not dead," Becca said. "You can stay here if you like, but I need to go to the ship. If you come with me, I'll explain what's happening. If you stay here, I suggest you brace yourselves. This is not going to play out the way you expect."

"What do you mean 'going to? It's already not what I expected."

"I know," she said, as calm as the surface of the lake, "are you coming with me or not?"

"Go with her," I growled at them, "we'll be here when you get back."

***

The crew on the bridge of the *Hyperion* witnessed what the landing party had experienced, transmitted via the helmet cams embedded in each pressure suit. Jones fought to hold back tears, as did Breuger. He moved to her side and placed a hand on her shoulder, saying nothing. Captain Roberts froze. When her shock gave way to reason, she gave her orders.

"Breuger, I need you at your station. Jones, give me a direct comm with Reggie."

"Yes ma'am, patching you in. You're set…"

"Reggie," the captain said, "do not go with her, we do not know what's happened to them. Retrieve Blake's body and get back up here, we're going home. We need to regroup."

"We need more time," the Major responded, "if Becca has an explanation, I want to hear it."

"You've got one hour. Then you launch or we're coming down to get you, *Hyperion* out."

The captain turned to Dex, who'd been sitting quietly at the nav station, staring at the view screen. "How soon can you plot our course back to Deimos?" she asked.

Dex, his eyes locked onto the screen, didn't respond.

"Dex," the captain said, "focus, we need you."

Dex shook his head, "What's happening…"

"Our return trajectory, how soon can you plot our course home?"

Dex moved his shaking hands over the nav console, "I can't do it from here… I… I don't have…"

"I know you're frightened Dex," the captain said, "but I need you to focus. Go to astrometrics, get started, give me an ETA, I need you to go, immediately."

"Yes…yes captain, right away." Dex rose unsteadily from his seat, still shaking. Captain Roberts grabbed his arm as he braced himself against the bulkhead. "I'm all right, thank you…I'll be okay…," he said, and left the bridge.

"Captain," Jones said, "you need to see this, sending to main viewer…"

"What am I looking at?"

"It's the feed from Blake's helmet cam, something is happening to her suit."

Blake's body lay on the beach, Captain Bimmy seated beside her on the sand, despondent. Blake's suit began to disintegrate, becoming bits of fine dust that vanished into the sand. The pressure suit disappeared.

The video feed jittered, then began to fade, until the screen filled with static, then cut to black.

***

Major Mulzac and Michael followed Becca through the forest. Her lack of a pressure suit allowed her to move more quickly and they soon fell behind. She felt no need to slow down. She assumed they knew the way. The distance gave her space to contemplate Bimmy's reaction to what had happened on the beach. She didn't know Blake, other than a few stories Bimmy had told of their time serving together during the Secessionist War. She began to question the nature of his relationship with Blake. She dismissed her darker thoughts and focused on her immediate goal.

She found her pangs of jealousy reassuring, a counterpoint to Bimmy's concerns about their humanity.

Before she climbed through the wrecked ship's airlock, she took a few moments to scan the mass of vegetation draped over the hull. She ran her hand over the rough ends of the vines that had been cut away from the opening. She heard a noise behind her and turned to watch the Major and Michael Jay emerge from the underbrush.

"Amazing how fast things grow here," she said.

The Major gave his brother a quick glance, "Becca, you've been missing for two years," he said.

"From your perspective, maybe," she replied, "for us, we've been on this planet for nine weeks, give or take. It's hard to keep track. Did you know a year here is less than nineteen Earth days?"

"Interesting, but not the information I need right now."

"He's wrong you know, about us," she said, "we're different, but still human."

"Explain. You said Blake wasn't dead...," Michael said.

"The atmosphere is laced with nanobots. Breathe the air, you breathe in the bots. They get in your bloodstream, enter your cells. Your cells multiply, the bots multiply. But first, I think, the nanobots spread through your entire body before they activate. Probably through the lymphatic system. I'm not sure if their presence in the air is by design, or the result of some of kind of accident. We saw them for the first time today, under a microscope. There's a lot more to learn."

"Blake...that's what happened to you and Bimmy?" the Major asked.

"Yes, but there appears to be a more controlled process. We found a room, in the city, with equipment designed to expose people to the bots. It seems to be a prerequisite to…something, I'm still not sure what it all means."

"How did you know we were here?"

"Coincidence. We were on our way here when we saw your ship come down. We came back to retrieve data on the other planets in the habitable zone. We scanned two of them when we arrived. It might shed some light on our situation."

"You're taking this a lot better than Bimmy," Michael said.

"He and I process change differently. Like I said, this is new information to us. But you're right, he's struggling with what it could mean, the broader implications for us, for others who might come here."

"And you don't feel the same?"

"I've learned not to worry about things I can't change. I can't change this," she said, waving a hand over her chest, "my body is different, but is my body all that makes me human? I think it's the least of it. If it weren't for your arrival, for Blake's exposure, he'd have already come to terms with the situation."

Becca paused, lost for a moment in the memory of her first encounter with Charlie, long before he became Bimmy, the day she traversed a wormhole for the first time, the day he saved her life. It felt like someone else's life, a long time ago.

"Can you help me pull the data I need?" she asked. "I'd like to get it and get back to the beach as quickly as possible."

"Are you worried about him?"

"He needs time," she said, "but he'll be okay. He's been through worse. He's tough, resilient. But I don't know how long the bots take to do their work. When Blake wakes up, she may be disoriented. We should be there to greet her."

"We've got one hour. Then we launch," the Major said. "We came here to find you, and bring you back."

"I'd say your mission has changed, given the circumstances."

"We have quarantine procedures, come back with us, we'll figure this out…"

"No way," Becca said, laughing, "you think I want to be someone's experiment? The answers are here, on Avalon."

"Avalon?"

"We named this planet Avalon," she said, "and we call it home. I understand you can't stay for long, but why rush back? There's a city to explore, other planets, did you see the orbital station? It's not as dead as it looks, be careful up there."

"We came here on a rescue mission; we didn't equip for more than a few days. If we didn't find you by then, our orders were to report back and let the higher ups decide the next move, based on what we find."

"We need to tell Bimmy. Help me in here. Let's get this done and get back to the beach."

***

I watched Blake's transformation with morbid curiosity. As much as I feared it, I wanted to see it, to understand the mechanics of what had happened to Becca and me.

Her pressure suit and helmet dissolved. The flesh of her face and hands became a yellowish color, like untanned hide, stretched tight over bone. With every passing second, she looked more like an exhumed corpse, like something from a horror movie.

Her clothing rippled like waves passing over the ocean on a windy day, each successive motion altering the fabric until it took on the same subtle iridescence of my transformed uniform.

Her fingers curled into her palms, forming tight withered fists, making sharp cracking sounds. The soft tissue of her body shrank into itself, leaving her ribs and shoulders and hips pushing up against her clothing. Her hair fell away from her scalp as if shorn by some invisible blade. Watching the rapid decay of her body, I found it difficult to believe she could return from such a ruined state. I became convinced that whatever had happened to Becca and me, Blake's process was different.

The fabric draped over her body stopped moving. It shimmered in the sun, clung to her as my soaked uniform clung to me when I crawled out of the lake. I held my breath, waiting for what would happen next. A minute passed with no change, then I glimpsed a minuscule movement on her face.

I leaned closer and saw her eyebrows growing back, her skin color changing, and the flesh itself expanding, thickening over her skull.

Her hair began to grow back, but not the color I remembered. Where it had been a light brown, with a hint of red, it returned a deep, rich auburn. She sprouted new eyelashes, then her hands opened, settling palms down on the sand.

Thirty minutes after she had died in my arms, or at least passed through a process I can best describe as death, her body was fully reformed. Her chest surged upward as her lungs filled with air. Her breathing intensified for a time, then settled in to a gentle rhythm, like someone in a peaceful slumber.

But she did not wake up.

I heard a rustling sound and looked up to see Becca emerge from the forest, carrying a digipad, followed by Reggie, with no sign of Michael.

I remained seated and Becca stood over me, looking down at Blake. I reached up and took her hand and she looked down at me and smiled sweetly.

"She's alive…" Reggie said, "how…"

"Yes," Becca said, "we still don't know why, but yes, she's alive."

"Did you get what you needed?" I asked.

Becca held out the digipad, "Got it all right here. It can wait, the Major has something to tell you."

I looked at Reggie, recalling the times we served together, how I felt I'd gained a brother on our mission to Mercury, and I felt a sense of dread. I resigned myself to it, whatever he wanted to tell me. After years of being in control, I knew I needed to let go; to try to accept what the universe presented me, to incorporate it into my life and make the most of it. Becca had been trying to teach me the lesson ever since our reunion, after the destruction of her university, where she'd been buried alive. I was still working to learn it.

"I'm staying here," he said, "with you." He nodded at Becca. Then he looked down at Blake. "And her. You can argue all you want; it won't change a thing. That's my decision, and it's mine to make."

I stood up, Becca pulling my hand to help me, and faced my old friend.

"Fair enough," I said, "but keep your suit on until we get to the city."

"There's more," Becca said.

"Hasn't there been enough for one day?"

"The *Hyperion* is leaving as soon as the lander docks," Reggie said. "We'll be on our own until they can come back."

"We've been on our own for weeks," I said, "we're not exactly roughing it."

Reggie looked at the city in the distance. "How long does it take to cross? My air supply is below three hours. When it's out, this helmet is coming off, no matter where we are."

"Less than an hour," Becca said, "plenty of time to get you to the welcome center."

"The what?"

"You'll see," I said. I looked across the lake at the city, our city, then back at Reggie. "The good news is, we have three ships, plenty of food and water, an entire city to ourselves. Bad news, we have more questions than answers, know next to nothing about the ships, and we don't know what any of this means."

Before Reggie could reply, Blake sat bolt upright, a blank stare on her face.

She looked down at her hands, dug her fingers into the sand, grabbed handfuls of the white crystals and raised her fists for a closer look, then let the sand sift through her fingers like an hourglass made of flesh and blood. She brushed her palms against her trousers, looked out at the city, then looked up at me.

"So, Captain Jerk," she said with a grin, "what were you saying about ships?"

I managed to smile back at her, grateful for her sense of humor. "Welcome back Blake. Get off your lazy butt, we've got work to do."

5

Reggie

If Blake was fazed by the nanobots swirling about inside the three of us, she didn't show it. "At least I don't have to wear that stupid suit anymore," was her lone comment on the matter. Our slow return across the lake gave her and Reggie time to take in the city. They stared wide-eyed and speechless at the gleaming towers flanking the harbor.

They were anxious to see the spaceport, but we had the matter of Reggie's impending loss of oxygen to contend with first. We arrived at the harbor, climbed the stairs and crossed the park, stopping at its edge, in front of the welcome center, to give Reggie and Blake a chance to take in more of their surroundings.

"How sensitive is the atmospheric sensor on your suit?" Becca asked.

"Not sensitive enough," he said, glancing at Blake, "it's reading all-clear. I doubt the designers ever expected it to check for molecular-scale nanobots."

"The ship's sensors were the same," I said, "they picked up an unknown element, but it wasn't flagged."

"That's what I'm reading," Reggie said.

"Good," Becca said, "I suspect you'll get similar data inside."

"What do you call this city?" Blake interrupted. "And welcome center, so boring. Why not something fun, like Valhalla, or Asgard, I mean look at the place."

"We named it Avalon, but the buildings haven't been a priority," I said, "call it what you want, looks like a welcome center to me. It will make more sense when we come back through. Everything between the spaceport and the welcome center is enclosed, separated from the planet's atmosphere."

We entered through the airlock, into the main hall of the building.

Reggie and Blake stopped and gawked up at the painted ceiling, as Becca and I had, its bucolic valley and curving river flowing end to end.

"This is some welcome center," Blake said, "looks more like a cathedral."

"Interesting point," Becca said, "we don't know the significance of this place, the city, the planet, it could have a religious element."

"I've never been to a cathedral," Reggie said, "but on Earth I went to an island called Ios. This building is nicer, but it reminds me of a building in Athens. We landed at the spaceport there and had to pass through a medical check before we could jet out to the island. After the first Marauder War, the Alliance wanted to send the troops home rested and recovered, especially the Colonial Marines. I spent a month eating seafood and getting sunburned. When I got home, everyone on Deimos thought the whole war had been one big party. If they only knew."

"What's your suit reading?" Becca asked, "We've got a decision to make."

"Yeah…looks like you were wrong, the readings are different, there's no unknown element in here."

"It could have been filtered out," I said, "but I'm not sure I trust the sensors."

"One way to find out," Reggie said, and began unlocking his helmet.

"Wait," I said, "you've got more air, let's go to the spaceport first."

He slid the latch on his helmet open. "We'd be delaying the inevitable, here's as good a place as any." He lifted the helmet away and took a deep breath. "Is the air outside like this?" he asked.

"Not even close," Blake said, "outside is nice. In here smells like the inside of a starship on a long duration mission. Recycled, used up, stale."

"How long does this usually take?"

"A few minutes," I said, "the faster you breathe, the faster it happens."

"It starts with a little scratch in your throat," Becca said.

"That's strange," Blake said, "I thought it started with Captain Bimmy screaming at you."

"Blake, I'm sorry…you, Reggie…after Becca, you're my oldest friends. I was…"

"Oh stop," Blake replied. "Do you remember the first time we met, on the Luna shuttle?"

"Yes."

"You were trying to fly, like a kid on a zero-g playground, and failing."

"I remember."

"You remember how many times I've made fun of you for it?"

"I've lost count."

"Yeah, well, let's treat this like then, and we'll be fine."

Reggie started taking deeper breaths, closer together. His face flushed, his ears turned red, and he became unsteady on his feet.

Becca took him by the arm, "Stop already, enough, you'll pass out, you're hyperventilating."

Reggie normalized his breathing but stumbled backwards. Blake, Becca and I each grabbed him. I couldn't help myself; I started laughing. Soon we were all laughing at Reggie, ourselves, the absurdity of the moment, the three of us propping him up. A feeling came over me, something special. I had an epiphany. I realized these people, my wife, my friends, they were my family, and had been for a long time, even before Becca and I got married and absconded with a starship. The realization led me to another. Despite whatever mechanism was at play inside my body, I was still me, and still mostly human.

Reggie regained his balance and laughed with us. I don't know why, but I hugged him, stretching to get my arms around his broad shoulders and his pressure suit. There was a powerful reassurance in that embrace with an old friend, and I felt better than I had in days.

"What, no kiss," he said, and we laughed again.

I turned to Blake and she backed away, grinning, "Oh no captain, last time you grabbed me I died, remember?"

I thought about Breuger, the way he had hugged me after my weeks-long stay in the hospital, recovering from my first taste of combat. I smiled, "Come on Blake, bring it in." I spread my arms and she punched me in the chest, then hugged me. "Call me Bimmy, there's no captain here," I said.

I heard Becca say to Reggie, "Like I said, he's resilient."

"Okay, moving on," I said, still grinning. "Reggie, you sure you want to do this? It's not too late to change your mind. You can get from here all the way onto the ships at the spaceport without going outside. There's food, water, shelter…"

"I didn't stay here to live indoors," he said. "I'm on an alien planet, in the heart of an alien city, surrounded by alien technology, and who knows what else. I'm not about to miss out on any of it."

"Then let's get to it," Becca said, "follow me."

She led us into the room with the glass enclosure, where I helped Reggie out of his suit. I hung it on the wall and leaned his plasma rifle against the cabinet. Reggie took a seat inside the chamber. Becca activated the control panel, closing the door.

"Here we go," she said, and tapped the panel. The mechanism turned on and the metallic mist flowed into the chamber. The nanobots swirled into a dark undulating cloud that closed in on Reggie. Then the cloud bolted away from his body in one sudden, coordinated motion, as if repulsed by a hidden force. The cloud formed a ring which spun around, then formed tentacles which reached out to touch his skin. They were all thrust back by whatever indiscernible force was at play. An orange light began to flash on the control panel, the exhaust icon lit up, and the mist retreated from chamber. When it was empty again, the door opened and Reggie stepped out, toward me. I took a reflexive step back, then stopped.

He looked at me, confused. "Looks like we'll be doing this the hard way."

"Or not at all," I replied, "you don't have to risk it."

"Already made my decision Bimmy, and my speech. I'm doing this. The method doesn't matter, as long as the result's the same."

"Then brace yourself," I said, "it's not as fun as it looks." I walked out of the room, toward the airlock, Reggie close behind.

"Wait," Becca said, stopping us in the main hall, "what if we picked the wrong room? What if we get a different result in a different room? Three different species, maybe there are three different processes, or bots."

"Sounds logical," Blake said, "but why would there be one outside, in the atmosphere? Is it dumb luck we got one that didn't kill us, I mean kill us for good? We're not members of any local species, unless there's something you're not telling us."

"For all their advanced technology, these people didn't leave a lot of instructions lying around," Becca replied.

Reggie nodded toward the corridor leading out of the far end of the building, connecting to the residential district, and the spaceport beyond. "Why don't we ask her?"

We turned in unison and saw a tall slender female standing in front of the arched opening to the corridor. Her flowing blue robes shimmered under the yellow light shining down from the fixture at the top of the arch. Her flaxen hair was pulled back tight against her scalp, woven into a large knot at the back, with three small silver rods pointing out from it, each a different length. Her eyes were larger than ours, and her ears were unusual, delicate swept-back curves flowing away from her face. Her skin, a reddish-brown tone, the color of dull copper, was smooth and reflected the glow of the light. She was not human, but overall similar in form to us.

She stood perfectly still, smiling. She held her hands down at her sides, palms forward, a few inches away from her body.

"Friend of yours?" Blake asked.

"Never seen her before," Becca.

Reggie lowered his voice and tipped his head toward the room where we'd left his suit and his weapon, "Plasma rifle, do we need it?"

Becca started walking toward the being, "Let's find out."

Then the being flickered, before returning to a steady image.

"Hologram," I said, "I don't think we'll need the rifle."

The four of us stood in a semicircle in front of the hologram, which continued to smile as it raised one hand, palm facing us, and held it in front of each of us until it got to Reggie.

The hologram's lips moved but we couldn't hear any words. Then it twirled its hand with a flourish, brushed a finger over Reggie's forehead, then tapped the air over a door in the far wall, as if touching an invisible button. A blue light came on over one of the doors. She lowered her hand and folded it over the other, spoke silent words again, then vanished in an instant.

"That's the wildest user manual I've ever seen," Blake said.

Becca took a few steps toward the door with the glowing blue light over it, then looked back at the three of us, "Blue means go. You coming or not?"

The four of us entered the room, identical to the previous one in appearance, a glass chamber, glass control panel, two benches along the wall, four transparent reclined seats in the chamber. Reggie stepped inside and sat down, Becca waved her hand over the panel, and the door to the chamber closed. She tapped the icon on the panel and the nanobots moved in, this time filling the chamber, until we could no longer see Reggie.

"You okay in there?" Becca asked.

When Reggie didn't respond, I called out, "Reggie, say something. We're getting worried out here."

Still no response. More bots poured into the chamber. What had looked like a mist, then a cloud, turned into churning fluidic mass, frantic movement flashing bright white, like boiling mercury.

The lights changed on the control panel and the chamber began to empty, the thick mass thinned away until at last we could see a shape reclined in one of the chairs.

"Something's not right," I said.

"Give it time," Becca said, "the process is different, maybe…"

Becca fell silent when the bulk of the material swirling in the room cleared, allowing a better view of the interior.

"Is he…who…what in the world…" Becca said.

The Reggie I knew, the grown man I had served with in the war, a man I thought of as an older brother, was no longer in the room. While I recognized his facial features, the man in the chamber was a much younger version of Reggie, perhaps eighteen, no more than twenty years old, sleeping peacefully, a faint smile on his face, breathing deep and slow.

Blake leaned against the glass, stared at Reggie for a moment, and grinned, "Oops."

6

Mission Report

President Jay paced along the wall of his office, a diagram of the Sol shipping lanes and the registered moons of Jupiter glowing on the screen behind. The *Hyperion* mission report had taken a sudden alarming turn. "What do you mean he stayed behind?" President Jay asked, incredulous, "Why? What purpose could it serve?"

"Father, you know Reggie," Michael said, "I think he felt like he owed it to them."

"It will make more sense when you see the cam footage from the lander team," Captain Roberts added.

"If it's important," Fleet Admiral Wilson asked, "why didn't you transmit it as soon as you made the jump back? You've kept us in the dark for a full orbit, no report, no logs, nothing. Why?"

"I can see you're both frustrated, but try to be patient. This data, what we found, it's disruptive…volatile would be an understatement. We wanted to collect it on physical storage rather than transmit it, it takes time."

"Explain volatile."

"To start," Captain Roberts said, "there's a semi-functional orbital station over the planet, and what looks like a modern city that's shielded from orbit…"

"A city," the admiral interjected, "and an orbital station? Are there people on the station? Is it armed? What sort of military capacity are we looking at?"

"It's all in my report. We don't know much about the city, it's shielded from orbit, we only saw it through the landing party's cams, scans from Michael's suit gave us limited data. As for the station, no known occupants, no identifiable weapons, no discernible offensive capability. It's old, damaged, it has power and at least enough propulsive energy to maintain its orbit. Its orbit brings it over Luyten b's landmass during daylight. That's all we can say for certain right now."

The admiral shook her head at the captain. "I can't deal with these vagaries…"

"We didn't spend a lot of time on orbital mechanics, but we've got the data, Dex is working on it."

The President sat down and Admiral Wilson stared across the table at him and shook her head again. "Peter, I have to take this to the Federation High Council. Four crew members stranded on an alien world, an alien space station, a hidden city, and we have one working interstellar ship. I can't keep this a secret."

"There's more you need to know," Michael said.

"Do tell," Admiral Wilson said, exasperated, "I've got nothing but time."

The President folded his hands on the table, projecting calm. "I don't think sarcasm improves the situation, Amanda." Out of the corner of his eye he caught a gesture, a small twitch from Captain Roberts, directed at his son. He knew Captain Sally Roberts well, his wife's step-sister, and he knew what the twitch meant. They were hiding something, and she wanted Michael to keep quiet. If true, he needed to get the admiral on her way and get the full story.

"The atmosphere on Avalon, their name for the planet, not ours," Michael continued, "there's something in it, something toxic. You'll see when you watch the mission log, it's…. bizarre. Bimmy and Becca looked perfectly normal, but when Blake took off her helmet, Bimmy, he lost it. Started shouting about not being human. Becca didn't appear fazed by it, but then Blake died…"

"She's dead?" the admiral shouted, "Is this your first mission debrief? How do you not lead with that information?"

"Admiral, she's not dead. But she died or…something happened. But before the lander launched from the planet, we captured cam footage from Reggie's suit, of Blake, alive and speaking, no suit, no air supply, comfortably breathing the atmosphere."

"All right, I've heard enough, transfer your data to the Arcturus, I'll review it with my team and we'll let you know if we have any questions. In the meantime, start prepping for a second mission, as soon as possible. I'm sending a team with you this time."

"To study the planet?" Michael asked.

"I care about the high ground, the station in orbit around the planet. We're going back and we're taking control of it. And if we can't, we're going to destroy it. Whatever its condition, we're not leaving it there for someone else to exploit."

The admiral surveyed the faces of the colonists around her. She sensed there was more, perhaps something she wouldn't find in the reports or logs of the mission. Peter Jay had a history of charting his own course through major events, the Colonial Rebellion and the Luyten project being the two most recent examples. She knew one thing for certain, President Peter Jay of the Deimos Colony, his interstellar ship notwithstanding, needed her and the Federation more than she or the Federation needed him.

When no one spoke, she knew the meeting was over and her senses went on alert. Whatever they were hiding, it had to be important enough for Peter to risk his colony's membership in the Federation, and to gamble with his own future. He knew as well as anyone, even the President of a colony could be replaced.

"I'm going back to my ship, then I've got business on Mars. I'd like your timeline for a second mission as soon as possible." She turned to Captain Roberts, "I want all your data, comms, video, scans, all of it, within the hour, understood?"

"I don't work for you," the captain said, offended by the admiral's tone.

President Jay moved his hand, the slightest of waves, enough to get the captain's attention.

Captain Roberts saw the motion, and understood the message: Let it go.

The admiral glared at the captain. She considered her options, whether she could discipline a Colonial ship's captain. She concluded she was within her rights, until the captain adjusted her attitude. Nevertheless, she tagged Captain Roberts as a potential problem she'd have to handle, sooner or later.

"The data packet is ready; it will be on your shuttle by the time you leave."

"Very well," the admiral replied. She marched out of the room, leaving the door open behind her.

"Michael, the door please."

Michael closed the door, then returned to his seat at the conference table.

"That could have gone better," the President said, "but we are where we are. One of you needs to tell me what's not been said."

"The city on the planet, it's a big one, bigger than this colony," Michael said, "Wilson will see the images when she reviews the mission logs. It's shielded, it has power, and lots of it, but as far as my sensors could tell, no people. I collected as much data as I could, but suits have limits."

"We got better data from the station," Roberts said, "turns out it has the same power signature as the shield."

"Why is this important?"

"Because we believe, Dex Farber believes, both are powered by a significant quantity of Promethium."

"We scrubbed the data we're sending to Wilson's people," Michael said, "no point mentioning Promethium until we're certain."

"That decision is above both your pay grades."

"Were we wrong?" the captain asked.

The President tapped his fingers on the desk a few times before answering. "You made the right call. If Promethium is abundant in the Luyten system, it changes everything. For us, for all of humanity."

"But mostly for us," Michael said, "if we can control it, mine it there and bring it back, or find a way to build ships there, or both, we could control interstellar travel."

"Slow it down Michael, wars are fought over this sort of thing, and we're in no position to fight the entire Federation. Control the supply, as much as possible, build the ships, definitely. Control all interstellar travel, absolutely not. There's no way we could pull it off. We can't muster the forces, and I'm not sure I'd want to if we could."

"They're going to figure out what we've figured out, once they take the time to look," the captain said.

"Then we'll have to make sure they're all looking at something else for a while. Where are Breuger and Jones? Can we trust them to keep this quiet?"

"They're a matched pair, got married a year ago" Captain Roberts replied, "one talks, they'll both talk, and we know Jones is close to the admiral, but we don't have to worry about them."

"Why not?"

"They don't know any more than the admiral will know; we didn't mention the Promethium. If they're part of the next mission we'll tell them, if it becomes necessary. If not, they don't need to know."

"I'm looking forward to reviewing what you found, but first things first. Michael, you need to visit your mother and explain to her why her eldest son didn't come back with you. And you," he said to Captain Roberts, "need to get started on mission planning. We don't want to leave our people alone on - what did they call it - Avalon? We don't want to leave them alone there any longer than necessary. Get some rest, then let's get busy."

***

Admiral Wilson's shuttle was touching down at the military spaceport on Mars when a blinking comm light signaled an incoming message. She touched the device at her wrist, "How's it looking?"

"It's a lot of data," a voice replied, "we'll need a couple days to go over all of it. What are your priorities on this? Where do you…"

"Don't start with the data," she said. "Forward a copy of the comm stream from Major Mulzac's helmet-cam to me, then dig into the package. Look for gaps, timeline, contents, anything suggesting tampering, understood?"

"You think they're hiding something?"

"Of course," she said, "it's common sense. I want to know what it is, what it's connected to, what type of information is missing. You know the drill. How soon can you get me a report?"

"It will be ready by the time you get back. I'll put our best people on it."

"I expect nothing less," she said, "Wilson out."

7

Jinx

"How long was I out, on the beach?" Blake asked.

"Less than an hour," Becca said, "but your transformation is the first event we've witnessed. It could be longer or shorter, no way to know without more data points."

"Feels like Reggie's been asleep longer than an hour," Blake said. "Should we try to get in there and wake him up?"

"We could damage the chamber," I said. "This could be the only one that works for humans."

"I'm hungry. Were you hungry when you woke up? I'm more than hungry, thirsty too. You said there was food and water?"

"I can show you around," Becca said, "there's a fruit tree in the garden, it's like an apple, crunchy, but sweeter. I think you'll like it. There's a drinking fountain out there too."

"I've never so much as seen a real apple. I'd also like to get a look at those ships. Bimmy, will you be okay without us?"

"I'll manage," I said, "we'll meet you at the spaceport. Becca can draw some blood while you're there."

"Not a bad idea."

"What are you talking about? I like my blood where it is."

"Don't worry, I've had some practice on Bimmy."

"Yeah, no, not gonna happen."

It was good to hear them laughing when they left. Becca's introduction to Blake wasn't ideal. I assumed she'd want to discuss it with me at some point. I was surprised by my own reaction to Blake's arrival, the depth of my emotions when I feared I might lose her. A few hours later, my fears felt overblown.

As for Reggie, the shock of seeing him thoroughly transformed was giving way to new worries. How would he take being changed? Was his transformation more than skin deep? Would he have the same memories, same feelings, same behaviors? The more I thought about it, the more my fears piled up.

In an effort to distract myself, I decided to look in the cabinet next to the benches. I assumed it would hold dried-up old snacks and bottled drinks, like the previous one, but when I opened it, I got yet another surprise.

The ancient supplies were there, as had been in the other cabinet, but there were also four objects arranged in a row. Small rectangular devices, each with a band curving away from the body of the device, all of them perched on a small stand connected to the shelf. They were black and shiny, with smooth edges and rounded corners. They looked similar to the comm link every crew member in Space Force wore, but somewhat larger.

I picked one up. To my amazement, the face lit up and a 15-centimeter-tall holographic figure rose up from its surface.

An undeniably human figure.

***

Becca was grateful to have time alone with Blake, to get to know her better and learn more about her relationship with Bimmy. While she showed Blake the gardens, and they collected a few pieces of fruit for 'the boys,' as Blake called them, she directed a significant amount of mental energy toward figuring out how to broach the topic. When they stopped to eat in the park between the garden district and the spaceport, it was Blake who took the initiative.

"I didn't see it coming, what happened back there, at the beach. Does he get like that much these days?"

"It's not the norm," Becca said, "Bimmy's all about emotional control, at least around other people."

"Other than you…"

"He's open about his feelings, but sometimes I have to prod him. What was he like, during the war?"

"That one? Hah, don't you ever tell him I said this, but his nickname was Captain Ice. Not his public nickname, we never came up with anything better than Bimmy. But his private nickname, he earned it."

"I don't understand."

"He can be ice cold, especially when the chips are down. He has no trouble with tough decisions, and I've never seen anyone as calm under pressure as him. The stuff at the beach, he was out of control, scary, it kinda has me worried."

"I'm sure it would scare anyone. But you get it, right? When Bimmy cares about someone, he cares with intensity."

"Yeah, I understand, I've seen his commitment firsthand, but never, you know, so…out in the open."

"When Earth was attacked, I was trapped in a bomb shelter for days, they told us it was eight days. The power died on day four. Everyone thought we were dead, but my best friend, Naomi, she figured out how to get a message out. Bimmy told me later he was ready to resign his commission and come back to Earth to look for me. Completely impractical, a little crazy, maybe."

"But, wow, romantic," Blake said. "How did you get a message out if you had no power?"

"Naomi found the main exhaust vent for the shelter. She set a fire inside it."

"That's insane."

"We did the calculus, the odds were against us if we didn't act, we had to do something. She lit the fire, the smoke made it out, two days later a crew dug us out."

"You and Bimmy were made for each other."

"I like to think so. Explain this private nickname thing. Some kind of codeword?"

"Sort of. Think about this, in Space Force you never knew when you might get transferred or get a new commanding officer. The cadre, all us officers, even the senior NCOs, we'd come up with a nickname for our commanding officers. For us to know, not them, hence the private part. The enlisted crew had their own nicknames for officers, I never heard any of 'em. It gave us a way to communicate what sort of person we were dealing with, without writing a book about them. Simple, direct, a sort of label for the package. For example, Admiral Porter, his was Lord Plush Bottom. He was an okay commanding officer, mostly left anyone below his direct reports alone. He was tolerable until he started committing war crimes, but he was…what would you call someone who thinks only officers are worth their time, only people of a certain sort mattered, and everyone else was a bunch of objects to get used up and tossed away when you were done with them?"

"Elitist, snob, rude, manipulative, cruel, lots of words come to mind, I'm not sure if any of them would be accurate, I didn't know him."

"Exactly," Blake said, "but you hear 'Lord Plush Bottom' and…"

"You get a picture of the man. I get it, it makes sense. Who came up with Captain Ice?"

"It started with me. I called him Charlie Cool, as a joke, the opposite of what I thought when we first met, but it didn't last. When we got bushwhacked by the pirate fleet and Bimmy saved the day, he became Charlie Ice. The captain part, you know, came later. At first it came down to him surviving a total inferno when the bridge of the *Arcturus* exploded. He might as well have been an ice cube in a volcano, but somehow, he survived. Be glad you didn't see it, the place was cooked top to bottom, bodies all over the place, the captain dead right in front of him, body parts everywhere, it was Gruesome with a capital 'G'…"

Becca stood and walked away. She recalled the long comm silence when Bimmy was injured, not knowing where he was, her fear he'd been killed, followed by her constant worry when he turned up on a hospital ship. He'd never shared details of what happened, and she'd never asked for them, even after seeing the graft scars around his back, the lone physical remnant of his burns. She fought back her tears at the thought of him in pain, suffering, and her own helplessness. The memories threatened to overwhelm her.

"Oh, hey, Becca, I'm…" Blake followed her, leaving behind their harvest. "Becca, I'm sorry, I'm an idiot, I'm supposed to be getting better at this. Please," she took Becca's hand to stop her, "listen to me, I'm sorry, I wasn't thinking. Please…"

Becca wiped away her tears before turning to face Blake. She considered Blake's facial expression - serious, concerned, earnest, no hint of guile, then asked "Do you love him? Does he love you?"

"What? Of course not…well, I mean, you get close to the people you serve with, I suppose you do love each other. It could easily become hate. It's more like brother and sister. Unless you're Breuger and Jones, but they're the exception, not the rule. I never…it would never occur to me to have any physical or, you know, romantic feelings for Bimmy. But, yeah, I do love him, in a different way. Am I making sense? Please tell me I'm making sense. For the record, Bimmy is not my type, not even close."

"What's wrong with Charlie Bimmy?" Becca asked. Blake's look of shock and confusion amused Becca and took her mind off her memories. It was what she was hoping for, a way to move beyond her own darker feelings, to put the conversation behind them. Becca wagged her finger at Blake. "Gotcha," she said.

"That's...you're..." Blake stumbled, "you're evil, not nice at all. Who knew under that pretty face there was this demon hiding in plain sight?"

"Yeah," Becca said, "who knew?"

***

I was fascinated by the hologram and wondered how such a small device could produce such an energy-intensive display. The fact it was human, and male, and dressed in what looked like a uniform, though the insignia was too small to make out. All of it was captivating. Yet no matter how I held the device or interacted with it, the man didn't react. He stood still, arms crossed over his chest, smiling and staring at me, unblinking and unmoving. Despite my concerns about the nanobots, this was a situation where some insight from them would be helpful, but there was no insight, no feedback, nothing.

I was seated, looking down at the device in my hand, when the door to the chamber opened and the new version of Reggie left the enclosure and stood in front of me, looking down with a smile from ear to ear.

I smiled back at him and stood up. "Welcome back. How do you feel?"

"Hungry, thirsty, I feel I might be a few pounds lighter, I feel great. Do I look okay?"

I pointed at the control panel, its dark surface the closest thing to a mirror in the room. "See for yourself."

When he saw his reflection, he stopped smiling and slid his hand over his smooth face, where hours earlier there had been a day's growth of beard. He ran his hand through his hair, still the same color, but thicker and longer. He looked at his left hand and said, "The scar is gone.... did your scars go away?"

"No."

"And you stayed the same, no rollback of the clock?"

"You can see for yourself."

He stared at his reflection a little longer, then turned around to face me, smiling again.

"Try putting it on," he said, pointing at the device in my hand.

"This is the least interesting thing in the room," I said. "This machine took twenty years off your life…"

"More like fifteen, maybe ten, but who's counting?"

"It's a number, my point is, every time we think we have something figured out, something new pops up. Why make a system like this? Why didn't the rest of us have the same experience? There are way more questions than answers."

"Where are Becca and Blake? I assume they know about this."

"On their way to the spaceport. They know about you, but not about these devices," I said. "What say we catch up to them?"

"Is there food at the spaceport? I'm starving."

"We can grab something along the way. Fair warning, Becca will probably want a blood sample from you, and she's still honing her technique."

"If that's the worst thing that happens to me today, I'm good with it."

"The day's not over. Don't jinx us."

8

A Few Answers

We were entering the park on our way to the spaceport after a detour to retrieve Reggie's plasma rifle. I'd taken one of the bottles from the cabinet, cleaned it out, then filled it at the fountain. We'd grabbed some food in the nearest garden, and Reggie was happily chomping on a piece of fruit and swigging water as we walked, his rifle slung over his shoulder.

"You should go through the tank too," Reggie said, "I feel like I'm eighteen all over again."

"No thanks," I said, "the way my luck's been running I'd end up being thirteen again."

"What's wrong with thirteen?"

"More than I care to say," I replied.

There was a lightness to his step I'd never seen before, a sparkle in his eyes, absent when we first met. His happiness was infectious and I found myself feeling gratitude for his presence, and a renewed sense of hope for the future. I couldn't help but wonder if it was all too good to be true.

Reggie pointed at the dome in the center of the park, "What's that?"

"Don't know, but it invited us to have a seat once. We think it may be some sort of theater."

"It invited you?"

"Yup, come on, I'll show you."

We passed under an arched opening with a glowing blue light at its peak. As before, lights in the floor traced a path to two adjacent seats in the interior.

"You gotta be kidding me," Reggie said, "you get *this* and you don't stick around to see what happens? Let's try it."

Before I could reply, he moved sideways to take a seat. The butt of his rifle collided with the seatback and slipped off his shoulder. It clattered to the floor, activating the charging bolt. In seconds, the path lights went out and doors descended over all the openings. The rifle began to vibrate, rattling and shimmying across the floor, before dissolving into a scattering of fine dust, which also soon faded away.

We stared at the empty spot where the rifle had been, then exchanged a dumbfounded look.

"This could be good, this could be bad," Reggie said.

"It might explain why we haven't found any weapons in the city."

"If we do find one," Reggie said, "I'll try not to drop it."

"Good idea."

A few minutes passed before a low tone sounded, the deep note of a bell tolling. The door we'd entered through began to rise back into the upper wall. As the opening grew, I could see two pairs of legs on the opposite side, casting shadows into the interior. I assumed it was Becca and Blake coming to find us.

Instead, the rising door revealed two individuals, similar in appearance to the hologram we'd met earlier, only these wore uniforms.

And they were *armed*.

***

 Becca and Blake sat in the first-floor lobby of the tower at the center of the spaceport.

"It's getting late, they should have been here by now," Becca said.

"What if Reggie hasn't woken up?"

"It's possible, or he did and they got distracted…"

"By what?" Blake asked, "A big ol' empty alien city?"

Becca forced a laugh, which failed to ease her concern. "We've got a couple hours of daylight left. We should postpone the tour and head back before it gets dark."

They retraced their steps toward the park and the welcome center.

"Have you been out after sunset before?"

"Yes, but we stick close to where we live. We've never seen anything unusual but…"

"You play it safe."

"Yes, normally. The time of day might alter our ability to get in and out of some of the buildings. I don't want to spend the night in the welcome center, or out in the open, if I can avoid it."

"Too spooky?"

"Too uncomfortable," Becca said. "You think the welcome center is nice, wait until you see where we live."

As they stepped out of the tunnel and into the open plaza, Blake grabbed Becca's arm and pulled her back into the tunnel.

"Look!" Blake said, pointing at four people on the far side of the plaza, beyond the domed structure at its center. Their backs were to Blake and Becca, but there was no mistaking Bimmy and Reggie, flanked by two armed and uniformed figures, walking away from the dome.

***

"Well, isn't this a pickle," I said.

"A what? Where do you get…forget it," Reggie said, "let's go see what they want."

"I'm pretty sure it's about your rifle."

"Ya think? Come on, looks like they want us up there."

"It could mean stay where you are."

Reggie started climbing the stairs, "One way to find out."

"Maybe now we'll get some answers," I said, and followed him.

We reached the top and the two beings stepped back a few paces. They were tall and thin, with the same eyes and ears as the hologram, but they had no hair. Their features differed from the hologram somewhat, square jaws where the hologram had been curved, broad shoulders, they were clearly not human. Then I understood, it went further.

"Androids," I said.

"With weapons."

We stepped into the waning light of the day and one of the androids spoke.

"Citizens," it said, a slight crackle in its deep voice, "the Protectorate apologizes for interrupting your entertainment. Only Guardians are permitted to bear arms within the city. If you wish to hunt in the forest, an appropriate weapon will be provided."

"Do you understand them? I understand them. How is it I understand them?" Reggie asked.

"How should I know? It's the bots, that's as far as we've gotten."

"We are not from here," Reggie said, "can I have my rifle back?"

"Of course, Citizen," the first Guardian said, "a suitable facsimile of your weapon will be provided at the time of your departure."

"We're not in a position to leave," Reggie said.

"Our ship crashed in the forest. We've been…"

The two Guardians turned towards each other in a sudden move, then looked back at us.

"Do you require assistance?" the first Guardian asked.

"Yes, as a matter of fact, some assistance would be nice," I said.

"Are you injured?"

"No…but we have friends waiting for us at the spaceport. Two females, same species…"

"We will send Guardians to retrieve them."

"Not necessary, we'll find them later," Reggie said. He looked at me and I nodded my head in agreement. No need to involve Becca and Blake. If our situation turned violent, they'd at least be removed from it.

"We will escort you to the Auxiliary Protectorate Interface in sub-precinct seven. Come this way," the Guardian said. The two of them turned smartly around facing away from us and took one synchronized step forward, then turned to look back at us. We started walking and the androids took up a normal pace.

"May I ask some questions?" I asked.

"We are here to serve; your queries are welcome."

"Do you have names? What do we call you?"

"Yes. I am Guardian Lef, this is my companion, Guardian Soong. You may call us whatever you like."

"Lef and Soong, nice to meet you," Reggie said

"Lef, where are we?" I asked

"You are in Plaza Two, Hospitality District, Sector…"

"No, bigger picture, where are we? Let's start with the name of the system, then the planet, and work our way down from there."

Lef looked at me and I could have sworn he was annoyed by the question.

"The system…planet…"

Soong spoke for the first time, and his voice surprised me with its tone. Softer, more refined, not at all mechanical, with a lilt to it one might hear when a father answers questions from small child.

"As there is one city on the planet, there is no distinction between planet and city," he said, "and its name is Sumera. Some call this the Eternal City, in the vernacular of the people of Ki, your people, the ones who built it, as a gift to all the people of Gha'ba."

"That clears it up," Reggie said.

"I am glad to be of service," Soong said.

"What is the purpose of this place, this city?"

"Purpose? Sumera serves many purposes, can you narrow your query?"

When we rounded a second corner I heard a noise behind us. I looked back and caught a glimpse of Blake ducking behind a wall.

"Your companions are unable to keep pace with us," Lef said, "shall we wait for them?"

"No," Reggie said.

"Always the tactician," I muttered. "Soong, what I want to know is why did… my people…build this place?"

"A peace offering to all the people of Gha'ba," Soong said.

"Was there a war?" Reggie asked.

"Yes," Soong replied, "there were many wars. We have arrived." Soong pointed down a narrow avenue at a wide door set deep in the thick wall of a windowless building made of large blocks of stone.

"Another question," I said, "why aren't there other people here? Where is everyone?"

"I am curious about this as well," Soong said. The door opened and we entered the building, followed by the Guardians. "We will awaken the Magistrate, if you have more queries, the Magistrate will provide additional data."

We stepped into an open, empty space. The floor was rough stone, the walls the same stone but smooth and polished to a high gloss. There was no furniture, no equipment, no decoration, and all the charm of a prison cell.

***

"Armed guards," Becca said, "what do we do?"

"We follow them, we keep our distance and see where they go, but all we do is follow, see how it plays out. Come on, stay close to me."

Blake ran from the tunnel, angling to the right to put the dome between her and Becca and the guards. Becca followed Blake around the side of the dome until they could see the guards again. They watched until the group turned the corner of a building on the far side of the plaza.

"Let's go, let's go," Blake said and began running. She reached the corner, Becca breathing heavily behind her. She peeked around in time to see the four turn down an avenue to the left. She ran again and looked around the next corner. One last turn and they watched the group enter a building at the end of the avenue. There were no more turns heading up to the building, and nowhere to hide if they stepped around the corner.

"What now?" Becca said.

"We need to think this through."

"Reggie didn't have his plasma rifle," Becca said, "maybe we should go get it."

"You want to go blasting away, like some kind of alien jailbreak? Really? We don't know what we're up against but if there's two of them with weapons there's probably a bunch more of them where they came from, and I'm betting they came from the building they just walked into."

"Okay, you're right. What do we do?"

Blake peeked around the corner, then looked up at the sun dropping toward the rooftops. "Stay here," she said, "If I'm not back by dark, get someplace safe and wait it out."

"What are you talking about? Back from…you are not going in there, not without me."

"Yes, I am, somebody has to stay out here, in case we do actually need a jailbreak."

"Then it should be you, I'll go in, I don't know anything about plasma rifles."

"What's to know? You point, you pull the trigger, blam, blam, you got yourself a gunfight."

"Blake, no, I'll go in, you stay out here. This idea is crazy but my version is at least more logical."

Before Blake could stop her, Becca stepped around the corner and started walking toward the building. Blake looked around and thought about going back to the welcome center, but instead hurried to catch up with Becca.

"What are you doing, I thought we had a plan?" Becca said.

"We do…we did. We're in this together. You, me, Reggie, Bimmy, all of us. Besides, I'm kind of turned around. I don't think I can find my way back."

Becca stopped walking, "What? It's easy, a left, a right…no, it's right, then left, another right, cross the plaza, one more left, through… okay, yeah, it's a lot to ask."

Despite their circumstances, Blake started laughing, then stopped abruptly when the door to the building reopened.

***

A panel to my right slid away, revealing a dark passage. Lef and Soong entered the passage. Then Soong turned around to face Reggie and me. "It has been a pleasure to serve you," he said. "If you have need of a Guardian in the future, it is my wish to be awakened to assist you." Then the panel slid shut and they were gone.

A dot of white light appeared in the far wall, like a train coming down a long tunnel. The light expanded and became a spherical mass of swirling white dots, a meter in diameter. It made no sound until a voice, deep and melodic, said, "Children of Ki, how may I serve you?"

"Ummm…," I began, "We crashed our starship…"

"I am aware. Do you require a replacement vessel?"

"That would be nice," Reggie said with a grin.

"You are Children of Ki, the fleet is at your disposal. How else may I serve you?"

"We have questions…"

"Wait," Reggie said to me, "I want to ask for a few things."

"Like what?" I asked

"We lack provisions. Where can we get food, water, packs to carry our supplies? We want to explore the city. Do you have a quartermaster, a commissary, a supply depot?"

The sphere pulsed brighter, then a thin tendril of light shot out like a whip toward the device on Reggie's wrist, "Follow your guide, it will lead you where you wish to go."

"I have no idea how to use it…"

"Your guide is a standard org-synth interface."

"Truly helpful, thanks," Reggie said. "Can we come back here if we need anything else?"

"Only a Guardian may awaken a Magistrate. Follow your Guide, it will lead you where you wish to go. If you require a Guardian, inform your Guide."

"Yep, got it," Reggie said. "Okay Bimmy, you're up."

"You sure, you got all you want? You want to order a cake, some new shoes, tell a few jokes while you're at it?"

"Nah, I'm good, go for it."

"Magistrate," I said, "where are all the people? I asked Guardian Soong, but he…"

"The Children of N'aha are dead, the Children of Kern are dead, you are all that remains of the Children of Ki. This is not for the Guardians to know."

"Dead," I said, shocked. I looked at Reggie and he shrugged his shoulders.

"How did they all die?" Reggie asked.

"They were slain by the Children of Kern."

"Then who killed the Children of Kern?" I asked.

"Justice was delivered equally to all by the Protectorate."

"How?"

"This knowledge is not for a Magistrate. Follow your Guide to the Temple of Time, seek Tomrin the Wise, and you will be enlightened."

"Sounds like a book I read when I was a kid," I said to Reggie. "Magistrate, what is the purpose of this city? Guardian Soong said the Children of Ki built it as a peace offering, what did he mean?"

The light grew brighter and churned as if agitated. It soon returned to its original intensity and said, "Follow your Guide to the Temple of Time, seek Tomrin the Wise and you will be enlightened. My awakening has come to an end…"

"Wait, please, one more question," I said. "How long has it been since you or the Guardians were last awakened?"

The ball of light again grew brighter and spun around faster and faster until finally the voice said, "My purpose is to serve, but I cannot exceed my authority, this knowledge is forbidden. You must follow your guide…

"Yeah, yeah," Reggie said, "time temple, Tomrin the smart guy, got it…"

"Reggie, please, give me…"

"My awakening is ended," the voice said. The sphere of light stopped churning and twisting. It coalesced into a flat unmoving disc, faded until it was a small dot again, then blinked out. The door we'd entered opened behind us, and we turned to leave.

"You know, Reggie, sometimes a little more tact…"

"What do you know about tact?" he asked.

"More than you, apparently," I said. I pointed through the door at Becca and Blake standing outside. "Look who caught up."

We exited the building and Becca turned to face us.

"You are not gonna believe what happened to us," Reggie said.

"Oh, ya think? You're half the age you were this morning, two armed aliens let you go after you did who knows what, and I see you've got some fancy new accessories, what am I not gonna believe?" Blake said.

"We are the proud owners of our very own fleet of ships and," I said, pausing for dramatic effect, "we're going on a quest to find Tomrin the Wise."

Becca looked at Blake, then at Reggie, finally back at me.

"What did you do?" Becca asked.

"Define quest," Blake added.

9

Return to the Stars

"Let me get this straight," Blake said, "we're supposed to put these on, and a little genie pops out?"

"The Magistrate called it a Guide," Reggie said.

Blake waved her hand. "Whatever. It's a little person who grants our every wish while we're here in…what did you call it?"

"Sumera," Bimmy said, "the whole place. The planet, continent, city, all one name, Sumera."

"Right…"

"I think what Blake is getting at," Becca said, "is do we trust this artificial intelligence entity and the little genie person. Am I right?"

"Yeah, no, I definitely do not trust either of them, because I haven't seen one yet, what am I supposed to trust?"

"We didn't get a lot out of the Guardians, or the Magistrate," Reggie said. "If we want more answers, this is how we get them. We've had the guides on for a while and they haven't done us any harm. We need to figure out how to operate them, then how to exploit them. These devices may be the key to figuring all of this out."

"Remind me why we care about any of this?" Blake asked. "And why we're not already at the spaceport preparing to launch."

"For one," I said, "we don't have anywhere to go, not yet. And second, we need some time to figure out how to fly those birds. If this Tomrin being is a higher-level AI, I think finding him should be our next move."

"I'm with Blake on this one," Reggie said, "we might need one of those ships, and the circumstances may not allow a lot of lead time to learn how to fly them. I say we grow our wings before we need to fly."

"Hard to argue with your logic," Becca said. "As for destinations, there are three planets waiting for us. I took a look at the data from the *Katie*. The other planets we scanned have atmospheres similar to this one, the nitrogen level is a little low for humans on one of them, but..."

"We're not human anymore," Blake said, flashing a grin in my direction.

I thought about our situation and realized my desire to be back in space outweighed our need for more localized information, at least in the short term.

"Okay," I said, "spaceport it is, but I have one condition."

"Of course you do," Becca said, "name it."

"We stay away from Zombie Station. Last time didn't go well for us."

"That I can agree with," Becca replied.

Reggie glanced at me, then looked at Becca. "How 'bout we get settled in for the night and leave at first light?"

***

We gathered outside our residential tower at dawn. Becca had spent the evening experimenting with her Guide and had figured out the basics.

"It's mostly touch and motion to access functions," she said, tapping the device, "then voice commands to use those functions. Tap the lower left corner and swipe horizontally and the genie pops up..."

"You mean Guide," I said.

"I like genie better," Blake said.

"To each his, or her, own," Reggie said.

"Once the genie appears," Becca continued, activating the hologram, "you interact by voice, but you have to start with the word 'Guidance'..."

"It understands English, or interprets it," I said, "which is pretty amazing."

"The implications are interesting," Becca said. "It couldn't handle every word I used. But it understood most, which makes me think there's some sort of common translation protocol between our nanobots and the devices. Keep it basic at first, see if we can apply more complex phrases later. A couple of important tricks, tap with three fingers and you get a map of your immediate surroundings, touch and hold with three fingers and ..."

Three small holographic heads appeared over Becca's device, one for each of us.

"We have comms," Becca said, and tapped my image.

The device on my wrist vibrated, then a hologram of Becca appeared over my wrist and a hologram of me over hers. When she spoke, the hologram repeated her words. When she gestured with her hands, the hologram did a reasonable job of keeping up with her movement. It wasn't perfect, but it was good enough to be useful.

"Can you contact all of us at the same time? Is there a conference mode or something?" Reggie asked.

"Let's try," Becca replied, "maybe if I tap and hold again...and there it is."

Becca's method opened a connection between all of us.

Becca tapped the device again, closing the connection. "If we're separated again, we can stay in touch."

"But we're not splitting up again, right?" Blake asked. "Doesn't seem necessary, you know, we're all going on this adventure together."

"Correct," Reggie said, "but it was luck you saw us when you did last night. This takes some of the risk out of the situation if we have to split up. Great work Becca."

"Thanks, I'll show you more along the way. Should we get started?"

"As long as the first order of business is food." Blake started walking in the direction of the spaceport. "I ate my last apple-thingy-whatever yesterday and I'm in dire need of calories."

We stopped in the gardens to eat and collect food to take with us, assuming there'd be nothing edible on the ships.

The transparent dome adjacent to the spaceport's main tower was filled with light from the fully risen sun, which also bathed the tarmac and ships in a warm glow. I stared up at them, all identical from the outside. They appeared to be roughly fifty times larger than the *Katie*. Unlike the *Katie*, their configuration was similar to a Federation battle cruiser, with thrusters beneath the main horizontal axis, as well as aft, although nothing like a battle cruiser had ever landed on a planet in the Sol Federation. I tried to calculate how much thrust the engines would need in order to take such a large ship to orbit, but I couldn't scale the numbers without knowing more about the ship. None of my rough estimates seemed practical, or even possible.

"Which one do you want, captain?" Reggie asked.

"I'm not the captain anymore, one of you take charge, I'll be on tactical."

"No sir," Blake said, "you're the captain. We've never lost a fight with you at the helm."

"We've come close," I said, "and I crashed our last ship, remember?"

"And we're still alive," Becca said, "because it wasn't a crash, it was hard landing."

I laughed, but no one laughed with me.

"You are our captain," Reggie said, "I wouldn't want it any other way. You defeated Cheng multiple times, defeated the rebels, captured Mercury..."

"You saved the fleet from a trap, you backed Rudnev down over Europa, and took on a battle cruiser without much more than a bad attitude," Blake said.

"You took a dead ship and used it to keep us alive," Becca added. "Your experience makes you the right man for the job."

Blake and Reggie came to attention and saluted, "Waiting for your orders Captain Bimmy," Blake said.

Becca looked at them, then me, "No, uh-uh, I don't do salutes."

I came to attention and returned their salute, then turned back to the three spacecraft. I pointed at the one Becca and I had visited and said, "This one is ours; I've already bled for it."

"All right then," Blake said, with a grin, "let's go light our purty little candle."

We rode the lift through the center of the tower to the boarding level and entered the ship through the gantry connected to its bow. We took another lift near midship up to the command deck. We headed forward to the bridge down a wide central corridor that ran parallel to the ship's keel for much of the length of the ship. Doors and smaller corridors were arranged at even intervals along each side of the main passage.

We reached the end of the corridor and the wall facing us slid aside, revealing the bridge. We walked in and took a few moments to puzzle out its configuration.

As I looked at each of the twelve operational stations on the bridge, their purpose came to me...tactical, communications, engineering. The same was happening for everyone.

Flight ops was located in the center of the bridge on a raised section of deck. Blake continued forward, "That would be me. It's gonna take some time to get used to this just-in-time info business."

"I don't like the idea of learning these systems as we go," Reggie added, "I need to understand them in advance, before I need to use them." He sat down at the tactical station and waved his hand over the smooth surface in front of him. A three-dimensional array of the ship's weapon systems rose up from the surface. Reggie ignored the rest of us and started exploring the holographic menu.

Becca made herself comfortable at the nav station and before long all three of them were becoming familiar with the ship's operation. With no obvious captain's station, I took position standing behind Blake at flight ops.

That's when the ship came to life.

Each station and system lit up and reported in, one by one.

"Communications, active," the ship said in a deep rumbling voice, "navigation, active, engineering, active," and on down the line.

Blake scanned the bridge, then looked over her shoulder at me. "What did you touch?"

"Nothing, I stood here and all the lights came on."

"Captain," the ship said, "all systems are active."

"Uhh, okay," I said, "and what is the name of this ship?"

"I was designated *Vali'maim'a Mulosoia* by the shipwrights of Ki. Would you like to alter my designation?"

"Yes," my crew answered in unison.

"Now we have to come up with a name," I said. "Any suggestions?"

"I got nothin' and I don't much care. So long as I can pronounce it, call it what you want," Blake said.

"Reggie," I said, "thoughts?"

"I'm busy, you and Becca come up with something," he said, without turning away from the weapons interface.

"There's nothing wrong with Katie," Becca said when I looked at her for an answer.

"With that voice? Bad idea."

"Katie isn't exactly a dainty lapdog…"

Blake started laughing, followed by Becca, while Reggie stayed focused.

I had to stifle my own laughter before I said, "Ship, your designation is now *Katie*."

"Acknowledged. What are our mission parameters?"

"What is the designation of the station orbiting this planet?"

"That vessel is designated *Talall Four*."

"Why four? We saw one in orbit."

"A Talall was constructed for each of the four inner worlds of the Gha'ba system."

Reggie swung around in his seat, "How many stations remain operational?"

When the computer didn't respond, Becca looked at Reggie and said, "Try saying her name first."

"Her? What…all right…Katie, how many of the four Talalls are operational?"

"Talalls One and Four are currently operational, however, I am unable to establish a communication link with either station."

Reggie looked at me, his eyes wide, a toothy grin on his face, "Looks like we've got ourselves a destination."

"Let's see if we can get to orbit first," I replied, "Blake, think you can fly the ship?"

"Heck no, I don't think I can, I know I can," Blake replied.

"Fuel status?"

"Based on these readings I'd say we're ready to fly."

"Then let's get going, take us up."

Blake swept her hand over her control panel. "Roger that, here goes nothin'."

A hologram of the ship appeared in the air a short distance in front of her station. She moved her right hand over a section of her console and the gantry retracted into the ship, then the hatch closed behind. Blake lifted her left hand and a blue cylinder of light rose up under it, growing by millimeters as the ship's engines came to life. She moved her hand higher and the superstructure of the ship began to shake and groan.

"Easy Blake," I said, "don't break the boat on our first voyage, this ship hasn't been up in a long time."

"This is takin' it easy, give me the green light and I'll launch us like…"

"Captain," the ship said, "would you like me to deactivate the terminal shield."

"Yes, Katie," I said, "please deactivate the terminal shield before we hit it."

"Sorry, forgot about the shield," Blake said.

"We both did, focus on your controls."

"Terminal shield deactivated," Katie said. "Would you like me to release the docking clamps?"

"Yes," I said, "release the docking clamps. Are there any other preflight steps we've missed?"

"I recommend activating inertial dampeners prior to a high-velocity launch such as the one you are attempting. Would you like me to activate inertial dampeners?"

"Yes, Katie, activate inertial dampeners. Do we have artificial gravity systems?"

"Gravity systems are automated and will engage once we have reached a micro-gravity state. We are ready for orbital acceleration, releasing docking clamps."

The clamps released and the ship shot directly up, tearing through the sky like a bullet from a gun. The inertial dampeners were all that kept us from being crushed by our ignorance of the ship's operation.

"Whooooo hooo," Blake shouted, "this baby's got some heat!"

Blake transitioned the ship from its horizontal landing configuration into an angular trajectory. We were blasting through the atmosphere fast enough to heat the ship's exterior. Our extreme acceleration told me our engines, and their fuel, were extraordinarily powerful. My early calculations started to make sense.

"Bimmy," Reggie said, "if the weapons are half as powerful as the engines, I'd say we've got quite the ship on our hands."

"Correction Reggie, we have three of them," I said.

The city and continent dropped away and the darkness of space loomed ahead. Our acceleration decreased and Blake rolled the ship, placing the planet beneath our feet, then brought us into a level plane as we moved away from Sumera. I felt a brief moment of weightlessness, followed by the familiar tug of artificial gravity, and the intense thrill of being in space again. I stared with renewed awe at the stars shining before me, billions of glittering diamonds tossed across an endless sheet of black velvet.

"Becca, can you show us the current planetary alignment," I asked.

"Give me a sec…yeah, got it, look at this," Becca said.

The hologram of the ship vanished and the four planets appeared, moving in their relative orbits around Luyten's Star.

"I like this ship more every second," I said. "Katie, display the location of *Talall One*, and label each planet with its name."

The hologram shifted ninety degrees, giving us a kind of 'overhead' view of the system. The outer gas giants appeared, then faded away.

The inner rocky worlds moved through their orbits, each with a label. Two of them, Kern and N'aha, were closer to one another than to us, while the fourth and largest planet, Ki, was a significant distance away. An icon representing *Talall One* appeared orbiting Ki.

"Becca, when can we expect the full conjunction? Ki looks like a longer trip than I was expecting us to take today."

"I did the calculations last night, but I can't be precise without more data. Best guess is another three years."

"Three years," Blake said, "we can fly to every one of these planets in three years, a whole bunch of times. Are we gonna sit around and wait…"

"Three years by Sumera's clock," Becca said, "about two months, Earth time."

"Oh, well, then, never mind," Blake said. "But then again, this ship could…Katie, how long would it take to fly to Ki?"

"The planet Ki," the ship began, "is two-point-two kazeks from our current location. Using standard propulsion, the journey would take one hundred and eighteen cycles."

"What's a kazek?" Blake said.

"We have more than one type of propulsion?" Reggie asked.

"What's a cycle?" I added.

"A kazek is a unit of measure equivalent to the average distance between the planet Ki and the Gha'ba Aszan."

"It's like I get a riddle instead of an answer every time I ask a question," Blake said.

"I imagine it's similar to an astronomical unit in Sol," Becca said, "the distance between Earth and Sol. Based on the data we gathered from orbit, Ki is less than 30 million kilometers from its star, which means it's about 60 million kilometers from us, which would mean our maximum speed is roughly five hundred thousand kilometers per hour, if we treat a cycle as a day, which on Sumera is 23.69 hours."

"Thanks for the lecture, Professor Becca, but you can't be right," Blake said, "no ship is that fast."

"Katie," I said, "based on the equivalent values Becca has stated, can you convert speed and distance to kilometers and hours?"

"Yes Captain. Based on the values and the nomenclature provided by the navigation officer designated Becca, I can concur. Our maximum speed, using standard propulsion, is 482,803 kilometers per hour."

"I was close," Becca said.

"Show off," Blake replied.

"It's math, not magic."

"You are all missing the point," Reggie said. "How many forms of propulsion do we have? And is there a faster one than 'standard'?"

"All you have to do is ask," I said.

"We need some kind of protocol for this.... Katie," Reggie said, "how many forms of propulsion does this ship have, and which is the fastest?"

"I am equipped with maneuvering thrusters, orbital insertion thrusters, landing thrusters, standard planetary transit propulsion and a sixth-generation Kelton drive. Kelton drives, by virtue of their ability to simultaneously contract and expand spacetime, are the fastest form of space travel yet devised."

"How fast?"

"Using your nomenclature and measurement, I cannot provide this value without knowing the term for the shortest whole unit of time measurement in an hour."

"That would be one second," Reggie said, "there are sixty seconds in a minute, sixty minutes in an hour."

"This is a curious form of measurement. Please standby... calculating...utilizing this new data and your standards of measurement, a Kelton drive is capable of propelling the ship at a speed of 281,682 kilometers per second."

"What?" Blake exclaimed.

"We have a warp drive," Becca said.

"If your smile gets any bigger, your face is gonna break," I said.

"Becca, work your magic, how long to get to Ki with a warp drive?" Reggie asked.

"That's easy, under four minutes."

I leaned back on the railing and considered the implications of a warp-capable ship. "Looks like we're going to Ki after all," I said.

"Hold on," Becca said, "the warp drive concept was abandoned by Earth scientists for a long list of reasons, including the amount of energy it would take to power one. We may have a drive, but how much fuel do we have to power it? How long will it run?"

"Katie," I said, "how much energy do we have to power the Kelton drive? How long can it operate before depleting its fuel?"

"The Kelton drive is capable of continuous operation for a maximum of one hour and forty-two seconds, by your measurement."

"Well then," Becca said, "Bimmy's right. We're going to Ki."

10

Ki and Prophecy

After a few test-runs around Sumera to familiarize ourselves with more of the ship's systems, we set our destination for Ki. What we discovered there was both intriguing and disturbing.

"From up here it looks like Earth," Blake said, "but a lot bigger."

"Sumera is three times the size of Earth," Becca said, "and Ki is about twice the size of Sumera."

"That's a big rock all right. Atmosphere?" I asked.

"It looks nice," Becca said, "blue skies, clouds, ocean, land, everything you'd expect, but I can't make sense of these readings."

"Remember, they released all sorts of nanobots down there…"

"That's not the issue," she said, "it's the names of the elements in the data. They're not translating. They might as well say seventy-eight percent 'Joe' and twenty-two percent 'Suzy.' I'll need to see molecular structures to build a translation table."

"Katie," I said, "is the atmosphere on Ki safe for us to breathe?"

"Yes captain, the atmosphere on Ki is safe for all citizens of Ki as well as all members of the Triad."

"I don't know Bimmy," Blake said, "I'm not sure I trust it."

"I don't blame you," I replied. "Take us in for a close-up with *Talall One.*"

"Roger that."

Things started to heat up on our approach to the station.

"It looks perfect," Becca said, "but it's in geosynchronous orbit. Why would the station over Sumera have an eccentric orbit and this one is parked?"

"The damage," Reggie said, "if it was knocked out of orbit, then all it's been doing is maintaining best-possible configuration. That's how the stations over Earth are designed, a failsafe protocol."

"Katie," I said, "are you able to make contact with *Talall One*?"

"Negative, captain. However, I am receiving an automated message. Would you like me to display the message?"

"Yes."

A hologram appeared, a human male, and delivered a warning.

"…this station has been declared off-limits. Any attempt to board this facility will be deemed a violation of the Hehzan Accords and may result in the destruction of your ship. Unknown vessel, this station has been declared off-limits. Any attempt to board this facility will be deemed a violation of the Hehzan Accords and may result in the destruction of your ship. Unknown vessel…"

"Katie, shut it down. We've heard enough."

"Yes, captain."

"Bimmy," Reggie said, "I'm picking up energy signals, high-frequency comms traffic, all sorts of EM signatures down there, but I don't see any large-scale defensive systems, not on the planet or the station, not anything that could threaten this ship."

"You have visual on anything? Cities, military installations…"

"Working on it, but we need to get closer."

"Katie, what are the Hehzan Accords?"

"I am unfamiliar with this term."

"Can *Talall One* destroy this ship?"

"I have scanned *Talall One* for offensive weapons and found none. However, the station is equipped with a self-destruct mechanism with significant capacity to inflict damage."

"Katie, is there a spaceport on Ki big enough for us to land this ship?" Blake asked.

"My records indicate I was launched from a facility on the planet, but I am unable to establish contact with that facility."

"How about a fly-by?" Blake asked.

"Good idea," I said. "Katie, transfer coordinates to flight operations."

"I got 'em," Blake said, then altered our course.

We passed from the day side of the planet to the night and could see lights gathered in groups along the coastline of a large continent. Cities, some large, some barely visible, dotted the planet's surface. The larger groupings were connected by streams of light.

"Somebody's down there," I said, "any contact, any response to hails?"

"Nothing yet," Becca said, "scanning alternate frequencies."

"Approaching coordinates," Blake said, "want me to take us down?"

"Might as well," I said.

We entered the atmosphere, setting the hull of the ship aglow, then made a wide turn toward our destination. We passed over an open plain and dropped to an altitude which enabled us to make out some of the larger lit-up buildings in the city we were approaching.

"Too low, Blake, give us some altitude. We don't want to scare the locals."

"Too late, incoming," Reggie shouted, "two missiles, on our flank!"

"Evasive, Blake, get us out of here."

"Brace for impact," Reggie shouted.

The missiles struck us aft at nearly the same moment. The explosions shook the ship, our lights flickered, but we continued to gain altitude.

"Katie, why didn't you warn us," I said.

"My sensors did not detect the weapons. I cannot explain this anomaly."

"Getting hit with missiles is not an anomaly," Blake yelled.

"Damage report," I said.

"Reactive hull plating has been depleted in sectors nine-four and nine-five and is functioning at forty percent capacity."

"Reggie, report," I said.

"Those missiles, they came out of nowhere," Reggie said. "Must be air-to-air, I didn't see anything launch from the surface."

"Are we being pursued?"

"Not by anything our sensors can detect."

"Blake, put us in orbit, directly over the city. Becca, any luck on comms."

"I'm in the higher end of the frequency range and I'm getting lots of noise, but nothing I can discern as directed at…wait…got something. I'm receiving…it's audio only, putting it through."

"…state your intent. Your presence is a direct violation of the Hehzan Accords. I repeat, alien vessel, identify yourself and state your intent. If you enter our airspace again, we will destroy you."

"Can we reply to this?"

"I don't know."

"Katie, can you configure our system to transmit back to the source of this message?"

"Please stand by."

"I thought they built this ship," Blake said, "how is it alien to them?"

"We don't know when they built it," Reggie said. "They don't seem to be space-faring anymore. Maybe they've forgotten their history, or they're in some kind of technological dark age."

"A connection has been established, you may transmit when ready."

"This is Captain Charles Bimmy, my apologies if our presence has alarmed you. We mean you no harm. We are on a mission of discovery and have no hostile intent. Do not fire on our ship again…"

"Alien vessel, we are receiving your transmission but do not recognize your language. Our first salvo was a warning, you must maintain your current position our we will be forced to fire on your ship again."

"This makes no sense."

"Yes, I think it does," Becca said. "This is a first-contact scenario. We can't know why they don't recognize the ship, but we know they have no context for understanding our language. We understand because we've been connected to adaptive systems, but not people."

"Katie, can you translate my message and resend?"

"Affirmative."

"Wait," Becca said, "Katie's voice is not one I'd like to hear coming from an alien ship over my city. Too menacing. Katie, can you modify the tonal quality of your audio output?"

"I am capable of unlimited variations."

"Good call," I said, "Katie, alter output, something similar to Becca's voice."

Becca shot me a look of disapproval.

"What? You have a nice voice, and we don't have time to experiment."

"I don't like it; you realize you'll be talking to them in my voice. It could be very confusing if we have a face-to-face meeting."

"I like it," Blake chimed in, "I think you have a downright sultry tone. People down there are gonna love it."

"We'll cross that bridge if we get there. Katie, transmit message."

"Message delivered."

"Captain Bimmy, we're reading you. Who are you and what are you doing in our airspace? The presence of orbital ships is unlawful under the Hehzan Accords..."

"We are unfamiliar with the Hehzan Accords. I'm sure you understand, we are not from this system."

"Ignorance of the law is not a defense...not from this system? Where are you from and why are you here? The military is on full alert. You've caused a global panic..."

"Again, sir...who am I talking to?"

"My name is General Reban Pileser, of the Republic of Envar, I report directly to the Imperium..."

"Good," I said, "then let me repeat, we have no hostile intent. We are here seeking information, nothing more."

"What information?"

"Our ship was built on this planet. We were hoping to learn more about its origins and the people who built it."

"You said you were not from this system..."

"Yes, I did, but we live here now. We came here from Earth, a planet in the Sol system, thirteen lightyears away. Our ship crashed on Sumera and..."

"Sumera? Sumera was destroyed centuries ago, there is no Sumera."

"If it was destroyed, it's been rebuilt, we call it home. That's where we got this ship, and this ship led us to you."

The General didn't reply, but instead started conferring with someone else. Their conversation was too low to be understood. When he eventually spoke to us again, he caught me off guard with his question.

"Captain Bimmy, do you have a landing craft aboard your ship?"

"We can land the ship..."

"No, do not attempt a landing. Under no circumstances are you to reenter the atmosphere. If you do, we will destroy your ship, are we clear?"

"We are not clear," I said, "why do you want know if we have..."

"The Imperium would like to meet you. He has authorized a one-time exception to the Hehzan Accords, under article fifteen, subsection twelve, regarding interstellar travel. If you have a lander, you, and you alone, are invited to meet him. Do not land in force or we will respond in kind."

"Don't do it," Becca said, "it's too dangerous."

"I have to agree," Reggie said, "you against an entire world, they've already been less than welcoming, not worth the risk."

"Blake, what do you think?"

"I say go for it. We can always come down there guns blazing to get you back."

"What kind of advice is that?" Becca said.

"It's reverse psychology," I said, "isn't it?"

"Yeah, you caught me, but I had to try. I say it's a no go on the meet and greet."

"My gut tells me to go. Becca said it, these are the first people we've come across. If they think we're aliens, and we are aliens, let's not forget, then it makes sense they'd be afraid. A ship like this swooping down on Earth wouldn't get a warm welcome either."

"You're not much of a pilot," Blake said, "just this morning you were bragging about crashing your last ship."

"Katie, do we have autonomous landing craft on board?"

"Four trans-orbital shuttles are located in launch bay eight. Would you like me to prepare one for you?"

"Yes," I said.

"This is a terrible idea," Becca said, "I'd say your worst."

She turned her back to me and stared at the surface of her console. I didn't want her to be angry at me, but I felt certain I had to make the journey, to learn as much as I could, before we returned to Sumera. I placed my hand on her shoulder and she placed her hand over mine. She looked up at me, her face resolute.

"I can accept your decision," she said, "without agreeing with it."

"General Pileser," I said, "what assurances do I have this will be a peaceful meeting and I'll be able to return to my ship unharmed?"

"You said you had no hostile intent and expect us to accept your statement as truth. I ask you to return the same courtesy."

"Fair enough, where would you like me to land?"

"There is a military base outside the city you flew over, with an operational landing field. We'll set up a beacon on this frequency, you can follow it down to the site. We will meet you there at dawn."

"Dawn it is, Bimmy out."

"When is dawn," Reggie asked.

"I was hoping you would know," I said, looking back at Becca.

"Based on the rotational speed of the planet and the source location of the transmission, I'd say it's about ten hours until dawn on the surface. From this orbit, you'll need an hour to make your descent and landing. You've got a little time to kill."

"Good, let's spend it coming up with a plan."

***

The ride down to the surface revealed what we had not seen during our nighttime flyover. For all the well-lit cities we'd seen, there were many more in ruins. Crumbling urban centers and collapsing infrastructure scarred the surface. The military base appeared to be of recent construction, as did the nearby city, but around both of them the land was a picture of destruction and decay. The current civilization appeared content to build itself amidst the bones of the previous.

My shuttle followed the signal to a landing strip at the base. We had debated the need for me to wear a pressure suit, but the argument was settled when we couldn't find any on the ship. Despite Katie's assurances, I was nervous and held my breath when the hatch opened.

I stepped onto the empty tarmac, exhaled, took a deep breath. The air was breathable, but unlike the cool crisp air of Sumera, Ki's air was warm and damp. It felt oppressive, and tasted of something chemical and burnt. But it wasn't killing me. "So far, so good," I said aloud.

I don't know what exactly I expected, but I didn't expect to be alone. The landing field was bordered on one side by an expansive field of tall brown grass, waving in the slight breeze. Beyond the field, the jagged skyline of a ruined city formed a bleak horizon. The nearer side of the tarmac was bordered by a series of buildings of varying sizes. Unlike military bases on Earth, there was no uniformity to the place. It was haphazard, as if cobbled together from spare parts over the years, built with materials scavenged from the ruins all around, as time, need, and resources permitted. It did not give an indication of a people who had the capability to build anything akin to Sumera. Whatever greatness they had achieved, their technological zenith was well behind them.

At the center of the collection of structures stood the largest of the buildings, a hangar. Its massive doors began to roll apart, but I couldn't see inside. A person, dwarfed by the moving panels, walked between them and toward me, a human male wearing a uniform. Black shoes, blue trousers, a long white tunic, and a blue scarf adorned with a silver band wrapped around his head and face. He was followed by three men in similar uniforms, but their scarves were red, and each carried rifles held at the ready. I was surprised to realize they were not energy weapons.

I began walking toward the officer and his guard until we met halfway between my shuttle and the building behind them. We stopped and, unsure what to do, I stuck out my hand. "I'm Captain Charles Bimmy," I said, "I assume you're General Pileser."

The General pulled the scarf away from his face and let it drop over his shoulder, revealing his confusion, "I don't understand you…and your voice…"

"Ah," I said, "I forgot to…" I raised my arm to activate my Guide to translate for me, which surprised the soldiers, who reacted by aiming their weapons at my head. I held up my hands, palms out. I pointed at my mouth, then the guide, then my ear, and finally the General. He understood and motioned for his soldiers to lower their weapons.

Once they were no longer aiming at me, I activated my device and my guide appeared, "Translation," I said.

"Translator activated," the guide said, then vanished, leaving a tiny blue light glowing on the screen.

I repeated my greeting, "Hello," I said, "I am Captain Charles Bimmy. The voice you heard before was our ship's translation. You must be General Pileser. I apologize for failing to activate my translator. This is a new experience for me."

"For you? It is not as if it happens every day here. Why are you holding out your hand?"

"It is a form of greeting," I said, "we clasp hands and shake, it's how we begin on a cordial note."

The General tipped his head to one side, grinned briefly, and grasped my hand. We shook and he said, "Welcome to Envar, Captain Bimmy. I hope you can explain to me how an alien, who looks exactly like my people, and can breathe our air, has ended up on my planet."

"And I hope an alien, who looks exactly like my people, can help me understand precisely these things, and more."

"Hmm," he said, "we will see. The Imperium is anxious to meet you. Please, this way," he said, waving his hand toward the open hangar doors.

We began walking at a leisurely pace. He was in no hurry, in spite of the comment about his leader. I was content with the slower step; it provided an opportunity for us to size each other up.

"Tell me, Captain Bimmy, how are things on Sumera? We understand the ecosystem is alive and well, but the remains of the city were long ago consumed by the forest."

"We live in the city," I said, "we're trying to learn more about it."

"You've occupied Sumera?"

"That is, strictly speaking, true. And in a way, Sumera has occupied us."

"I do not understand this turn of phrase."

"The atmosphere on Sumera is laced with nanobots, trillions of intracellular machines. They invade the body, and replicate to the point where they seem to kill the host. Then, for reasons we do not understand, the host is remade, alive and healthy, but with some changes, some augmentations."

The general stopped and placed his hand on my arm. The color had drained from his face, his eyes were wide, his voice dropped to a whisper. "You died," he said, "on Sumera, and you are here before us today…"

"That's it, yes, in a nutshell. A lot has happened…"

The General removed his hand from my arm and placed it on his chest, "The Hehzan Prophecy," he said, "I admit, at times I have lost faith, as have many of our people, convinced the prophecy is no more than a myth from antiquity. Hehzan the Healer tells us, one day the children of Ki will return home, to bring us forth from the darkness, after they have been struck down and reborn on Sumera…. you are the fulfillment of the Prophecy of Hehzan."

"No, I'm not. Not even close," I said, "our ship crashed on the planet, we didn't know anything about Sumera, nothing about Ki, weren't aware of the nanobots, we were looking for a home for our people, the people of Sol, we're not part of any prophecy."

"How can you know?"

"Because I know who I am, where I'm from, and these nanobots, they're endemic to the planet, anyone who lands there and breathes the air…"

"But it was you who arrived there, and now you have arrived here."

"I have no connection to this world beyond this meeting today."

"There is a way to be certain," the General said, "but first, the Imperium is waiting."

We hurried across the remaining distance to the hangar and did not speak again. Inside, a rotund man sat facing me at the center of a long table. A second table sat facing him, with one empty chair pulled back from it. The Imperium was flanked along the table by a retinue of well-dressed officials, backed by a contingent of a dozen armed guards.

"Please do not proceed beyond this point," the General said, pointing at the table. He left me behind and hurried toward the leader. The Imperium stood, and his entire table stood with him. He leaned forward and the General spoke to him, his voice too low for me to hear.

It was the worst possible First Contact scenario, arriving on a new world and being viewed as part of some religious heritage, or worse, seen as some sort of divine being. The mere concept of First Contact was laughable to me when I studied it in Officer Candidate School. I always believed humans were alone in the known universe, until we arrived at Sumera. Here I was, faced with a new reality. I began to question the logic in being there and felt an urge to leave, immediately. I reminded myself of our purpose, and my nerves began to settle.

"Captain Charles Bimmy," the Imperium said, "welcome to Envar. It seems we have important matters to discuss. Shall we begin?" He motioned to the chair beside me. Once I was seated, he and his retinue took their seats.

The soldiers who'd taken aim at me on the tarmac remained standing behind me. I looked back at them, then at the Imperium. I pointed over my shoulder. "This makes me uncomfortable," I said, "maybe they could relocate."

He waved his hand and the guards moved to the side where I could see them.

"Thank you," I said.

He smiled, but it was forced, more a grimace than a grin. "Your arrival has alarmed my people. The leaders of our military and our scientific community are in a collective state of shock. General Pileser informs me you have occupied Sumera, a world we once held as our own..."

"I'm sorry, excuse me, perhaps it's a problem with the translation. We haven't occupied the planet, we've taken up residence in the city. We never intended to land there..."

"The translation is accurate. You have admitted it yourself. You live on Sumera, in the City of Eternal Peace, you drink from its fountains, eat from its gardens, do you not?"

"Yes, but..."

"Then Sumera is yours, we relinquish our claim to it."

I was at a loss for words. We'd come seeking information, answers to our questions, not the deed to an entire world. Then again, we did consider it our home, and the people of Envar didn't seem to have a means to evict us from it.

"Captain Bimmy, I would like you off this planet as soon as possible. Your presence threatens the very order I and my forebears have spent generations creating. I will not allow your arrival to destroy the world my people have built. You came here seeking information, what is it you want to know?"

"I appreciate your directness," I said. "I will be direct as well. First, why did you allow me to land?"

"To get the measure of you," he replied.

"Interesting choice of words."

"Perhaps it is the translation."

"Ki was one of the most advanced and powerful planets in the Gha'ba system, what happened?"

"You have your history wrong."

"Do I?"

"Ki was, and still is, the most powerful world in the Gha'ba system. Our ancestors ruled all the worlds of Gha'ba. Kern and N'aha were controlled by our ancestors by force of arms, for thousands of years. Our ancestors elevated their technology, gave them purpose, gave them a future, gave them hope to rise above their wretched existence."

"You colonized the planets."

"We occupied them."

"I ask again, what happened?"

"A bloody and protracted revolt. The two worlds joined forces, used Ki's own technology against the ruling houses, expelled our ancestors from their planets. The rebellion went on for centuries, until our ancestors grew tired of the endless cycle of slaughter and vengeance. They gave the people of Kern and N'aha what they wanted, a life without the people of Ki to guide them."

"On Sumera, we were told the city was built by your ancestors, as a peace offering."

"I am not familiar with this story. It does not ring true for me. It was millennia ago, there are gaps in our knowledge of the past. We know our ancestors created the Triad, a fourth tribe, to rule the worlds, to unite them under a common government, with a common language, a shared history. Sumera was built to facilitate unity. It was a failure. History has shown, an excess of freedom and prosperity will inevitably give rise to leaders with dictatorial tendencies. The last war, the one you should ask me about, ruined all our worlds. Kern is devoid of anthropoid life, N'aha fared worse. But I do not believe you are here for a history lesson. If you have terms, let us hear them. Otherwise, do your worst. Bring down your troops, bomb our cities, we will fight you, and defeat you, as we have every enemy across all of time. The people of this world are bred for war, they are not afraid to die."

"We have no hostile intent. We came here hoping to understand what has happened to us on Sumera, and to learn more about the worlds in this system. We didn't know anyone was alive here. We are not interested in conquest; I've had my fill of war. But one day, more of our people will make the journey here, seeking a fresh start on a new world. I can't speak for all of them, but it is my hope we can share this system in peace. It seems to me we have a lot in common."

"You're an alien species, you've already occupied one of our worlds, you know we cannot stop you from taking more. Take them, they are dead worlds, of no use to us, we have all we need, and more. This is my warning to you, if your people try to take this world, we will bury them here, to a person. We are not inclined toward mercy."

The Imperium glared at me, his face red, teeth clenched, I could see sweat forming on his brow. His rage, his hostile stance, mystified me. I realized I was glaring back at him and forced myself to smile.

I stood quickly, startling the leader, and his guards. "It's unfortunate our first meeting has gone this way. I had hoped if we found other people, we could form a bond of friendship. That we could live together in peace, help each other prosper. I think you could use our help, based on what I've seen of your world. If you have a change of heart, you know where to find us. Until then, I wish you well."

The Imperium didn't stand. He pointed at the General, and snapped his fingers. "Escort him to his ship."

The General hurried to my side, then walked with me back the way we came, followed by the three soldiers. As we neared my shuttle, he turned to the guards and said, "Wait here," then continued walking with me.

"Do not concern yourself with this man," he said, "he will not be in power forever. When my fellow Hehzanites learn the details of your journey, his time will grow shorter still."

"I told you, I am not a part of your prophecy, our presence here is coincidental."

"There is not enough room in the universe for a coincidence of this magnitude. It is not necessary for you to believe. We have been waiting for our ancestors' return, and now you are here."

"We are not returning, we…"

"But you are," he said. "I cannot prove it to you today, I need time to search the archives, but I believe my ancestors have been to your world, and you are their descendant, as am I. If this is true, it will upset the political and social order across the world, but it might also usher in a new age of peace and prosperity."

"I can't accept this."

"I ask you to keep an open mind, and when you return to Sumera, seek out a synthetic named Tomrin. If he still functions, he will have your answers. But history tells us he is both dangerous and deceitful. Do not let your guard down when you find him."

"I'm more confused than when I arrived. Coming back here would be a bad idea. Your leader is out for blood. We meant well by coming here, we're not here to invade your world, but we've obviously done plenty of harm already."

"You have done no harm beyond what is necessary. You have given me hope. You will return, and when you do, you and all of your people will be welcomed, this I promise you. We can discuss it further, on Sumera, I will bring you the proof of what I say."

"You don't have any ships."

"We have ships, few in number, hidden away and cared for by the Keepers, waiting for this day to come. I will see you on Sumera, when the planets align, until then, find Tomrin, get the answers you seek, and wait for me. The day will come when the Triad of Gha'ba will be restored, and you will lead us into the dawn of a new age. I will bring you the proof, at the next conjunction."

He turned smartly and marched away, taking his guards with him.

I stepped into the shuttle, strapped into my seat, and placed three fingers on my guide, bringing up holograms of Becca, Blake and Reggie.

"Did you get all that?" I asked.

"Boy did we," Blake said, "fifteen minutes on the planet and they want to give you the whole system."

"It sure felt like it," I said.

"It may have," Reggie said, "but why? And do we want it? And who's to say it's theirs to give?"

"Those," Becca said, "are the right questions."

The shuttle's thrusters fired and I rose into the muddled light of a world I came to seeking answers, and was leaving with even more questions. I looked out at the landscape, the ruined and new cities alike, and thought for certain I would never return.

11

The Triad Lives

"I don't think we should leave right away," Reggie said, "let's linger here and see how they respond."

"Respond? How?" Becca said, "Shake their fists at the sky?"

We were seated around a table in the galley, working through our next move over a hot meal. To our surprise, the ship's food supply was perfectly preserved and edible, though meager in quantity. After hearing the name Tomrin for the second time, I decided to put finding him at the top of my to-do list. I was ready to get back to Sumera.

"I don't see the point in provoking them any more than we already have," I said. "You heard the general, they've got us mixed up in some kind of religious prophecy. The longer we stay in orbit, the more people might get a first-hand look at the ship. If we leave soon, we might minimize the damage. Let's finish the atmospheric analysis and move on."

"I agree," Blake said, "and this time I mean it. But we shouldn't go straight back to Sumera. We're out here, we might as well visit the other planets. It's barely a detour with the engines we've got."

"She's right," Reggie said, "we should gather what intel we can, while we can."

"We keep ending up with more questions than when we started," I said.

"True, but it's how we learn, until we find a library loaded with history books," Becca replied.

"Or find this Tomrin person," Reggie said.

"Let's do the flybys," I said, "but let's try to keep our distance. No more communication with alien civilizations."

"Come on Bimmy," Blake said, "where's your sense of adventure."

"I've had my fill of adventure for the day, and of whatever this is we're eating."

"Who cares what it is, it tastes good and it's hot," Reggie said, "I don't know how the two of you made it on raw fruit and vegetables all this time."

"Don't think I haven't considered a hunting trip, more than once. There are these little deer in the forest, they look delicious."

"When have you ever been hunting?"

"I could tell you stories."

"Bimmy," Becca said, offended, "I told you we're not eating the baby deer."

"We don't know they're baby deer, they could be very small full grown…"

"We are not eating them," Becca said, "figure something else out."

We continued our meal, putting aside the strangeness of our day for a little while, until the ship interrupted us.

"Captain, atmospheric analysis is complete. Also, there is a message for you from the surface. Would you like me to transfer the data to you?"

"We're coming back to the bridge," I said, "you can play it for us there."

On the bridge, a hologram of the four inner worlds and their star, the Gha'ba Aszan, was frozen in place in front of the flight ops station.

"Katie," I said, "is this the message from the surface?"

"Affirmative."

"Is the source the same as our previous messages?"

"This message was sent utilizing a more advanced form of radio telegraphy. Would you like me to activate the message?"

"Yes." I said, and turned to Becca. "This one's all yours."

The planets orbited their sun several times in rapid succession, then slowed as they came into alignment over Sumera. The hologram then repeated three times before zooming in to isolate Sumera and its star. Each time the planet completed an orbit, a counter advanced by one increment. The pace of the orbit increased until the counter reached fifty-nine, at which point the image zoomed out again, revealing the planets in conjunction.

"Looks like we've got ourselves a countdown," Becca said.

"I don't like it," I said, "but there's not much we can do about it. What's our flight time to…what's the next planet on our itinerary?"

"N'aha is the logical next stop based on our current location," Becca said, "but if it's a desolate wasteland, maybe we skip it and move on to Kern."

"Let's stick with logical, N'aha it is. Blake, fire up the warp drive."

"It's a Kelton Drive," Blake said, "show some respect for the person who invented it."

"How do you know Kelton is a person?"

"Fair point," she replied, "firing up the warp drive, setting course for N'aha."

Minutes later we were in orbit over the planet and got yet another surprise. On arriving, we saw no signs of cities or any indications of an advanced civilization, but the planet was far from dead. Streaks of grey and white clouds wrapped around the world, casting shadows on the dayside, speckling the surface with light, alternately hiding and revealing lakes, rivers, rocky mountains and green valleys arranged in jagged parallel swirls around the planet, alternating stripes of green and blue, like a giant marble floating in space. The poles were capped with ice, and we could see island chains scattered across a small southern sea.

"This place is teeming with life," Reggie said, "readings are off the chart, but I can't find any sign of cities, no comms, no e-m signals, nothing to indicate a civilization down there."

While the planet moved below us, more land mass came into view. The lush green surface gave way to a vast yellow-brown desert region, covering more than a third of the planet. It was marked in numerous places by extensive areas of glittering black.

"This doesn't look good. What are we seeing?" Becca asked.

"Hard to say for certain," Reggie said, "these readings, take a look at this. Does this remind you of anything?"

I looked at the data Reggie displayed over his station. At first, I didn't understand it, then it dawned on me.

"Nuclear war," I said, "on a scale I've never seen before."

"Are you saying they were nuked into oblivion?" Blake asked.

"These areas," Becca said, pointing at the blackened areas of terrain, "could these have been cities?"

"Looks that way. The yield of the weapons had to be extreme to vaporize everything to this extent," I said. "Can we overlay this onto a topographical rendering?"

"Let me see…. got it, here ya go."

The image changed and we could see what our eyes couldn't fully appreciate from orbit. The lighter-colored areas of the desert sat much lower than the blackened areas, which were in turn arranged along tall ridges in the planet's surface.

"Islands, big ones," I said. "Looks like somebody found a way to boil the ocean."

"And nature found a way to fix what it could," Becca said, "impressive does not begin to…wait…I'm reading…there's something down there. It's a repeating signal, getting stronger…"

"A message?"

"A ping, a regular repeating signal, a beacon of some kind."

"Coordinates," Blake said, "send 'em when you get 'em."

"All yours…"

"Takin' us in…"

"Not too low," I said, "no contact if we can avoid it."

"Roger that, no buzzin' the rooftops."

The beacon led us to a location at the heart of the desert, near what appeared to have been one of the larger islands in an archipelago. Deep in a low valley, between broken lines of towering stone, we found the source of the signal. A series of domed metal structures, scarred by oxidation, arranged in concentric circles, partially buried by drifts of sand.

The sand at the center of the innermost circle started to move. A tower rose up from the desert floor. It reached its apex and the domed covering began to open, sending sand pouring off its sides. When the platform was completely revealed, faded markings became visible on its surface.

"I'll bet a month's wages we're lookin' at a landing pad," Blake said.

"Wages," Reggie said. "We're getting paid for this?"

"How big is it?" I asked

"Too small for this ship, plenty big for a shuttle," Blake answered.

"You said we weren't doing this again," Becca said.

"Not exactly…"

"Captain," the ship said, "we are receiving a message."

"You said we would fly by, and keep moving," Becca insisted. "Last time could have turned out much worse."

"We're here, they've seen us, I think we need to take the call," Reggie said.

"Katie," I said, "is the message automated or live?"

"I am receiving an open line communication from a synthetic designated Barzon Seven. Barzon Seven appears eager to speak with you captain. They are emphatically requesting a response, by name. They are not alone in the installation. My sensors indicate the presence of both synthetic and hybrid life forms."

"How many?" I asked.

"Two thousand one hundred and fourteen synthetics, eight thousand, nine hundred and twelve biologics, eighty-two percent of which are hybrids. Approximately eighteen percent of the population is comprised of non-hybrid children."

"An unusual fact to point out."

"Such data can prove useful, should the encounter become antagonistic."

Becca rose from her chair and looked at me. "Katie, define hybrid."

"Synthetic-organic hybrids are biological anthropoids enhanced with embedded micro-cellular technology."

"That's an interesting population. Sounds like the Triad isn't dead and gone after all."

I looked at Becca and her expression made it clear she was becoming excited by the turn of events.

"This could be what we've been looking for, what we need," she said. "They can explain this, what it means. If they want to talk, we should talk. If you go down there, I'm going with you."

"We've got a mutiny on our hands," Blake said, grinning.

"Katie, put the comm through," I said.

An image of an individual coalesced in front of us. The individual struck me as male, tall in stature, broad shoulders, square jaw, large eyes and swept-back ears. With the exception of a full head of close-cropped hair, he looked remarkably similar to the Guardians, Lef and Soong, who we'd met on Sumera.

"Triad vessel," he said, "welcome to N'aha. This is a momentous occasion, I am designated Barzon Seven, what is your ship's complement, we will prepare for their arrival…"

"Katie, do not respond, mute the comm," I said. "Reggie, what are you seeing?"

"I'm picking up weapons, but nothing planetary, nothing to threaten us, the structures are well protected, they've got shielding, but…this is strange…I'm seeing weapons installations along the outer perimeter."

"Seems like a smart place to put them," Blake said.

"Yeah, genius, but these are aimed at the ground, and none of them are operational. They're some kind of projectile weapons, but they're inactive, rusted over, no threat to us."

"Katie, does this facility appear in your data archive?"

"Affirmative. This facility was built by order of the Triad Assembly. Upon completion, it was designated Scargg Zendi Three."

"Not exactly helpful…"

"Katie," Becca said, "we are not familiar with the term 'Scargg Zendi,' please define."

"Scargg Zendi has many meanings in the Triad lexicon. These include refuge, shelter, safety, hiding place, and asylum, among others. Scargg Zendi may also refer to the Fourth Dynasty architect of the same name, who pioneered the development of subterranean and suboceanic structures designed to protect civilian populations during times of conflict."

"It's a bomb shelter," Becca said, "but the war is long over, why are they still in it?"

"Let's find out," I said. "Katie, open comm."

"Barzon Seven…," I started, but was cut off by the source of the message.

"Is your communication system malfunctioning?" Barzon asked. "We seem to be experiencing some intermittent outages."

"Yes, we're working on it," I said. "I am Captain Charles Bimmy, our ship is designated *Katie*, we are on a mission of discovery…"

"Captain, it is a great day, we had lost hope we would ever see a ship here again. Generations have been born and died since the last sighting. When can we expect your arrival?"

"This one understands us," Reggie mumbled.

"We were not planning to land," I said, "we did not expect to find anyone alive on N'aha."

"We are the last survivors of the Triadic Usurpation," Barzon said. "Scargg Zendi One and Scargg Zendi Two were destroyed. We are the last, but we have thrived here in our refuge. We have ample supplies to host you and your crew. Captain, the people, they are anxious for word."

"Word of what?"

"The Prophecy. Is it true? Our contacts on Ki sent a message, the prophecy will be fulfilled at the next conjunction. Hehzan The Merciful…"

"Not this again," I muttered.

"Oh boy," Blake said, "looks like your rep has preceded you."

"You don't have to look happy about it."

"Roger that, not looking happy," Blake said, pretending to focus on her flight controls.

"Barzon..."

"I am designated Barzon Seven."

"Barzon Seven," I said, "we are not part of any prophecy. We are travelers from a distant world. We arrived on Sumera by accident, we never intended to land there, this is all a..."

"Your story sounds a great deal like the Hehzan Prophecy."

"I know, but..."

"Please, Captain Bimmy, let us meet in person, you and I, as well as the leaders of our community. Let us judge for ourselves if what we see is, or is not, what we believe. We have prepared a grand welcome for you and your crew."

"My crew will remain on the ship, my wife and I...."

"Ahhhhh," Barzon said, more a long exhale than an identifiable word, "that would be most delightful. The prophecy speaks of two who are as one. Yes, yes, when can we expect you?"

I looked at Becca who was trying hard not to laugh. "Well Commander Gorgeous," I said, "ready for a ride?"

"Why not Captain Handsome, let's do this."

"I thought we weren't supposed to talk like that," Blake said, smiling at Reggie

"Apparently the rules are shifting," Reggie said, smiling back at her.

***

Unlike my arrival on Ki, Becca and I did not leave the shuttle right away. After landing in the center of the platform, the dome closed over us, and our ship was lowered into the tower beneath the platform, then the entire structure sank down below the sand, with the top of the dome exposed to the sky. A hatch, twice the size of our shuttle, opened in the side of the tower, followed by a second hatch, which opened into the interior of the underground structure. Barzon Seven stood waiting for us. Behind him, hundreds of people greeted us, festooned in colorful outfits, some waving banners emblazoned with the silver sphere and three rod assembly also found on our ship. They jostled for position, each trying to get a glimpse of us.

When we stepped out of the shuttle, Becca took my hand and smiled at me. The crowd erupted into an ear-splitting frenzy of cheering and shouting. I was miserable and she knew it.

"Come on handsome, lighten up. This is a lot better than the last place."

"Roger that," I said. "Reminds me of back on Earth, Arcadia, when I was home on leave."

"When you came home to marry me, steal a starship, and take me on a never-ending honeymoon across the far reaches of the galaxy?"

"Exactly."

We laughed and I immediately felt better. We stepped hand-in-hand through the double portal and approached Barzon, who spread his arms wide, shimmering folds of his robe hanging down to floor, catching and reflecting the light. The people fell silent, and waited.

"Children of Ki, Bringers of Light, Vessels of Joy, welcome to N'aha."

The crowd erupted once again. I could feel the structure around us vibrating with their energy, and in the moment, I could not help but smile. The absurdity of it, the idea we would traverse the galaxy, arrive in an alien system, thinking we were alone, and find ourselves the center of attention from the remnants of a civilization which had collapsed centuries earlier.

I looked at Becca and she nodded her head. The crowd fell silent again. I turned back to Barzon and began, "Thank you, Barzon Seven, and the people of N'aha, for this warm welcome. We have many things we'd like to discuss with you and your people."

"They are not my people, Captain Bimmy, they are your people," he said. With a grand flourish he swung his arms and torso around, smiling at the assemblage behind him. Once again, they began to cheer and shout, applause thundering against the metal roof high above us.

"I don't know what to say."

"We are honored," Becca said, "to be here today. We look forward to hearing about your lives on this planet, in this place. We have stories of our own to share. But our time here is short…"

"Time? We have waited generations for your return, today is but a moment, a fleeting thing. Surely you can spare more than a moment."

"This is our first visit to N'aha," Becca said, "I'm certain there will be many more."

Barzon looked at me, cocked his head to one side and raised his eyebrows.

"If she says it will happen, it will happen," I said. "Barzon Seven, this is my wife, Becca Kiel, and you already know my name."

Barzon turned and motioned at a trio of people standing at the front of the crowd. One of them appeared human, like us. The other two, representing the people of Kern and N'aha, were more similar to each other than to the councilor from Ki. With their darker skin tone, delicate swept-back ears, and on the male of the pair, short hair style, they had more in common with Barzon Seven than with their co-council from Ki. The implication was clear. Android design had not been centered on Ki, and perhaps other advanced technologies were similarly devised, far away from the supposed center of power and technology in the system.

They approached, smiling, nervous.

"I present to you the Council of the Triad," Barzon said, "Councilor Unthen Arne, Child of Ki, Councilor Agrund Drensol, Child of Kern, and Councilor Masley Korst, Child of N'aha."

"It's a pleasure to meet you all," I said, "You know my name, and this is Commander Becca Kiel, she happens to be my wife as well."

"It's an honor to meet you…"

"The pleasure is ours," Councilor Arne said, "the honor is ours. We have heard of your visit to the home of my ancestors. It is our hope we can present a more hospitable welcome than they, in their ignorance, provided."

"We appreciate the warm welcome," I said, "but you didn't have to go to the trouble. We came here to learn and…"

"And they shall be humble and seeking."

"Please, we are not part of your prophecy, we're…"

"And yet," Barzon said, "every passing moment confirms you are. Come, the people long for a closer look. We must oblige them, then we will dine, then we will confer."

Barzon led us through the crowd, which parted to form a narrow lane in front of us. The people fell silent as we passed, some of them reaching out as if to touch us, but none of them made contact. It was unsettling to be surrounded, to have a large crowd pressing in on us.

I kept looking at Becca, to see how she was holding up. She kept her head held high, and her smile never wavered. She occasionally nodded toward someone with whom she made eye contact, or waved at the children raised aloft by their parents, who gleefully waved back. I thought again about how she'd been trapped in the bomb shelter at her university during the war and realized the experience, as terrible as it must have been, had made her stronger. I forced a smile, and tried to relax.

We moved through the large space at a leisurely pace, and left the crowd behind. We entered a corridor, brightly lit, painted pale blue. Our footsteps echoed against its metal walls. Despite being in a smaller space, the color and light mitigated my sense of oppression.

A set of double doors slid apart. Beyond the doors, a table had been arranged with food and drink. It was not a round table, like a disc, but circular and open within, the shape of a ring.

We were guided to two chairs, where we stood waiting for our hosts to make their way to their respective seats. "Please," Barzon said, "be seated."

The others waited for Becca and I to sit down, then did the same. There was no pretense or formality once we were seated. The Councilors started to eat while Barzon sat quietly with his hands folded on the table. I stared at the food in front of us, then looked at Becca. "Would it be rude to analyze it first?"

"I think in this case, caution is more important than politeness."

I used my Guide to scan the food and beverages. Everything checked out except one glass of a bright green liquid, which was identified as 'Dulsin, a common celebratory beverage made from the fermentation of any number of fruits found on the planet N'aha.'

"I think I'll skip the Dulsin," I said to Becca.

"Likewise," she replied.

Barzon had watched me closely as I scanned our food. When we started to eat, he smiled, then asked, "Captain, are your internal systems malfunctioning?"

Becca stifled a laugh and I smiled.

"Internal systems?"

"You are using an external device, but my scans indicate you are both Triadic hybrids, endowed with our most powerful technology."

"You scanned us," Becca said.

"Of course. It is an autonomous process, much as breathing is for you, or our mutual ability to understand one another's language. If repairs are in order, we have the most skilled technicians available to assist you."

"Repairs," I said, "we're not synthetics…"

"I meant no offense," Barzon said, "Triadic hybrids, of the highest order…"

"None taken, I…it's…the word repair has a different meaning for us. What sort of repair?"

"It's not a malfunction, strictly speaking," Councilor Arne interjected, "it's an activation issue. I can show you, or Barzon Seven can, or any of us. A series of gestures, a basic command sequence. You'll have full access to your internal systems in no time at all."

The two other Councilors nodded their heads eagerly, "Of course, we must show you," they said.

I looked at Becca whose smile vanished for a second, then returned as quickly. "Yes, we would appreciate your assistance with this matter, before we leave," she said.

Her sudden formal tone put me on alert. Without taking her eyes off Barzon, she leaned in close to whisper in my ear, "If they can scan us, they can probably hear what I'm saying to you."

Barzon's expression never changed, but the grin on Councilor Arne's face gave it away. They could definitely hear us.

"Genius, and gorgeous," I said.

Becca laughed and pushed at my elbow, making a show of being lighthearted. We were alone, isolated below the surface of an alien world, uncertain if our friends in orbit were receiving the transmission from our guides. If they weren't receiving, and the situation turned sour, there was nothing they could do to help us. I followed Becca's lead and remained calm, but on alert.

We didn't talk much for a time, and instead focused on eating our meal, occasionally asking or answering questions, nothing more serious than "What sort of vegetable is this?"

Until I asked, "Why do you remain in this facility when most of the planet is lush and green? Whatever happened here, it either didn't happen everywhere, or most of your planet has recovered."

The question brought the table to a dead stop.

Barzon Seven looked at the Councilors, who nodded their heads in approval. He turned back to us and said, "This is a question we have debated for many years. Barzon Five, and Barzon Six, both believed the world had recovered enough for our people to reclaim their lives upon the surface, to rebuild their cities, and once again enjoy the beauty of their world. Each of them set out to find the truth, and neither of them returned. I was then activated, and sent in search of my predecessors, both of whom I found. Their memory cores were intact and I was able to experience what they had experienced, namely, the distance across the desert is too great for our people. If such a trek is treacherous for a synthetic, it is beyond the capabilities of even the most capable hybrid. We are, in a sense, trapped in a cage of our own making. But we are safe. Our people are happy and healthy. It is a trap we are content to endure, until such time as our circumstances change."

"You have no aircraft…," I said.

"We never did," one of the Councilors said, "this facility was underwater, our vehicles were designed to fly under the ocean, not in the sky. We repurposed all of them, ages ago."

"If Barzon Five and Six failed to make it back from their expeditions, how did you make it back," Becca asked.

"My predecessors," Barzon said, "agreed to go as far as they could go, to serve as waypoints for any who followed. My mandate was to find them and return, which I did, on two separate journeys. You can still see them, the desert is exceptionally arid, they will be there, standing on the dunes, or in the case of Barzon Five, atop a rocky knoll, for generations to come."

"Sounds like a lonely vigil," I said.

"Without their memory cores, they have no concept of the passage of time. They know their mission, to stand and wait, until we come for them, or until hey are destroyed by the environment, whichever happens first."

"How do they function without their memory cores?" Becca asked.

"There are certain base-level functions which do not require a memory core," Barzon said, "much in the same way as your heart beats without a conscious effort from your mind, a synthetic has numerous functions operating in a similar fashion."

"I like the analogy," Becca said, "but if we continue with it, there's no way to remove a biological's memory without destroy the being. It's possible to keep the body alive, but the essence of the person is lost."

"This is where the nature of our existence, of synthetics and biologicals, diverges. My sense of being is not bound to my physical body. Although, I should point out, my memory core does not house my sense of self. That is held in a separate component, my neuro-core. If you separate the two, the memory core is nothing more than data. An extraordinary amount of data, to be true, but data nonetheless."

"Then if you don't separate them, the synthetic person can continue to exist, even without a complete body?"

"Yes."

"I'm confused," I said, "are Barzon Five and Six still aware, do they know they're standing out there in the desert?"

"On a certain level, yes."

"Do they suffer?" I asked.

Barzon looked at the Councilors, then back at me. He lowered his eyes; a frown replaced his smile. He looked as though I'd hurt him in some way.

"Please do not judge me harshly," he said, "I could not carry them back. I had to make a choice, and I chose based on what I would want, were I in their place. The removal of a memory core is a simple task, but removal of a neuro-core is exceedingly complex, difficult under the most ideal circumstances. Barzon Five and Barzon Six are aware, but they do not retain awareness. They exist in each individual moment they experience."

"Like the beating of a heart," Becca said.

"More like the sounding of a single note continuing without end, changing in minuscule ways over great stretches of time, where those changes go unnoticed because there is no memory of the note as it was before."

"Why is a memory core easy to remove?"

"I said it was simple, not easy. There is a quantifiable difference. My memory core is here," he said, pointing at his chest, near where a human heart would be, "while my neuro-core is here," he continued, pointing at the base of his skull. "One is designed to be removable; the other is not."

"How long will they last out there?" Becca asked.

"I cannot say, but I believe they will still be there when our people embrace their destiny and return to the surface of our world, to the light, and the green, and the blue of what was arguably the most beautiful world of the Gha'ba system."

"Then if you could leave, and start over in some other part of the world, you would?" Becca asked.

"Many of us would," Councilor Arne said, "others would remain here. Despite its outward appearance, this city is quite comfortable. We have farms, factories, schools, ample resources, including energy to power all of it, indefinitely. Quite a few of our people would not want to give up such comforts to start over in the forests beyond the desert. And this is good. Scargg Zendi Three is the last facility of its kind. It would be unwise to abandon such an important refuge, given our history."

"Speaking of history," I said, "could you tell us about the war? The President on Ki told us about a rebellion, against his ancestors, but it was a one-sided history to me, and we never got around to talking about the last war, the war that…"

"Lay ruin to our worlds, all of them," Councilor Arne said. His fellow Councilors nodded their heads in agreement.

"Our ancestors," Councilor Drensol said, "have never been able to stomach peace for very long. The Triad was created to end war, once and for all. Instead, it brought about the greatest conflagration ever known. Everything you see, the ruin, the destruction, the pathetic state of our worlds, all of it stems from the evolution of the Triad from a unifying force for good, to a ruling body controlled by elitists with a penchant for tyranny."

"And yet you would see the Triad reborn?" Becca asked.

"Reborn? It never died, we are living proof, all of us seated at this table, we are Triadic, through and through. But we have learned the error of our ways."

"The new Triad is better than the old Triad," I said.

"It will be," Barzon said, "with you to lead us into the New Dawn."

"I don't see leading the people as our purpose."

"Great leaders rarely do," Barzon said, "they become what they are meant to become, by virtue of their deeds."

I was about to protest again when Becca leaned forward and said, "Tell us about the Triad, and the last war, we'd very much like to know this part of your history."

Councilor Drensol waved her hand. When she spoke, her voice was laced with bitterness. "My ancestors would tell you the people of Ki started the war, the people of Ki will tell you N'aha started the war, the people of N'aha will tell you they were victims of the war. Only the people of N'aha would be telling you the truth. We can dispute the facts forever. But one fact we all share in common; it was Tomrin the Wise of Sumera who ended it."

"This is the third time we've heard his name," Becca said.

"Our own war, between the planets of Sol, ended with a new political order, by agreement between the warring parties," I said. "How did Tomrin, an individual, accomplish this?"

The Councilors again fell silent and turned their collective gaze to Barzon. He closed his eyes, bowed his head briefly, then looked at Becca and me for several seconds before speaking.

"Tomrin the Wise," he said, "unleashed a plague upon all the worlds of Gha'ba. Indiscriminate mass murder, his way of ending war for all time. His idea of peace was to kill all creatures capable of waging war. The Triad, backed by the military forces of Ki, was about to defeat Kern, to restore the Triad to power, when Tomrin let loose a swarm of molecular devices, a few atoms in size, but more powerful than any natural plague in existence. It infected everyone in its path, spread from person to person, ship to ship, world to world, until the very moment the Ruler of Ki was about to claim his victory, the restoration of the Triad. It was then Tomrin intervened, then released his killing machines. Billions died before anyone understood what was happening. The people of Ki managed to devise a countermeasure before all was lost, but their world, as you have seen, descended into an age of protracted war amongst the ruling houses, until little was left of their civilization. They had done as much to ruin their lives as had Tomrin. In the end, Tomrin's plan failed, he did not kill us all. But it succeeded in one important way."

"It ended interplanetary war in the system," Becca said.

"Yes," Barzon said.

"What about your people, how did they survive?"

"We are members of the Triad," Councilor Korst said. "For a synthetic, Tomrin has many traits in common with biologics. Arrogance is one such trait. He used our own technology to develop his weapon. He never expected us to be immune, by virtue of…"

"The nanobots," Becca said, "they were already inside you."

"I am unfamiliar with this word…"

"The molecular devices, inside your cells, they make you, us, Triadic Hybrids, they kept you safe from the plague."

"Yes, I understand now. You are correct."

"What about the people on Ki," Becca asked, "are they hybrids as well?"

"All but the Hehzanites, who live their faith in secret, turned away from the Triadic path long ago," Councilor Arne replied. "After the Great Purge, our kind died out on Ki within a single generation. The nanobots, as you call them, unlike genetic material, do not transfer from parent to child."

"Can you imagine," Councilor Korst said, "a child imbued with such capabilities? A terrifying notion."

"Which brings us to each of you," Barzon said. "Tell us of your experiences on Sumera."

"We'll tell you," I said, "but please accept we are not part of your prophecy."

"Did you die on Sumera?" Barzon asked.

"In manner of speaking, yes…"

"One is either dead or not dead, there is no middle ground," Councilor Arne said.

"That's debatable," Becca said. "For us, in our way of thinking, as long as the brain is alive, the person is alive. Once the brain is dead, the body generally follows. Conversely, if the body dies, the brain will follow. The fact we are still here means we didn't experience true death."

"Or," Barzon said, "it means the prophecy is being realized, and you are both part of it. Tell me this, how long can the brain linger after the body expires?"

"I don't understand the question."

"For example," Barzon said, "if my energy core is destroyed, my memory core will remain functional as long as the energy already delivered to it remains. The memory core has its own capacity to retain energy long after the supply of energy to it ceases. The same is true for my neuro-core. I have seen this, I told you about my predecessors. We have ample scientific evidence this is also the case with the biological memory, the brain. Energy lingers there for some time after a body has expired. Scientifically speaking, it is possible, even probable, you did die, but enough energy remained to sustain your brain until your body could be repaired."

"If we concede your point," I said, "it doesn't mean we're… whatever it is you think we are in terms of your beliefs."

"Nor does it preclude the possibility."

I felt cornered, defeated. There was no convincing the survivors of an interplanetary catastrophe their dreams of a better life, a new start, were being pinned on a prophecy involving people who had no interest in being part of it.

Becca and I sat quietly, looked at each other, then it hit me. We had been saying we wanted to live in peace with all the people of the Gha'ba system, how we wanted to bring others along to live here, to help them rebuild their worlds. We wanted a new home for the people of Earth, and the greater Sol system. We'd been telling them exactly what they'd hoped to hear, and in return, they had offered us everything we wanted.

Prophecy or no prophecy, our goals were aligned. I remembered the lesson Becca had been trying to teach me, to accept what the universe gave me and make the best of it. I concluded it was exactly what the situation required.

"For the sake of argument," I said, "let's say we are part of this prophecy, and all of this is part of some grand plan. If that's the case, what is it you expect from us?"

***

"That's it?" Blake asked, incredulous. "All they want is for us to reunite three planets, restore their civilizations, make peace with some guy named Tomrin, and serve as their benevolent rulers until the end of time. Sounds great, let's do it."

We had returned to the ship to discover Blake and Reggie had not been receiving our transmission. It took some time to bring them up to speed on the situation, and what we had tentatively agreed to do.

"Your sarcasm is duly noted," I said, "I know it sounds like a lot. We have to take it one step at a time."

"We're not baking a cake," Blake said, "there's no recipe for something like this."

"Actually, there is," Becca replied, "sort of. Their prophecy has some rather specific elements we can use as a map, a plan for the future."

"We're not going to pretend we're some sort of deities, I'm not signed up for that," Reggie said.

"Agreed," I said, "but Becca makes a valid point. If we view their prophecy as a set of goals, we should be able to help them achieve those goals, while we're achieving ours. It won't be easy, but given the state they're in, the good and the bad, I'm counting on plenty of help from the locals, assuming we can get more people here from Sol."

"What we need is help from Deimos," Reggie said. "Engineers, techs, designers, you name it, Deimos has it. We could set up shop on Sumera, and send ships to all three worlds."

"Which would be easier," Becca said, "if I could figure out how to convert the Kelton drive into something more like our Gateway system."

"What's the hold up?" Blake asked. "I thought you were a genius."

"I'd have to understand how it works in the first place," Becca replied, "before I could even start trying to modify it. It's a matter of time. Between the ship's knowledge and our super-bots, I can figure it out, eventually."

"Speaking of super-bots," Blake said, "when are you going to show us how to upgrade?"

"You mean activate. It's the one easy thing we've learned," Becca said. "Hold out your left hand, make a fist. With your other hand, activate your Guide, but don't say Guidance, say 'System Menu.'"

Reggie and Blake followed her instructions, and were both looking at the interface Becca and I were shown by Barzon Seven, a conical spiral of icons and characters in the now familiar script we'd first seen on the hull of the space station, *Talall Four*, over Sumera.

"You swipe any of the curved lines in the menu and it spirals up or down. But you don't have to if you know the submenu you want. In this case, say 'Internal Systems' and once it pops up, say 'Activate.'"

"Woah, man is this wild," Blake said, "it's like I'm inside a sim, and outside a sim, at the same time, like augmented reality dialed up to the max, but better. We've been livin' under a rock."

"I'm not sure I like this," Reggie said, "it's an overload of data. How do I shut it off?"

"You can shut it off by saying 'Deactivate Internal Systems' while you have the menu open," Becca said, "or you can send all of it to the background, or you can set it to autonomous operation."

"We chose the last option," I said. "It works a lot like the information we see, the systems activate when you need them, or at least when they think they're needed. Councilor Arne says it doesn't take long for it to become second nature, and I think he's right. On the flight back I was able to view the planet's surface in multiple modes, infrared, topographical, false light, by thinking about what I wanted to see."

"Wait, everything's gone," Blake said. "What'd I do?"

"Did you think about autonomous functionality?"

"Yes, but…"

"Welcome to the world of super-bots."

"Deactivate internal systems," Reggie said. He looked at me, then Becca and finally Blake. "I think three ultra-cyborgs is enough for one ship."

"All this data," Blake said, "it's incredible a bunch of nanobots floating around in the atmosphere can carry it all."

"There's more than enough capacity, when you add it all up. But it would make sense if functional capabilities are there, or they develop over time, and the data itself is coming from external systems, through some kind of near-range telemetric interface."

"I don't know what a tele-whatever is," Blake said, "but if it's sending data to us, what are the chances it's getting data back?"

Becca frowned and looked down at her hands, reading whatever her systems were displaying.

"I hadn't considered it."

"Add it to the list for later," I said, "let's head to Kern. Barzon said there was nothing left of it, but I want to see it for myself."

"Roger that, Captain Cyborg, setting course for Kern."

"Don't call me a cyborg," I said, "I am a Triadic Hybrid, of the highest order."

"As are both of you," Becca said. "Cyborgs are yesterday's news."

***

When we entered orbit over Kern, we saw no evidence of nuclear conflict, no sign of wide scale destruction. Also missing was any sign of civilization. But the continents, like much of N'aha, were filled with life, as were the oceans, according to our scans.

Kern appeared to be devoid of people. We spent several orbits scanning for signals and found nothing. With each pass over the night side of the planet, we looked for the glow of cities and saw complete darkness.

"It's our turn to visit a planet," Blake said, "fair is fair."

"What's the point, there's nobody there," I said, "and if animals have ruled the world for centuries, there are probably a few that would happily make you their next meal."

"Way to kill the joy, captain, outstanding job," Blake replied.

"An entire world without people," Reggie said, "imagine what we could do with it."

"Not much," Becca said. "Barzon thinks the atmosphere is still laced with Tomrin's bot plague."

"Wouldn't it show up on our scans?" Reggie asked.

"We didn't pick it up on Sumera either. Better to be safe, wear a pressure suit, or make a visit to Sumera, before any people go down there."

"That's the plan," I said, "bring our people to Sumera first, enable them to survive on all the worlds."

"Until we can get them here," Becca said, "there's not much of a plan."

"We need to figure something out sooner, not later," Reggie said. "Things have gotten worse since you two have been gone. Between Earth and the Venusians, there's not much left but scraps for the colonies."

Reggie's comment took me back to the war, what some called the Secessionist War and others the Colonial Rebellion. At the time, I thought I knew which side I was on. In hindsight, the picture blurred rather than clarified. One thing was certain, our mission hadn't changed. Find a new home for people from Sol, and soon enough to relieve the pressure. If the inner planets were hoarding resources again, another war was inevitable. And like Gha'ba, the next war was likely to be the last.

"I want to have a word with this synth, Tomrin," I said. "Let's see if we can come to terms with him. If not, all of this may be for nothing."

12

Tomrin the Wise

Our return trip to Sumera was uneventful. The ship landed itself, which disappointed Blake but not the rest of us. Uneventful was exactly what we needed after our multi-planet excursion. We came down with the setting sun and agreed to rest for the night, then head out in search of Tomrin the following day.

When we met in the morning, Blake made her priorities known right away.

"I know I sound like a repeating signal," she said, "but I need to eat before we go marching off into the unknown again. And we'll need food for the trip, any thoughts?"

"Already on it," I said, "look at this." I activated a holographic map over my Guide and pointed at a series of blue dots hovering over buildings. "I asked the Guide for a map to the Temple, and for locations of food and water, then asked it to overlay the locations on the map. This is what it gave me. No matter which direction we walk, we'll pass at least one of these. It might even update with more locations as we travel, we'll have to check again once we've covered some distance."

"How far are we going?" Blake asked. "Is this a one-day event, are we camping out, what's your genie-woman got to say for herself?"

"It's half a day's walk," Becca said, "but if we spend any time there, we'll probably want to find lodging for the night, rather than walk back in the dark."

"Okay," Blake said, "which way?"

I pointed toward the foothills rising in the distance. "That way," I said, "beyond that ridge."

"Half a day, uphill, on foot," Reggie said. "You'd think they'd have vehicles, an aero-car, something better than walking."

"What are you griping about," Blake said, "you're a spring chicken. None of us got a full fountain of youth treatment out of this."

"Like it or not, we're walking," I said.

"Food first, then hike, right?"

"Yup," I said, "let's go."

"Wait," Becca said, "did either of you bother to ask the Magistrate if there were vehicles, or are we assuming we have to walk? Because it seems to me…"

"As a matter of fact, no," I said.

Becca tapped her device and her Guide appeared. "Guidance," she said, "we need transportation to the Temple of Time, where is the nearest vehicle?"

"The nearest personnel transport is located in the subterranean storage facility at Dahoj."

"What's a Dahoj?" Blake asked.

"A Dahoj is an avian species native to the planet Ki. It is the central iconography of the ruling house of Ki, and is known for its graceful flight, dark plumage, and extraordinary size. It is an apex predator, capable of capturing and consuming…"

"Guidance," Becca said, rolling her eyes at Blake, "show me where the transport facility called Dahoj is located."

A map of the city appeared over Becca's wrist, then a section of the map expanded, showing a route from our location to Dahoj.

"The spaceport," Reggie said, "that makes sense. But can we fly it, whatever it is?"

"It is unwise for passengers to attempt to pilot a personnel transport," Becca's Guide said. "Such behavior may interfere with the transport's autonomous systems. Would you like me to summon the transport?"

"Yes," Becca said.

The Guide paused briefly, then said, "Your transport will arrive momentarily."

"For the record," Blake said, "if something goes wrong, if I need to take the controls, you can count on me."

"I'm with the guide on this one," Reggie said, "let the aircraft do the flying."

"No fun, no fun at all."

A few minutes after we requested the transport we heard a noise overhead. I looked up and was surprised by the appearance of the craft. It was small, sleek, wedge-shaped and decorated in swirls and geometric shapes, in bright luminous shades of green and blue against a white background. It looked more like a giant toy than a proper aircraft. It set down on the paved avenue in front of us and a door slid open along the side facing us. It had four rows of seats, two seats in each row.

"Remind you of anything," Becca said, pointing at the aircraft's side.

"The station, *Talall Four*," I replied, "the interior walls have similar decoration."

"What does it mean?" Reggie asked.

Blake climbed aboard and took one of the front seats. "Who cares, let's go," she said.

A smooth, dark, reflective surface curved across the front of the interior below the forward window, which wrapped around the entire bow of the craft.

Becca took the seat next to Blake while Reggie and I piled in behind them. Blake busied herself waving her hands over the surface in front of her, then tapped it in various places trying to get a response from the machine, but to no avail.

"How are we supposed to…" she began.

Becca raised a finger, cutting her off, and said, "Transport."

A voice replied "Destination."

"Temple of Time."

"That destination is not permitted."

"Great," Blake said, "back to hoofing it."

"Not so fast," Becca said. "Transport, what is the nearest permitted destination to our requested destination?"

The window became a view screen, and filled with an image of rolling hills and stone structures, connected by a cobbled path. "Comfort Station Nine is the nearest permissible landing site to your requested destination."

"Show me relative distance," Becca said.

The image adjusted, displaying our current location, the comfort station, and, a short distance from the station, the Temple.

"It looks like a temple all right," Reggie said, "those columns are a lot like ones I've seen on Earth."

I brought up my own map and compared it to the larger one in front of us. "We can get supplies there," I said, "and walk the rest of the way in ten minutes, give or take."

"Transport, our destination is Comfort Station Nine," Becca said with a smile, "let's get moving."

The door slid shut and the transport rose into the air. The motion was smooth, without the normal vibration or shuddering I'd grown accustom to on Space Force shuttles, or those on board our ship.

"Feel that?" Blake asked.

"I don't feel anything," Becca said.

"Exactly," Blake replied, "you should feel something, an increase in gravitational force, a sense of vertical motion, something."

"Inertial dampeners," I said.

"Why are you surprised?"

"Because inertial dampeners take up a lot of juice," Reggie said, "we never put them on shuttles, you'd run out of fuel trying to launch the things, they eat more power than gravity plates."

"When we're finished with this little side trip, we need to get back to the spaceport and see what other surprises we can find," Blake said.

We flew over the city at low altitude, our speed increasing as we approached the mountains to the East. We passed over a dense forest which soon gave way to rolling grass-covered hills. Our route carried us over the cobblestone path we would have been walking, until the transport crested a ridge, revealing a wide paved oval and a series of one-story stone structures. The buildings were covered in flowering vines, with an overgrown garden in a courtyard within the compound, and a large fountain flowing at its center.

The transport made a perfect soft landing, and the door slid open.

"Transport," Becca said, "remain here until we return."

"As you require. It is my pleasure to serve."

We entered the main building, and checked a few of the rooms. They were of varying sizes, but of the same design, with plain but comfortable-looking beds and chairs in each. We came to a large open room looking in at the garden, a series of long tables arranged at right angles to the open arches leading into the courtyard. A glass cabinet along the back wall held plates, cups and utensils, the first we'd seen outside of the apartment we had taken in the city.

"Does this all seem a little primitive?" Blake asked.

"Compared to the city, yes," Becca replied, "but it seems of the place, rustic and homey."

"Not sure homey is the word I'd use, but rustic, yeah, it fits," Blake said.

We gathered food and filled a pitcher with water from the fountain and ate our fill before continuing on toward our destination, picking up the stone path as it curved up the side of the hill, through an open field covered in tall green grass laden with bolts of grain at the top of each slender stalk. We stopped and looked back at the city when the path crested the next ridge. I could see the lake glittering beyond the harbor, the spaceport standing to our south. I couldn't help compare it to Arcadia.

"It reminds me of home," Becca asked.

"It is home," I replied, and continued walking.

The path transitioned to steps leading up the ridge, through a dense patch of low trees. We ascended through the tree line and a roof appeared, peeking over the edge of the hilltop. We reached the top, then surveyed the scene below.

The Temple was a large but simple stone structure, fifteen meters across, half again as tall, with a peaked roof. A set of four tapered columns lined the facade, a single metal door between the middle two columns. Other than the columns, the building had no ornamentation or decoration. The door lacked a handle and it did not open when we approached. A large metal ring hung in the center of the door.

I activated my guide and asked, "How do I open the door in front of me?"

"You cannot open this door to the Temple of Time," it replied.

"How do we enter the Temple of Time?" I asked.

"Through the door at the front of the Temple."

"The door is closed," I said, "how do I open the door and enter the Temple?"

"This is not the front of the Temple," my Guide replied, "you must approach the Temple from the East and awaken Tomrin the Wise."

"This is ridiculous," I said. "What I'd give for a plasma torch."

We followed the path around the building to the eastern facade, which mirrored the western one, except it had a paved terrace laid out in front of the building. It provided a commanding view of a wide valley, with a river meandering through its center. Trees and stone structures of varying size and shape dotted the landscape. A light mist hung over a waterfall at the far end of the valley. I could see animals grazing in the distance and felt a strange sense of familiarity.

"Wow," Blake said.

"Wow is right," Reggie said, "I've never seen such a beautiful place."

"The welcome center," I said, "the ceiling..."

"You're right," Becca said, "this is it. This is the scene on the ceiling, but the perspective is skewed in the painting, it's not from this position. But this is definitely the place."

"You are correct," a voice behind us said.

We turned to see a figure, human in form, standing in front of the open door of the Temple. He was tall and slender, with bronze skin and short hair, he reminded me of Peter Jay, Reggie's father. Like the hologram at the welcome center, his robes shimmered, and his eyes glinted green in the sunlight.

"Welcome to Namya Anamu, Valley of Peace."

"You must be Tomrin," I said, "we were told to find you..."

"Yes, I know," he said, "and you are Charles Lee Bimmy...and you would be Rebecca Claire Kiel, the captain's wife...are you enjoying your journey together?"

"It's Becca, and I'd say yes, for the most part," Becca said.

"It's been a ride, I'll say that much," I said.

"And you would be Reginald Perseus Mulzac..."

"Perseus," Blake said, "who names their kid Perseus?"

"And you, at last, are Charlotte Lucía Blake."

"Finally, we know your full name," I said.

"Yeah, it's Blake, you've always known it."

"Welcome to my home," Tomrin said, "please, come in."

He waved his hand back toward the door, then turned and walked inside.

"Lucía?" Reggie said.

"Well at least it ain't Perseus," she replied and followed Tomrin through the door.

"Tomrin," I began, "we have a lot of questions."

"Yes, I am aware," he said, "the challenge for you, is where to begin."

"I won't argue," I said. "Let's start with how you knew our names."

"Your identities are bound to the things you carry, or those things which carry you. Reginald's weapon, Charlotte's..."

"It's Blake," Blake said.

"Apologies," Tomrin replied, bowing his head with his hands clasped, "your name, Blake, was bound to your suit. Charles and...

Becca, your names were bound to your spacecraft. These objects and systems are accessible to me…"

"You look like us. Were you designed by the people of Ki?" Becca asked.

"I designed myself," Tomrin said, "I am able to take on the likeness of all of the species in the Triad, as needed, or desired."

"Why would you need the ability to change form?" I asked.

"You will understand, in time," Tomrin said. "You seek enlightenment, enlightenment you shall have."

We entered the building and passed through an antechamber, which opened into a large hall. Broad beams crisscrossed overhead, supporting the wooden ceiling high above. Light came from flaming torchieres evenly spaced throughout the hall, providing a dim glow inside the windowless building. A low set of cabinets ran the length of one wall, with a polished stone countertop reflecting the light of the lamps. Art objects, sculptures and glazed pots, were placed at regular intervals on the counter, with bundles of flowers piled high between them. Tables were spaced throughout the hall, with long benches pushed up underneath them. It looked more like a dreary banquet hall than a temple.

"Cheery place," Reggie said.

"If you think a tomb is cheery," Blake replied.

Tomrin laughed softly and walked further into the hall, "I have no need of light, or furnishings, or food. I have attempted to prepare the Temple for your arrival, if it is not to your liking…"

"It's not a problem, it's all very," Blake glanced at Becca, "of the place, you might say. Thanks for going to the trouble."

Tomrin led us through a narrow passage into a smaller chamber illuminated not by fire, but by lights embedded in the walls. Instead of stone, the walls and ceiling were made of a black glass, reminiscent of the smaller control panels at the welcome center, but without glowing symbols or apparent function.

"What is this place," Becca asked, "why is it called the Temple of Time? Did the people here worship time?"

"Worship time?" Tomrin laughed again, a laugh that carried with it a distinct element of condescension, and a hint of something sinister.

"Time is not to be worshiped," he continued, "it does not require faith in order to exist. But time is to be revered, this is true. This place was never called a Temple when the people of the Triad were still alive, it received that designation after the last war, when the Protectorate was all that remained of the civilization that had gone before."

My instincts had me on edge, but I couldn't say why. "We were told you ended the war, by trying to kill every living person in the system. You accomplished one goal, but failed in the other. There are still people on Ki and N'aha. They asked us to help them…"

"They see you as the fulfillment of their dream, no doubt, the embodiment of the Hehzan Prophecy. They wish to restore the Triad. Of course, you know such a restoration would be unwise."

"They've been suffering a long time…"

"They brought their suffering upon themselves. It pleases me some still live, but there has been peace here since I brought an end to their violence."

"They want peace, prosperity, a future without fear, to travel between worlds again, to…"

"In other words, they want to go back in time, to start their madness again, with you to guide them."

"They know they can't go back in time," I said, "they want to move forward, to…"

"Your understanding of time is primitive. You think of time, you experience it, in a way that makes explanation difficult."

Reggie crossed his arms behind his back and leaned forward, "We may be more clever than you think, try us."

"Difficult is not the same as impossible," Tomrin said. "However, a demonstration is more effective. Witness for yourself how they lived, how they killed, why my actions were the only logical choice."

Tomrin waved his hand and the room vanished, as did Tomrin. We found ourselves on the bridge of a ship in orbit over Sumera. A bridge larger than any ship's bridge in the Federation fleet. The forward bulkhead was transparent, curving from side to side through an arc ten meters across. Outside, dozens of spacecraft engaged in a pitched battle, some were destroyed, others damaged and burning but fighting on. Smaller ships darted in and out of view, firing on the larger ships, and each other. Explosions and weapons fire threw bursts of light into the bridge where we stood. Bodies of the various species of Gha'ba drifted across our view. The crew of the ship, made up entirely of people from Ki, rushed about the bridge while commands, competing with the sounds of the battle for attention, were shouted by officers. The ship was struck and I felt the explosion shudder through it. I recalled the bridge of the Arcturus, my first battle. If we were in a simulation, it was more realistic than any I had ever experienced.

"What's happening?" Blake shouted.

A man stepped next to me and stared out at the conflagration. He was the essence of calm in the midst of a brutal and terrifying storm.

"Are you the captain?" I asked, "What are we watching? How is this possible?"

"It is the end of days," he said, "and the beginning of your future."

"I don't understand…"

"I am not the captain, she is dead. Today I am no one, though I was once the ruler of Ki."

"Tomrin said…" Becca began.

"Tomrin," the man scoffed, "we created Tomrin to maintain Sumera, nothing more. A synthetic to command all synthetics, and they made him their god, or perhaps he made himself one. It does not matter. He evolved, and he will be the death of all of us, you will see. Watch…"

"This is supposed to teach us about time, I don't get it," I said.

I saw Reggie walking slowly through the bridge, watching the crew at their stations. A crew member turned abruptly and bumped into him.

"Excuse me, sir," the young man said and hurried away.

"What are you doing?" I yelled over the growing noise.

He looked at me, his face gone pale with sudden understanding, "Bimmy, this is real, I can feel the ship, I can smell the fear, this isn't a sim."

"No way," Blake replied, "it's gotta be a sim, a damn good one, but it's gotta be a sim."

"She's right," Becca said, "time travel is not possible."

"Your companion," the man said, "is a soldier. He knows the smell of fear, the stench of despair. He is correct, this is happening. You know nothing of time. I have borne witness to the death of my people, the end of my world and all the worlds of Gha'ba a thousand, thousand times over. You know nothing of time."

"Then enlighten us," I shouted.

"What is time to the clockwork?" he said, raising his voice. "Motion and weight, with purpose, but no meaning. A world moves around its star, you call it a year. A planet turns upon its axis, and you number your days. You stand in your city in the light of the dawn and call it morning even as other eyes in other cities see the setting of the sun.

The time you measure is an artificial construct, a method, a primitive framework. That framework is a prison."

He paused and looked out at the battle. I saw the space station over the planet, a scattering of ships fighting to protect it. A large ship, similar to the one under construction at the spaceport on Sumera, was pulling away from the station, protected by a phalanx of smaller vessels, maintaining a desperate rearguard. It was clear they were in danger of losing.

"For you," he continued, "time can be measured, the same as energy and mass, but in measuring it you constrict it to your own limited understanding of the universe. You give it direction where there is none, and a meaning which diminishes its true nature, to something small and digestible by your minds."

"Time is a continuum," Becca shouted, "an irreversible succession of moments, events, from the past to the present to the future."

More explosions rocked the ship. "This is what prevents you from grasping the truth," he shouted back. "The very core of your belief is a fallacy. There are events and there is motion and there is energy. You move through these, watching your lives wither away, and you think every passing moment is gone forever, washed downstream by the rivers of time you yourselves created. This is not true. When you move beyond the rivers of time, you discover time is an ocean, endless in all directions. And when you touch upon its true nature, then you gain access to all of it, everywhere, anywhere, at any moment."

A final tremendous explosion ripped the ship apart. I saw Reggie enveloped in fire; Becca crushed by a section of the ship's superstructure. Blake and I were expelled from the ship and I could see her face, her terror and agony reflecting my own. And in the millisecond before I died, I was saved.

We were no longer hurtling through space in the midst of a battle. But we were not back on Sumera. We were on another ship, this time over N'aha. I recognized the species crewing the ship. They were from Kern, and I knew what we were about to witness.

The ship was smaller than the one we'd left. Where the previous had a bridge crew numbering in the dozens, this one was occupied by eight individuals. One of them approached us, her uniform different from all the others.

"You again," she said, "have you not seen enough? Are you so enamored of our atrocities you wish to witness them yet again? I told you before, you cannot stop the past..."

"I don't know what you're talking about," I said, trying to keep my voice calm, "we…"

"We've never been here before," Blake insisted, "Tomrin sent us…"

"Of course Tomrin sent you, I know the way of things. If this is your first, you are ignorant of many things. Look then, witness for yourselves the last days of N'aha, the death of the Triad."

She stared at me and pointed toward the fleet of ships assembled around us, then swept her arm down toward the planet, before turning back to look down at N'aha. The ships let loose their volleys of mass destruction. City by city, the civilization on N'aha was destroyed. The explosions grew in frequency and intensity until the atmosphere itself appeared to be on fire. Eventually, we could no longer see the surface of the planet, nothing but boiling black, red, and grey. A world become flames and smoke and death. Of all the horrific things I'd experienced in my life, this was far and away the most soul crushing act of violence I'd ever witnessed, beyond anything I had ever imagined. I recalled my own willingness to use nuclear weapons on Mercury, and made a vow to myself to never again consider such a heinous act.

"Why…why would you…" I began.

"He didn't tell you? I will destroy N'aha and all those who support the Triad, this is my mission, my dream of a world free from their tyranny. I will take Sumera for Kern, and all of my people will bathe in its waters, drink from its fountains, and I will control its true power. My people invented the portal, my people gave it life. If I must kill every living soul on this world, or any other, for my people to have what is theirs by right, I will do it."

"You're going to get your wish," Reggie said, "but not the way you think."

"You fool, I know what lies ahead. Here, in this glorious moment, I am triumphant. Tomrin can never take this victory from me."

"Then you're the fool," Becca said, "and we have no further business here."

Becca turned to me, a grim expression etched on her face. "How do we get out of this?" she asked.

"Tomrin controls the portal, you are here until he…"

Before the ruler of Kern could finish her sentence, our environment changed again. The ship over N'aha was gone, replaced by a lush garden. The sound of water splashing in a fountain echoed off the high stone walls surrounding us. The sky above was pale blue and streaked with clouds. The light of Luyten's star, Gha'ba Aszan, shone through the clouds, casting dappled light over the garden. Somewhere in the distance a person was singing, but I couldn't make out the words.

"This is an improvement," Blake said.

"I don't like it," Reggie said, "what if we're on N'aha?"

"I don't think this is N'aha," I said, "I'm betting this is Kern."

"You are correct," a male voice said, "come, come around where I can see you."

We walked through a gap in a tall thick hedge, then through a stone archway, and entered a corridor bound on one side by vegetation and on the other by a building. A long colonnade held a roof three meters above us. The overgrown spaces between the columns concealed most of the structure from within the garden. Flowers and fruit hung heavy and filled the cool air with a sweet scent. An old man sat in a motorized hover chair, a blanket across his lap. He smiled, filling his face with creases. His eyes were ice blue and his skin deeply tanned, paling to light pink around his eyes. His thinning black hair was perfectly combed and I found myself thinking he must have been a handsome man when he was young. Putting aside the non-human ears and the shape of his head, his smile and demeanor reminded me of my father, Henry.

"We're on Kern," Becca said, "but when?"

"Right to the point," he said, "I see the scientist in you."

"Have we been here before?" Blake asked.

"Wouldn't you know if you had?"

"Apparently not, seems like…"

"Oh, things are never as they seem," he said. "Tell me, what have you learned on your journey thus far?"

"Let's start with names," I said, "I'm Charles Bimmy…"

"Captain Charles Bimmy," he said, "more accurate, yes? And you would be Becca, Blake, and finally Reggie, I know all about you, all of you. My name is Sherab Rudane Bista, but there is no need to be formal, you may address me as Sherab."

"How do you know us?" Reggie asked, "Did Tomrin…"

"Tomrin did not send you here," he said, "I brought you here. It is a distinction without a difference, from your perspective. I wanted to meet these young people from a distant world who had managed to conquer all the worlds of Gha'ba in a single day."

"No sir," I said, "we haven't conquered anything, we didn't come here to…"

"Do they not have humor on your home world?" he asked, smiling again.

"We do," Blake said, "but the captain doesn't always get the joke, especially after we die in battle."

"I see," Sherab said, "he is as described then, a serious young man."

"Described by who?" I asked.

"Why, by your wife, of course," he said, "but this is a story for another time. Come, we must not linger too long, Tomrin cannot be kept at bay forever."

Becca reached a hand out toward him, "Wait, tell us what's going on. This is…it's intensely frustrating, confusing. Did we get blown up on that ship? Are we jumping through time and space?"

"Why is this hard to believe? You have yourself experienced similar wondrous things, long before you arrived here. Was it not your own technology that allowed you to fold space, to traverse the interstellar void in the blink of an eye?"

"Yes, but…"

"Then why should you refuse to accept these experiences?"

"It defies logic," Becca said, "the idea of time as an ocean…"

"The idea is not the logic, Becca," he said, "it is the philosophy. Logic is one of the greatest powers any being can possess. It is what allows us to unlock the mysteries of the universe, and beyond. Logic empowers us to turn ideas into science."

"What is there beyond the universe," I asked, "isn't the universe… everything?"

"The beauty of your life, young captain, is you will live long enough, travel far enough, and learn enough truth, that you will one day answer this question for yourself, as will all of you."

"How do you know?" Reggie asked.

The old man shrugged and tilted his head to one side. "If we had more time together, perhaps I could devise a way to explain these things to you in a manner suited to your developing minds, but I am already using far too much energy to keep you here. Please, come with me, there is something you must see before you go."

Sherab manipulated a control on the arm of his chair, turning it around and moving away from us, through an open door and into the building.

For a moment we stared at each other and didn't move. "In for a dime, in for a dollar," I said, and followed Sherab through the doorway.

We passed down a wide hallway and entered a room noticeably different from the rest of the building. While the garden and the interior of the building were made of stone, with no obvious technology, other than Sherab's chair, the room we entered was filled with metal tables covered in devices and equipment of such varying design, it was impossible to know exactly what we were looking at. At the far end of the room, wooden crates held open a pair of doors.

The next room was as spare as the previous was cluttered. A simple curved console occupied the middle of the room, its sloped surface gleaming under soft overhead lighting. A large view screen was embedded in the wall a few meters in front of the station.

Sherab maneuvered his chair into the center of the console and activated its controls. "This," he said, "was the prototype for the temporal system Tomrin controls, the one he utilized to send you into the past. The portal here no longer functions, but the controls still work, and give me access to some of the primary systems on Sumera. This is how I brought you here, to my humble home. But first, a lesson in the history of Ki."

He tapped the console and a hologram of Ki appeared. A light flashed on the planet's surface and a small ship rose into the sky, and kept going until it reached orbit.

"The people of Ki were the first to break free from the bonds of their world," Sherab said. "When they grew adept at space travel, they used their technology to subjugate the other worlds of Gha'ba. I believe you know the history that followed. What you do not know, is how you are part of that history. Tomrin will not tell you of this, he has other plans, other motivations, than to truly enlighten you."

Sherab touched the panel again and the small spacecraft was replaced with a much larger one, shaped like a giant wheel, spokes emanating from a long cylinder, an axle with a single wheel positioned at its center.

"This," he said, his voice filled with reverence, "was the greatest adventure ever attempted. This was Velyk Nadiya."

"A space station?" Blake asked, "what's the big deal?"

"It's a ship," Becca said, "a generation ship by the looks of it."

"No way," Reggie said, "generation ships can't work. You can't keep a ship running that long."

"Once again, you refuse to accept what you do not understand," Sherab said. "Becca is correct, the Velyk Nadiya, the name is in the ancient tongue of Ki, from before the first dynastic period. An approximate translation would be 'Enduring Hope.' Thousands of years ago, during a period of constant war, the followers of Hehzan the First built this ship and set out for a distant world. They hoped to find a new home, a world where they could live in peace and harmony."

"Sounds familiar," I said. "Did they make it?"

"I believe they did," Sherab said, "and I believe you are the proof."

"Are you saying…do you mean they were trying to get to Earth?" Becca asked.

"Yes, the world you call Earth was to them called Nebo, in the ancient tongue. In your language, it would be joyful place, our perhaps joy."

"There have been humans on Earth a lot longer than a few thousand years. We are not descended from the people of Ki, it's a coincidence…"

"Of astounding proportions," Sherab said. "Two worlds able to support an identical species from across the galaxy, yes, it seems unlikely, improbable perhaps, but not impossible. Do we not all share a common origin, if one looks far enough into the past? Consider Gha'ba. All three species are virtually the same, their worlds have atmospheres with relatively minor differences. You must allow for the possibility, the logical potential, of a single type of world, a common set of conditions, which enable the development of advanced anthropoid species. Have you considered this? And if it is coincidence, does it not become a greater mystery still?"

"I've never had reason to consider any of this," Becca said.

"It is time you should," Sherab said, "and prepare yourself for your role as the living fulfillment of a promise, one which has evolved over the intervening millennia, into a prophecy. The Hehzan Prophecy."

"The children of Ki would one day return and lead the people into a new age of peace and prosperity," I said, failing to contain my sarcasm.

"You learn quickly," Sherab said, "as quickly as you dismiss ideas you do not like."

"General Pileser," Reggie said, "on Ki, he said he could prove it."

"He lives, in your time? Good for him. Hehzanites were persecuted on Ki, driven into hiding, quite tragic. Yes, if he can survive until the next conjunction and make his way to Sumera, he can compare your genetic material to samples archived on Ki, and you will all know the truth."

"We should go back to Ki and fetch him," Blake said.

Sherab waved a boney finger in the air, "You must not," he said, "he must make the journey himself. To him, it is his destiny, part of the prophecy itself."

"I don't get it," Blake said, "how does a guy named Hehzan, who lived thousands of years ago, and blasted off into space never to be seen again, how does that guy have a set of laws created after he left, banning people from building spaceships?"

Sherab smiled and shook his head. "You truly are confused, but it is a simple thing. Hehzan the First was succeeded by Hehzan the Second, who was succeeded by Hehzan the Merciful, who was succeeded by Hehzan…"

Blake raised her hands, "Hold on, I don't need the entire family tree, I get it. How many Hehzans have there been?"

"There have been forty-two, by my count. The people of Ki, the believers, have been waiting many generations for the forty-third manifestation of the Hehzan."

"Manifestation? That's a strange word."

"Not to Hehzanites."

"It's time we got back to Sumera," I said, "if I'm reading the history correctly, Tomrin is not going to sit back and let all this happen."

"You are, and he will not. But you will know what to do about Tomrin, when the moment arrives."

"You know this?" Reggie asked. "Why not tell us?"

"I do not know what you will do," Sherab said, looking at me. "But I do know you will face a choice, and you will make a choice, and you and all who come after you will live with your choice. Alas, as you said, it is time for you to go."

"Last question," I said. "You told us this system didn't work, you had to tap into the one on Sumera. Why? What happened to your portal?"

"The power source," he said, "there is but one in existence. When I built the portal on Sumera, I installed the power source there, now it is lost to me forever. I cannot fabricate another."

"Forever," Becca said, "how can you say…"

"Your time here is at an end."

He tapped his console one more time and the room around us faded away. We found ourselves standing in the room Tomrin had led us to in the Temple. But Tomrin was not there. When I reached out to take Becca's hand, someone began pounding against the door at the end of the room.

A voice outside the door shouted "Take cover," and a moment later, the door exploded inward, sending chunks of shattered stone flying around us. The concussive force knocked us all off our feet. I looked at Becca and saw the shrapnel wounds on her face and arms heal, felt my own healing. But I was too stunned to stand.

Two beings, armed soldiers clad head to toe in black articulated tactical armor, faces covered by helmets with darkened visors, rushed into the room. Through ringing ears I heard them shouting, "Let's go, let's go."

One grabbed Becca, lifted her roughly to her feet, and dragged her toward the door. The other grabbed me by the arm, pulling me up, "Get moving, or you'll never get out of here."

I was dizzy, my hearing was shot, it was difficult to follow what was happening. "Who are you? Are we back on Sumera…."

"There's no time to explain, you have to trust me Captain Bimmy, you have to get moving."

"Who are you?"

Two more soldiers entered the room and half dragged, half pushed Blake and Reggie through the doorway. "Move, move, move," they shouted.

In the corridor we were encircled by soldiers in the same black armor. The soldier behind me kept a constant grip on my back, shoving and directing me as we all careened through the passageway and into the main hall of the Temple. I saw Tomrin fighting with two of the soldiers. I tried to stop and watch what was happening, but I was shoved toward a jagged opening where the main door to the Temple had once stood. It now lay crumpled on the floor. We were pushed and dragged across the terrace outside, down an uneven path leading into the valley, until we came to a bizarre suspended doorway, three meters wide, a large circle of metal hanging in the air inches over the path.

The door was attached to nothing, no building stood behind, nothing but empty space and the valley beyond. It opened like the iris of a camera, similar to the iris protecting the dock on Deimos. But this door revealed the multi-colored swirling vortex of a wormhole. We were pushed through, into a ravaged wasteland of burnt forest and smoldering earth. The acrid air burned my lungs. I once again flashed back to my injuries during the attack on the *Arcturus*, and the smell of the burning wreckage and bodies around me, the excruciating pain of my scorched flesh. Becca was coughing, Blake and Reggie struggled to breathe.

A soldier shouted, "Clear, clear," and the iris closed behind us.

"Standby, recalibrating," the soldier said, "transit in three, two, one, go, go, go."

The door opened again and we were rushed back through, back into a world of sunlight and green fields, a river meandering through a broad valley, animals grazing nearby, a light mist over a waterfall. We were in the valley we'd seen from the temple, but at the opposite end. It was dawn and we were standing on a flat area of ground, a stone path led away to an arched opening tucked in behind the waterfall. A dozen heavily armed combatants surrounded us.

"All clear," the soldier said. The doorway closed, then vanished with a loud 'snap.'

When I stepped toward the soldier who was giving the orders, Becca gripped my hand. I was angry and frightened. I wanted answers and was in no mood to wait for them. Becca recognized my intentions. She pulled back on my hand to stop me. I continued forward and felt Blake take my other arm.

I looked back at Blake and saw she was holding onto Reggie as well.

"Read the room," she said.

The soldiers encircling us were not menacing, their weapons were held down, at ease, completely in charge.

The soldier who'd been giving commands tapped his helmet and his visor became transparent. His face was human, his eyes dark, a scar across his forehead, another along his jawline. He was smiling.

"How do you like being a time traveler?" he asked. The other soldiers laughed, and one came forward.

The second soldier's visor cleared, revealing a woman, smiling, a shock of red hair scrambling in tangles around her face.

"Captain Bimmy, it's good to meet you, it's an exciting day for us. Shall we?" She pointed down the path toward an opening behind the waterfall.

"We're not going anywhere," I said, "until you tell us exactly what is going on."

"Listen, captain, we can't stay in these suits forever. We need to get inside, get through decontamination, maybe grab a drink and some food, and when we're done, we'll debrief. What do you say?"

We needed to understand our situation, we had little choice but to go along with the soldiers, not knowing if they were our saviors, or our captors.

"Let's go," I said.

We entered a tunnel and the stone path gave way to a structure of metal walls, polished floor, lights embedded in the walls and ceiling high above. The soldiers talked quietly among themselves, while we remained silent. The series of events had left me, and I assumed my friends, in a state of shock.

We came to a wall with two large doors, one of which was open. The open door and the wall containing it were at least two feet thick, reminiscent of a blast door. I heard Becca mutter the words "another bomb shelter."

"You're on the right, we're on the left," the red-haired woman said, pointing at the open door. The soldiers opened the left door and began filing through. We entered a well-lit rectangular chamber, the walls coated in a dull green paint, peeling and chipped, visible rust in several places. The door remained open behind us. A table with four chairs facing a transparent wall sat at the end of the chamber. Platters of food and glass pitchers of water were arranged in front of each of the chairs. The clear wall offered a view into the room beyond, an empty dining hall. One by one, the soldiers entered, without their weapons and armor.

"What do you think," Blake asked, "should we eat while we wait?"

"You think it's safe?" Becca asked.

"If they wanted us dead, we'd be dead," Reggie said.

"And if they wanted us unconscious…"

One of the soldiers walked up to the transparent wall, waved his hand, and a speaker overhead crackled to life.

"We're not the enemy." he said. "You should eat, this could take a while."

He waved his hand again and walked away.

"We've been bounced around time like a bunch of…I don't know what…and we're supposed to eat," Reggie said. "Doesn't feel right to me."

"I'm still as hungry as I was yesterday, or I am the day before…or was this morning…whatever, I'm having some food. Who's joining me?"

I looked at the spread before us. Not since my breakfast with Chairman Gorman on Venusia had I seen such an abundance of food on one table.

"Is that what I think is?" Becca asked.

"Yes," I said, "meat, real meat."

"How would you know," Reggie asked, "when was…"

"When I was a kid, before my parents died, we ate like this sometimes, I'll never forget it." I saw no point in mentioning my meals while traversing the wastelands as a boy, eating whatever game Katie and I could catch to keep us going when our packaged food ran low. I didn't care to remember those days.

In the room beyond the wall, the soldiers were sitting at tables like ours, gathering in groups of three and four. Another door opened and a series of machines entered, carrying trays filled with food similar to what had been placed before us. They were robots, not androids. They lacked the refinement and humanoid form of the synthetics we'd met previously.

I used my internal systems to scan the food, then pulled back a chair. "It's safe, let's eat."

We sat facing the transparent wall, watching the soldiers, who mostly ignored us, other than the occasional glance our way. They did not eat until the red-haired woman entered and addressed them. We couldn't hear what she was saying, but it was obvious the soldiers found it amusing. They turned to their meals and the woman turned to face us. She waved her hand, activating the speaker, and said, "I know this is strange, disorienting, but I promise you things will be much clearer before the day is over."

A soldier came up behind her and spoke to her, but we couldn't hear what he said. She nodded her head and turned back to us, "Enjoy your meal," she said, "we went to a lot of trouble to get it here."

"What's your name and where are we, it's the least you can tell us," I said.

She grinned and said, "I think you've been through enough for now. Eat, relax, we'll talk soon." She waved her hand and the conversation was over.

"Terrific," Blake said, "can't wait, we've got more crazy coming."

As it turned out, Blake wasn't far from the truth.

When they finished their meal, the soldiers departed the dining hall until two remained, the red-haired leader and the scar-faced male. They sat across the glass from us and the female activated the comm.

"Did you enjoy the food?" she asked.

"Let's skip the pleasantries and get down to business," I said, "Names, location, situation, I…we… want answers."

"Directness, to a fault, exactly as promised," she said to the other soldier, who smiled and remained silent. "We'll go first, but hold onto to your hats, it's gonna get wild."

I looked at my friends and their faces echoed my concerns. I had a powerful urge to get away from these people as soon as possible. I had to fight the urge to walk out.

"You seem to think this is funny," Blake said. "I don't see anything funny. Stop dancing around and start talking or we're outta here."

"There she is, the warrior Blake, at last," the woman said. "We know all about you, all of you. We've been raised on the stories of your exploits. I'm Captain Richards, Head of the Temporal Guard, you can call me Red. And this handsome devil," she said, placing a hand on the back of the young man sitting next to her, "is none other than Lieutenant Charles Lee Bimmy, the fifth. I'll let it sink in for a minute."

I looked at Becca, my mind reeling. She smiled, shook her head side to side, and started laughing. She laughed until tears started rolling down her cheeks. It reminded me of the day I proposed to her, but this was not joyful laughter. "We always said we wanted a family," she said, "looks like we can go ahead and check that off the list."

"How can you laugh," Blake said, "this is nuts, but it's not funny."

"If they're from the future, our future, and they're descended from us, and they've come back to save us from Tomrin, I mean, how can you not find it funny?" Becca said, her voice rising, "It's completely preposterous," she shouted, her face crimson red.

"Like traveling through a wormhole when you're twelve?" the lieutenant asked.

Becca stopped laughing. "You know about the wormhole?"

"Know about it? It's in the opening paragraph of your biography, 'the impetuous young genius wanted to travel through a wormhole, so she did.' It's required reader for mid-graders."

"You're from the future," Reggie said, "and you…"

"We're from a future that may or may not happen, based on what you do next," the captain said. "We didn't come back to save you. We came back to save all of us."

"If you're from the future, if this is actually happening, then you're intentionally triggering a grandfather paradox," Becca said, "that's a big risk to take. You can't predict outcomes when…"

"Says the girl who uses the fabric of space-time as her own personal playground," the lieutenant quipped.

"What is it with you and the wormhole thing?" Blake asked

"Enough," the captain said, "I hate to say it, but we don't have much time. Temporal displacement is a massive power suck, and as you point out, loaded with risk. We have to jump to this time during specific narrow windows, when the portal in the Temple is active. The longer we stay, the more power we need to get back, and the higher the risk grows. You wanted answers, you're about to get them. You might want to take notes, we're gone in ten minutes."

The captain's mood had turned tense and serious. The young lieutenant's as well.

I looked at my friends, "Let's hear them out. We can decide what to do with it later."

"The burned-out hell-scape we dropped into," the lieutenant said, "make the wrong choice, and that's the world you'll leave behind."

"If time is short, let's stop wasting it," I said, "start with this planet..."

"A history lesson would take forever. There's a data archive on each of the ships at the spaceport, you can study it to your hearts' content. In our timeline, you never went to the Temple, you never saw Tomrin, he never had a chance to send any of you back in time. The shift happened when you dropped your rifle in the amphitheater," the captain said, pointing at Reggie. "Otherwise, you would have seen the presentation in the theater, then gone to the spaceport in time to join the battle over Sumera."

"What battle?" Reggie asked.

"The one that's about to happen," she replied, "between the Hyperion and four ships from Sol, led by your old friend Grace Cheng. But she's not the problem, Captain Rudnev is the problem."

"From the *Drache*..." Blake said.

"Yes, he and Cheng are part of an alliance, we don't know all the details, but we do know their objective."

"Which is?" Reggie asked.

"To take over Zombie Station, commandeer the Hyperion, and effectively control the entire star system. He's going to double-cross the Federation. If he succeeds, the Sol Federation will arrive in force and destroy the station. That won't sit well with the locals."

"Zombie station," Blake said, "who named it zombie station?"

"Bimmy did. Tell me you don't call it that, not officially," Becca said.

"Not officially, but I like it, and you're familiar with it."

"The locals? What locals... none of them seem like much of a threat. And why would Tomrin send us to the past to die, why not have one of the Guardians shoot us," I asked.

"Guardians can't exceed their mandate to protect life unless a life is threatened, or you try to destroy one of them, in which case you'll have the entire force gunning for you. And despite being a synthetic, Tomrin has a lot of human capabilities, not the least of which is cruelty."

"We're separated because of the bots," I said, "we're infested with bots and you're not."

"Not exactly. You're infested with the reactive bots, they're similar to the ones in the Major, modified for enhanced rejuvenation. As the war dragged on, the planets were in disarray. Tomrin created his mechanical plague, we call it Tomrin's Menace, to purge the entire system. It spread like a regular virus, then activated once it had reached critical mass. Billions died, until a counter-agent was developed on Ki. By then it was too late for Kern, and N'aha was a smoldering wasteland. The survivors fought back, Ki lived on, and they sent their last serviceable ships here to release the counter agent. They were too late, but it's the reason the three of you are still alive. The counter agent is triggered by an active infestation of the Menace bots. Once they activate, the counter agent responds."

"Why three ships?" I asked. "They look to have ample cargo capacity for a..."

"We don't know. Maybe it was excess caution, or maybe they intended to send one ship to each planet, and something went wrong. There's no record of their intent, other than the release of the counter agent."

"None of this explains me, why I'm physically younger, or the chambers at the welcome center," Reggie said.

"You got the original nanobots used to create the Triadic Hybrids, in a controlled environment, at high infiltration levels. You didn't have to wait for your bots to replicate," the captain said. "Sumera was originally designed as a resort city, built by the people of Ki after the third interplanetary war. The people of Ki were warriors, through and through, it was their third attempt to retake control of the entire system. The combined forces of Kern and N'aha fought them to a stalemate, but the cost...let's say remorse doesn't come close to describing their motivation for peace. They built the city, used nanotechnology to enable a common experience for the three species, and artificial intelligence systems to maintain everything on the planet. They created a kind of paradise, a playground for the people of Gha'ba, but a relative few ever got to see the place. They created the Triad Assembly, to prevent future wars. Sumera was supposed to be an everlasting symbol of peace and unity. And it was, for centuries.

Citizens from each world were chosen to come here during the conjunction of the planets, to become members of the Triad, a rite of passage for the young, a fountain of youth for everyone else. Those chosen shared this marvel of engineering until the political wind on Kern shifted, and a totalitarian dictator came to power. She decided Kern should have Sumera, and all that came with it, including the Temple. She started another war, the one you witnessed, to take it from the Triad."

"We've heard the history, some of it," I said. "What I don't understand is how Tomrin figures into the current state of things. Why does everything keep pointing back to him?"

"No one counted on Tomrin evolving. When the war was nearing its end and Ki was on the verge of victory, Tomrin made his first move. He gained access to Ki's ships, took down their defenses, disabled their weapons. He held his final weapon back until the three armies, and three civilizations, were close to ruin, then he made his second move. Three planets desperately trying to recover from the most brutal war in their combined history, they hardly stood a chance. Ki got lucky."

"Talk about kicking someone when they're down," Blake said.

"That's one way to put it. The original nanobots were designed to be restorative, and to make the three species in the system compatible with a common atmosphere and language. It's how you can read the language, understand it. They're interconnected with planetary and shipwide data systems. They learn, evolve, the longer they're in you, the more their capabilities grow. All other nanobots are based on those original models, but only the counter agent is more advanced than the original."

"Nothing you've said explains this separation," I said, pointing at the glass wall between us.

"We've eliminated the plague in our time, but there's always a chance we could pick up some of the killer-bots and bring them back with us. It's unlikely, but if we did, and brought it back, we could start a new pandemic, millions could die. We can't take any chances, and without sealed environment suits, we can't take you through the decon chamber. But I might be telling you too much."

"We're way beyond too much," Blake said.

"I'd say this is most definitely too much," Reggie said.

"We're running out of time, we need to talk about the battle," Captain Richards said. "Someone, probably on Deimos, has leaked news of what was found here, and the timing of the transit. Four ships will come through the wormhole with the Hyperion, they plan to ride the slipstream. Their trick is going to work, to a point. Some of the ships, we're not sure which, will be damaged. The *Hyperion* will be packed with Federation soldiers and equipment, their aim is to take the station, repair it, and hold it. Without your help, the *Hyperion* will lose and our history, your futures, may never happen."

"You said the Federation would come back in force," Becca said, "that's not possible without Promethium, unless they've found another way."

"The Federation is going to acquire more of it," the lieutenant said, "we think from one of Saturn's moons, a small one in the outer ring, it's not big enough to have a name. But this entire system is awash in Promethium, relative to the Sol system, some of it on Ki, plenty more on Kern. It became central to the power systems on every planet, and to their spacecraft."

"Their ships are impressive," Becca said, "and with Promethium, they should have developed hyper-luminal capabilities. They had warp drives, but nothing like our Gateway system."

"They did have it," the lieutenant said, "near the end of the war. They managed to build one ship, and were working on a second. The first one launched, then Tomrin activated his plague and that was it, game over."

"We saw the second one at the spaceport," I said. "Where did the first one go?"

"Earth," the lieutenant said, "over three hundred years ago, by your clock."

"They went after the *Nadiya Velyk*," I said.

The lieutenant's face twisted, his eyebrows raised, "After the what? We don't have data on anything with that designation."

"Doesn't matter, sounds like they didn't make it," Blake said. "Even I would have read about a giant spaceship arriving at Earth in the… what was Earth like three hundred years ago?"

Blake looked to Becca for an answer. In return Becca shrugged and said, "It tracks with what I know about an object entering the Sol system, the timeframe might match, but if they landed on Earth nobody made a record of it. As far as I know, the ship, if it was a ship, flew right on by. You can't blame them; it was a bad time to visit Earth. It hasn't gotten much better since."

"Sumera is old, and civilization on Ki is many millennia older than Sumera," the captain said, "and Tomrin is prideful. He keeps the place pristine with all his subordinate synths. It was his original mandate, a base-level function, and he can't let it go. It's also why we let him stick around as long as we did, until we figured out how to neutralize his higher functions. I know we've given you a lot to take in, but there's no time to explain any further. The archive on the ship will fill in the blanks for you. You need to get moving, the *Hyperion* will be here soon."

"Will we meet again?" Reggie asked.

"We may, but a lot has to happen between now and a possible then." The captain turned to me, "Unless you get the bots out of your system, and as far as we know you can't, you're going to live exceptionally long lives."

"How long?" Becca asked.

"I can't answer that," she said.

"I've summoned your transport, it's waiting for you outside," the lieutenant said, "it will take you directly to the spaceport. You must launch within two hours."

"You've brought us to our past," Becca said, "what if we run into ourselves, won't..."

"That's not how this works, but yes, you're in your past, one day, give or take. Remember, if you don't intervene, everything we've built, everything we've accomplished, every person alive, none of it happens."

"I guess the guy on the ship was right," Becca said.

"About time?" Reggie asked.

"Yes," she said, "the way we think about time. It is a prison."

"You're not trapped there anymore," the captain said.

"No," Becca said, "instead we're drowning in the ocean."

***

Blake ordered the transport to fly back to Dahoj at maximum speed. The faster and lower it flew, the more her mood brightened. I was content to keep a tight grip on the harness holding me in my seat, while Becca did her best to grin and bear it. Reggie took it in stride, and spent the flight staring out at the landscape below. When the spaceport came into sight, he shifted into battle planning mode.

"I've barely scratched the surface of the weapons systems on the ship," he said, "even if they're autonomous, we'd need at least two people on each ship, one to pilot, one on tactical."

"I don't think we should split up," I said, "even after our recent trip, they're still new to us. It's going to take all of us working together to…"

"Yes, exactly my point," Reggie said, "but if the weapons systems have low-order capabilities, or they're degraded, we'll need numbers to even up the fight."

"I get to do some more flyin'," Blake said, "and this time it won't be a point-to-point, but some honest to goodness flyin'…"

"I hear you like to fly upside down a lot," Becca said, "that's not for me."

"There is no upside down in space," Blake replied, without cracking a smile.

The transport descended through a gap in the rolling mountains and reduced speed before dropping to a waiting landing pad near the unfinished spacecraft. It made a gentle landing and powered down.

"Booorrring," Blake said.

"Which is perfect," I said.

Once the four of us stepped off the landing pad, machinery below the tarmac activated and the vehicle was lowered out of sight.

As we rode the lift up to our ship, Becca asked, "What do you think our odds are, two ships against four?"

"Impossible to say right now, it depends on the ship's full potential. Based on what we've seen so far, I'm feeling confident we'll be okay."

Blake had been lost in her thoughts since landing. "Isn't it kinda weird," she said, "to have a conversation with somebody who says you're their great-great…how many greats do I need here?"

"Kinda weird…way to keep things in perspective," I said.

"It's what I do, Captain Bimmy, it's what I do."

Back on the bridge of our ship, Reggie went directly to his station to review weapons and defensive systems. Blake did the same with flight ops, while Becca went to the comms station and began scanning for ships in orbit over Sumera.

I gave Reggie a few minutes, then asked, "How are we looking?"

"Based on what I learned on our first flight, I thought our odds would be about even. At this point, I'd say they're looking better. I'm starting to understand the menu structure. The submenus are pay-dirt. We've got multiple energy weapons, guided missile systems, some kind of EMP weapon, fully charged, and a couple of things I still haven't figured out, but I will by the time we need them. We're definitely armed to the teeth, and battle-ready."

"Good," I said. "Katie, our mission parameters are as follows. A friendly ship, the *Hyperion*, will be arriving in orbit shortly after we launch. There will be at least four enemy ships in pursuit. The enemy ships will attempt to take over both *Talall Four* and the *Hyperion*. We are to protect the *Hyperion* and destroy the enemy ships. The enemy must not be allowed to board the *Hyperion*, or *Talall Four*. Do you understand these parameters?"

"Affirmative," the ship said. "Shall I configure an automated attack strategy?"

"Reggie, care to let the ship do the shooting?"

"Let's see how I do first. I'd rather trust my instincts than rely on a ship I barely know."

"Roger that," I said, "Katie, deactivate terminal shield."

"Terminal shield deactivated…"

"Blake, do your thing."

"Yes sir," Blake replied, "Katie, release docking clamps."

"Docking clamps released…"

"Activate inertial dampeners."

"Inertial dampeners activated…"

"And do whatever else needs to be done to let me launch this bird."

"The ship is prepared for launch."

Blake again took full advantage of the ship's immense power and shot us into the sky. The city and continent dropped away, and the familiar dark expanse of space enveloped us. Artificial gravity engaged, and Blake rigged the ship for high orbit.

"Becca, can you give us relative position to the station?"

"Standby…"

The hologram of the planet and two symbols appeared, one for our ship, and one for the station.

"Blake, what's our best intercept point?"

"We can meet it post-apogee, hide in its wake until the *Hyperion* arrives."

"It's got a massive EM shadow," Becca said, "even as big as we are, if we position our ship inside it, we'd be as good as cloaked."

An outline of the ship appeared in close proximity to the station, a curved trajectory lit up, connecting our current position to the outline.

"There's your marker Blake, put us in the shadow, and keep us there."

"Marker set, taking us in."

Approaching *Talall Four*, I was reminded of our near fatal first encounter.

"Becca," I said, "the docking bays, they make sense now."

"The gantry," she said, "the ships go nose-in,"

"What about freight," Reggie asked, "you can walk three or four people abreast through the passage, but it'd be a terrible way to move cargo."

"Let's add it to our list of mysteries and…"

"You guys have no imagination. Look," Blake said, "a ship like this, you think they load and unload by hand?"

A schematic of the ship replaced our trajectory and Blake highlighted a section and enlarged it.

"What are those?" Becca asked.

"Cargo drones," Blake said, "which means there must be other bays on the station for them to access."

"If those are cargo tugs," Reggie said, "then those four smaller ones aft of them must be…"

"More drones," Blake said, "and by that, I mean combat drones."

Reggie turned back to his station and moved his hands through the controls with ever-increasing speed until he had a larger array of controls in front of him, then turned back and looked at me, smiling broadly.

"Bimmy," he said, "with all this firepower, the odds are absolutely in our favor."

13

Betrayal

Peter and Leticia Jay opted to watch the second transit of the *Hyperion* to Luyten b from Deimos Control, deep within the shell of the moon, rather than the observation deck on board the orbiting dock, where the ship had been prepped for the mission. It was a chance decision, one that saved their lives.

The launch was proceeding smoothly, until the wormhole was open and the ship was approaching the event horizon. The President, his wife, and members of their family were unprepared for the conspiracy of former enemies coming to fruition over their colony, as the *Hyperion* passed the point of no return.

A voice cried out across the control room, *"Abort! Abort! Twenty-four targets inbound, sector one-five-one, bearing two-two-seven. Repeat, abort, abort!"*

"What's happening?" the President shouted. "Are we under attack? Give me a visual!"

The main viewer in Deimos Control filled with pulsing light as inbound missiles began to strike the orbital dock, where minutes earlier the Hyperion had been at rest. Muffled explosions could be heard within the room as shockwaves from surface impacts rolled through the bedrock, shaking the solid stone structure.

"Look," Letitia said, pointing at an auxiliary view screen. Four bright orange icons swept across, telltale markers for pirate frigates. "They're going for the wormhole."

"Where are our surface batteries, why aren't we firing on those ships?" the President shouted.

"Batteries in sectors four, five, and six are down, sir. Fighters from the *Arcturus* are…this is insane…. Federation ships are firing on us, they're trying to take out the comms relay."

The *Hyperion* passed into the vast cauldron of the wormhole, and the four pirate ships entered with it, melding into the vortex. They became indistinguishable from the color and light and motion, then the wormhole collapsed, and the five ships were gone.

And the Federation attack on Deimos escalated.

Small fighters dodged in and out between the blasts from the colony's remaining defensive systems, until the *Arcturus* maneuvered in order to train its forward plasma cannons on the colony, after obliterating the docks that had, until that day, made Deimos the wealthiest colony in the Sol Federation. With a single blast, the flagship of the Federation vaporized the primary communications array.

"We have to stop the rotation," Thomas said, "all they have to do is wait, and the secondary array will come into range."

"Too late, we can't stop it in time, even if we had all our thrusters online," the President said, his voice hardly more than a whisper. He looked at his wife, his youngest son Thomas, then around the room at his staff, all expecting him to bring clarity to the moment, order to the chaos. Normally, he would have his military leaders there to take charge of the colony's defense, but his forces were spread thin in the maddening search for Grace Cheng and her remaining allies. While his ships and soldiers were scattered throughout the moons of Jupiter, he now knew, the Pirate Queen had been at his doorstep all along.

He glared at the images of the destruction being inflicted on his colony. For the first time in years, the President felt a murderous rage rise up from a dark place within, where he'd learned to keep such feelings in check. He felt his wife's hand on his forearm and looked into her eyes. His rage became a fierce determination to extract whatever he could from the day, before more was lost. He turned to his staff and gave his orders.

"Close the dock. Concentrate whatever weapons we have left on the primary approach. We can't lose it. I want those surface weapons back online, move back-up systems into place. Patch our comms through one of the ships in the dock, use whatever it takes. Get it done, and recall our ships, all our forces, I want everything we've got back here at

Deimos as soon as possible. Route casualty and damage reports directly to me; keep me updated."

"Father...Dad, you know," Thomas said, "our ships will never get here in time, the battle will be over by the time they make it back."

"I know," the President said.

"Then why…"

"Because without our ships, we're at the mercy of the Federation. If we lose this day, the best we can hope for is to evacuate the colony, save our people and our ships. And if we win it, if we can hold out until the fleet arrives, our people will be here to rebuild. Either way, our days in the Federation are over."

***

The *Hyperion's* second transit to Luyten b began the same way as the first, with alarms blaring throughout the ship. "Comms," Captain Roberts shouted, "did you receive an abort code? Was the message complete?"

"There was no way to stop the launch," Jones said. "What difference does it make?"

"I need to know why," Captain Roberts demanded, "did you get a code?"

"No, captain, the comm made it, but no code was issued."

"Tactical, unless we're in immediate danger, kill those alarms," she said. "And find those ships, give me number and status."

"Already got 'em," Breuger said, "four pirate frigates, two disabled. The others are holding position near the damaged ships, but they are operational. I'm picking up thruster activity and steady energy readings, multiple life signs."

"Keep me posted. Any movement, I want to know about it. Be ready, they didn't come here to make nice, and neither did we. Dex, time to intercept the station…"

"One hour at present speed and course," Dex replied. "We can cut it in half with…"

"Do it," the captain said. She considered her bridge crew, a team of Deimosian civilians and a pair of former Federation officers. She wondered if one of them had a hand in the debacle they were facing, then dismissed the notion. Traitors rarely put their own lives at risk. Whoever betrayed them was back at Deimos, and there was nothing she could do about it.

"Jones, get the commander of the assault team, Captain…"

"Caria," Jones said.

"Get her up here, and get my nephew up here as well."

"Yes, captain."

Dex rose from his seat to leave the bridge, "I'll start plotting our return trajectory," he said.

"Your place is right there," she said, pointing at the navigation console; "I didn't say anything about leaving. Our mission is to take or destroy the station, and we're not going anywhere until the job is done, understood?"

"Yes, captain, understood."

***

"The planet is of no interest to me," Grace Cheng shouted, "you think I want to crawl around in the jungle for the rest of my life?"

"Madame Cheng, we cannot survive on these ships forever, we will need supplies, food, water, fuel, we have lost two of our ships."

"Do you think I'm an idiot? Do you? Who else thinks I'm an idiot, go ahead, speak up." Grace Cheng, the Pirate Queen, glared at the men and women who had followed her into the unknown, on their illicit journey to the Luyten System.

"Anyone? Anyone? Apparently not." She returned her attention to her first officer, "You appear to be alone in your assessment of me."

"Madame Cheng, you know I have the utmost respect for you, my apologies if I am stating the obvious, but I wonder if you have considered the fact the planet may be our best hope for survival."

"There is nothing there for us, no population, no technology, nothing to raid, pillage, not a scrap of wealth. Once we land, we can never leave the surface, we would be no better than animals. I would rather starve. Or perhaps I will add you to my menu, we could make a few meals out of you, I think."

"If you wish to be a cannibal, I suggest you begin with our disabled ships."

"Madame Cheng," the comms tech interrupted, "I'm picking up a signal. It's weak, but I'm tracking an object approaching the planet."

"What are you waiting for? Put it on the viewer. Let's have a look at the prize we've come to take."

The station orbiting Luyten b appeared on the screen and Grace Cheng laughed, then shouted, "Who's the fool?" She slapped her first officer on the shoulder, before firing off her orders with glee. "Intercept course to the *Hyperion,* weapons on ready, assemble the boarding party, get Rudnev on the comm."

Captain Rudnev appeared on the viewer, "I take it you're tracking it," he said.

"Of course, prepare your crew for…"

"What about our other ships?"

"What about them? They're of no use to us in their current condition. We'll take the *Hyperion* and come back for them later. We have the advantage, the ship and the station will be ours. You will lead the attack, those are your orders, *Cheng out.*"

"You trust Rudnev?" Her first officer asked.

Cheng spit on the deck of her bridge, "Once a traitor, always a traitor," she said. "After we have taken the ship, as soon as the shooting stops, I want him dead."

"Yes Madame Cheng, I will see to it."

***

Captain Rudnev entered the cargo bay, the staging area for his boarding party. He stepped over the bodies of the dead pirates, and his soldiers parted to let him through as he sought out his first officer.

"You understand your orders?" he asked the young man. Lieutenant Tames had served him loyally on the *Drache,* to the bitter end. Of all the officers who'd ever served under him, Tames was the only one he'd ever trusted.

"We take the *Hyperion,* wait for Cheng to board. Once she does, we kill her and the rest of her crew."

"Good," Rudnev said, "excellent. This should all be over soon. What's our status on the other ships?"

"Our people are in control of both, minimal casualties on our side. The *Scorpion* is combat ready, the *Hawk* still needs work, but they're making progress."

"Outstanding," Rudnev said, "everything is going to plan. How's it feel to be an interstellar warrior?"

"Beats prison," Tames replied with a grin, "and it's looking less like a suicide mission by the minute."

"Indeed, it is."

Rudnev turned to his soldiers. He scanned the faces of the men and women he'd chosen to make the journey with him. Admiral Wilson had given him license to select his crew from his fellow inmates confined in the military prison on Vesta, and he hadn't wasted the opportunity.

"All right people, this is it. This is where we find out what we're made of. Do your job, trust each other, stick together, and remember, everyone on Cheng's ship is your enemy, regardless of anything you've heard me say before, or hear me say going forward."

He let his words hang in the air, then continued. "We board the *Hyperion* and eliminate the crew, if our team there hasn't already done the job. We'll have the advantage in ships, personnel, and operational capacity. If Cheng doesn't board after we take the *Hyperion*, we take out her ship. We will win this battle, and no one will ever enter this star system without our permission, and those who do will pay dearly for the privilege."

"Ten-shun," shouted Tames. The soldiers snapped to attention. One by one, Tames and the other soldiers saluted Rudnev as he left the cargo bay.

Rudnev swelled with pride. Not for his soldiers, but for himself. He'd made a deal to get out of prison for his assault on Europa, pulled together a loyal crew, infiltrated one of the greatest criminal organizations in history, and stood poised to control the richest prize humanity had ever known, an entire star system.

It didn't matter to him how many people had to die, as long as he wasn't one of them.

***

"Madame Cheng," the comms tech said, "something is wrong. The *Scorpion* has powered engines, but Captain Tulles is not responding to comms."

"Are their comms working?" Cheng asked. "Did you make sure…"

"Yes, Madame Cheng, I received the reply ping, I know they are hearing us."

"Try the *Hawk*. Get me an update on their repairs."

"No response from the *Hawk* either."

"Rudnev," Cheng muttered, "what are you up to?"

Cheng weighed her options, which she knew were few, then landed on a course of action.

"How long will it take us to intercept the *Hyperion*?"

"Less than one hour, Madame Cheng."

"Plenty of time. Contact our ships again, inform them that if they do not reply I will destroy them both."

"Captain Rudnev will hear your message as well," the first officer said. "He may take issue with your threats."

"I do not care about Rudnev's precious feelings," Cheng said. "I care about my ships. If they have turned against us, we must destroy them before we are destroyed. How do you not see this?"

"I do see it Madame Cheng, but I believe there is an alternative to destroying the ships, if you're willing to entertain the notion."

"I am all ears."

"It's a simple idea. We have two possibilities. We can get there first, try to board the *Hyperion* and hold it. I think this would be more difficult, with a higher degree of risk. Conversely, we hold back, let Rudnev think we've fallen for his subterfuge. Once his team is aboard the *Hyperion*, we take his ship, then withdraw and address the situation on the *Hawk* and the *Scorpion*. They will reconsider their objectives when their leader is outgunned. It levels the risk, but it also increases the reward."

"You may finally be earning your pay," Cheng said. "It seems Captain Rudnev is about to be caught in his own trap."

***

"Two ships on approach," Breuger said. "Weapons armed. Intercept in forty minutes."

"Arm weapons, bring us alongside the station, we'll have to move fast," Captain Roberts said. The hatch to the bridge opened and Commander Michael Jay entered, followed closely by Captain Caria of the Federation Special Forces. The look on her nephew's face was all Captain Roberts needed to know something was wrong.

"I'm sorry…," Michael began.

Captain Caria pushed him aside, revealing the sidearm she'd been pointing at the Commander's back, now aimed at Captain Roberts.

Captain Roberts instinctively reached for her sidearm, before realizing she wasn't wearing one. "What's the meaning of this? What do you think you're doing?"

"You're not in charge here anymore," Caria said. "This can go easy or…"

Before Captain Caria could finish, a burst of plasma flashed across the bridge, striking her in the chest, sending her body crumpling to the deck.

Captain Roberts turned to see Rachel Jones securing her own sidearm to a holster under her duty station. "You said it, we have to move fast," Rachel said. "They think they can get ops control from engineering. We've already locked them out, but…"

"They…," Captain Roberts said, "who is…. what is going on?"

"Captain Caria planned to take the ship," Jones said.

"Take the ship?"

"She brought us into the plan right before we departed Deimos," Breuger said, "but we won't be part of a mutiny. We have contacts on her team, we spoke to them, they agreed to stop her, looks like they failed. Seems her team is ready to fight."

"They locked about a third of their forces in the infirmary, the ones who refused to go along," Michael said. "It's pretty crowded in there. I tried to warn you, but they disabled ship-wide comms."

"Wait, back up, all of you. Start from the beginning, and be quick about it."

"Admiral Wilson found something in the data you sent to her, I don't know what, but it must have been big. Caria was supposed to kill you, and take over the ship. She told us Rudnev was in on it, and Grace Cheng."

"Rudnev is in prison."

"Not anymore," Breuger said. "He's here, on one of those ships."

"What do pirates have to do with this," Roberts asked, "this is…"

"If I know Wilson," Jones said, "she set this up to pin it on the pirates, one of her classic disinformation stunts. Cheng is here, and Wilson can use her as cover, then have Rudnev get rid of her at the first opportunity."

"Why didn't you tell me about this? We could have stopped the launch."

"We were hoping we could avoid bloodshed," Jones said. "And we couldn't be certain who was involved, or if we were being manipulated. We did what we could, when we could. Now we know who's on our side, and who isn't."

"To be honest," Breuger added, "we've been making this up as we go. We weren't brought into the plan until after we boarded the ship at Deimos."

Captain Roberts looked between the two officers, wondering if she could trust them. She knew she had little choice. "We have to go back," she said, "Dex, get to astrometrics…"

"We can't," Jones said, "Caria's team holds critical sections of the ship. And we don't know the situation at Deimos, we could drop into the middle of a fire-fight."

"Then what do you suggest," Captain Roberts shouted, her anger spilling over, "we're dead if we stay, damned if we go…"

"The hostiles are on decks two and three, we've isolated them there," Breuger said, "we've bought some time to deal with the ships…."

"They can do a lot of damage from where they are," Commander Jay said, "blast their way through a hatch, disable our engines, they're probably already working on it…"

"He's right," Jones said, "you have to…"

"Space the bastards," Roberts replied.

"Exactly."

"We have another problem," Dex said.

"What is it?"

"There's a ship, a big one, or maybe more than one, running dark in the EM shadow of the station. If we maintain course and speed, we'll have visual on it soon."

"If you can't see it," Commander Jay asked, "how do you know?"

"Mass," Dex replied, "I'm reading a significant increase in the mass of the debris field around the station, well above our previous encounter. It has to be a ship, and the one place a ship could be is inside the EM shadow, that's where I would hide."

"I've had enough, we're getting out of here, we'll take our chances back at Deimos. Jones, are we ready to vent the ship?"

"Almost," Jones replied.

"I've isolated the infirmary, we don't want to space the good guys," Breuger added.

"Captain," Dex, his voice quiet, asked, "are you sure this is the right thing to do? If we're going back anyway…"

"Buck up, Dex, consider yourself at war. Those people wanted us dead. Their mutiny opened the door to this. Mutineers don't deserve your sympathy. And if you think they'll let you waltz into astrometrics and plot our trajectory, you need to thicken up that skin and think again. I need you to rise to the challenge, can you do that?"

"Yes ma'am, I can do it."

"Good man Dex. Breuger, the moment…"

"Captain…we're being hailed…it's…," Jones paused, perplexed.

"Rudnev?"

"No, ma'am," Jones replied, "it's…Becca Kiel."

***

"Madame Cheng, the *Hyperion* is moving away from the station, weapons are armed, but something strange is happening."

"Show me," Cheng shouted, "put it on the viewer you nitwit."

Even the space-hardened members of Cheng's crew were shocked to see the *Hyperion* power away from the station with multiple external hatches open, venting atmosphere, and battle-equipped soldiers, their arms and legs flailing, then going still, dying within seconds of being expelled from the ship.

Cheng leaned toward the screen, watching the soldiers die. "My kind of captain," she said with a grin.

"What do you think this means," Cheng's first officer asked.

"It's your job to figure it out, is it not?" Cheng replied.

"I'm merely seeking your opinion."

"Look at the uniforms," Cheng said, "those are spec-ops, cream-of-the-crop assault team. You don't space such a potent weapon without good reason."

"Then I would think there's been a mutiny on the *Hyperion*."

"You're brilliant," Cheng said, "of course it's a mutiny. The question is why, with ships bearing down. And who's in charge now?"

"Rudnev," the First Officer said, "they're with Rudnev."

"Get him on the comm," Cheng said.

When Rudnev appeared on the view screen, his demeanor was not as calm as it had been during the previous conversation.

"Why have you stopped your ship? See something you don't like?" Cheng asked, "Your plan is beginning to unravel."

"I don't know what you're talking about."

"Admit it," Cheng said, "you thought you would outsmart me, take the ship, the station, all of it, for yourself. You've forgotten who you're dealing with, Captain Rudnev. I have ruled the moons of Jupiter for twenty years. I have plundered the interplanetary shipping lanes, I instill terror in the hearts of those who…"

"You're not in the Sol system anymore," Rudnev said, "and by my calculation, you've got one ship to my three. I suggest you listen carefully because I'll make this offer once. We go forward with our plan, but with one alteration."

"I'm listening."

"We're not taking the *Hyperion*, we're destroying it."

"Then how do we get back to Sol?"

"We don't," Rudnev said, "there's no need. Everything we need to survive is on the planet below, a city, a spaceport, equipment, riches beyond your imagination."

"There is no city! I can see with my own eyes!"

"It's there," Rudnev said, "whether you believe me or not, I've seen the images. There's a large city down there, ours for the taking. It's shielded, but I know it's there."

Cheng looked at her crew and despite their situation, she felt a degree of hope, even excitement, at the idea of a city waiting to be taken. Leaving space wasn't such a bad idea after all.

"We are twelve minutes from weapons range," she said. "I suggest we review our new battle plan."

14

Return to Sol

"Should I contact the *Hyperion*?" Becca asked.

"Scan the pirate frigates first, we need to know their status."

"I don't have sensor control at this station." Becca said, "I'll need to move ..."

"Stay on comms," I said, "Katie, run a sensor sweep of the enemy ships, I want operational status, life signs, anything you can get me."

"Yes, captain," the ship replied. "Three of the four ships are fully operational, the fourth has minor damage and is undergoing repairs. I read multiple life signs on all vessels, and multiple casualties on three of the ships, there are..."

"Casualties," I said, "how can you read casualties?

"The deceased carry a unique signature. It is likely they died from the discharge of energy weapons, the signature of which I am reading on each of the ships where the dead are present."

"Sounds like your typical day on a pirate ship," Blake said, "but why come all this way to kill each other off?"

"I say we kill 'em all and sort it out later," Reggie said, "Grace Cheng and her pirates are the last thing we need in this system. What happens if they make it to the surface?"

"The shield," I said, "Katie, is the shield over Sumera activated?"

"Yes captain, the city is hidden and protected."

"Two ships on intercept course for the *Hyperion*, moving slow and steady," Blake said.

"Lots of comm traffic from one of those ships over to the two ships hanging back," Becca said.

"I'd expect cross talk."

"Yes," she said, "but the other ships aren't responding. They were communicating with the other ship…"

"Blake," I said, "bring the ships up on the display, show me relative positions. Becca, show us which ones are talking and which ones aren't."

Becca left her station and pointed to one ship, "This one," she said, "was in comms with these two, the ones that aren't heading toward the *Hyperion*. This other one tried both of those ships and didn't get a response from either, even though comms are obviously working on all of them."

"Is this relevant to our mission?" Reggie asked. "If we're planning to destroy all of them, who cares?"

"We care," I said, "because it occurs to me there's a lot more happening here than meets the eye. The *Hyperion* launched from Deimos, which means these pirate frigates entered the wormhole at Deimos…"

"Which means something is very wrong at Deimos," Reggie said, "and it's found its way here."

"Exactly," I said, "and we're stuck hiding behind space junk."

"Bimmy," Becca said, "I'm not a military strategist, but do you think if the entire city of Sumera can be shielded, cloaked, maybe the ship could have something similar? Should we ask, maybe?"

"Why didn't I think of that," Blake said.

"Katie," I said, "please describe any stealth systems available to us, any shielding, cloaking mechanism, cloaking systems, anything similar."

"Standard ship-wide shields, effective against energy weapons; reactive systems in strategic sectors, effective against kinetic weapons; automated firing systems, effective against guided propulsive weaponry; an automated drone swarm, effective against small attack vessels; two platoons of defender synthetics, effective against boarding parties…"

"Katie, stop," I said, "I want to know about cloaking mechanisms for the ship, do we have a way to hide the ship the way the city is hidden?"

"The shipwrights of Ki deemed such systems unnecessary for Kazan-class vessels."

"That explains the firepower," Reggie said. "Katie, can the defender droids be used in offensive operations?"

"Negative. The use of synthetics in offensive operations is banned by the First Treaty of Sumera."

"Too bad," Reggie said, and turned back to his controls. He looked back at me. "Bimmy," he sighed, "the ship rattled off a list of systems I haven't found yet. I'd like to reconsider my earlier position. I think we should let the ship do the shooting. There's too much at risk."

"Blake," I said, "your thoughts?"

"As much as I'd like to do the flyin' on this one, Reggie is right, we should let Katie run the show this time."

"Becca?"

"I'm on comms, all I care is we win."

"Okay then," I said, "Katie, please prepare an automated attack strategy and…"

"I am unable to comply," the ship said. "Proximity of combatants, and relative flight patterns, restrict firing sequences to manual."

"Oh boy," Blake said, "he who hesitates."

"Captain," the ship said, "an energy weapon has been discharged on the bridge of the ship designated *Hyperion*, one biologic is deceased."

I considered the implications of weapons fire on the *Hyperion* and came to what I thought was the most plausible conclusion.

"Someone on the *Hyperion* may be working with the pirates," I said, "we need to know what's happening. Becca, hail the *Hyperion*. If anyone we don't know responds, cut the comm."

"You got it, hailing the *Hyperion*…no response. Resending. Stand by. I'm getting a data packet, no audio or visual…unpacking…I…I don't know what to do with this."

"What is it?" I asked. "Are they warning us off?"

"It's one line of text, a question. They want to know how you and I met."

"Mikey," Reggie said, "that would be his way of verifying our identity without a known ship transponder. Clever kid, that one."

"Watch who you're calling kid there buster," Blake said.

"Point taken," Reggie said.

"Send the reply," I said, "those frigates will be in range soon."

"Okay, updating the data packet with 'we met in the middle of the street after I traversed a wormhole' and sending."

After a brief delay, a static image of Captain Roberts replaced the hologram of the ship. The image filled in with color to give the approximation of a three-dimensional hologram, but the result was incomplete.

"Katie," I said, "what's wrong with the transmission?"

"The ship designated *Hyperion* is primitive, its communication capabilities are limited."

"The newest ship in the fleet," Reggie muttered, "is not primitive."

"By the standards of the shipwrights of Ki," Katie replied, "the ship designated *Hyperion* is, in every measure, primitive."

"Remind me… how old is this ship?"

"Captain Bimmy," Captain Roberts said, "I did not expect to see you, and I've got loads of questions about that ship of yours, but we've got more important issues to address at the moment. I'm sure you've seen the approaching vessels. Admiral Wilson has betrayed us…"

"Whoa, stop," I said, "those are pirate frigates. What makes you think…"

"I don't have time to debate it with you, I need you to trust me, trust us. Cheng and Rudnev are working together, and Wilson is behind it."

"Why?" I asked. "Why would Wilson betray Deimos? It's…"

"Criminal," Captain Roberts replied, "outrageous, heinous, pick a word, she's doing it for control of this system. There's enough Promethium here to build a fleet of Gateway ships. We discovered it on our first trip, but I scrubbed it from the data we shared. She must have figured it out, and blamed Peter for the snub. We can't risk going back with hostiles bearing down on us. I need to know your offensive capabilities."

"Reggie, you're up."

"Roger that," Reggie said, "we've got at least as much fire power as three Deimosian battle cruisers, maybe more. I'm still learning the systems. We should be able…"

"Who are you?" Roberts said, "Bimmy, where's…is he…"

"It's a long story Aunt Sally," Reggie said, "let's say the climate on Sumera agrees with me…"

"Sumera…what have you…when this is over…"

Captain Roberts looked over her shoulder, then turned back to me and said, "We're out of time, you can't hide from the enemy anymore, and I've got a problem to sort out before we engage. I'm sending course and speed data; can you use it to…"

"We can coordinate our attack strategy from your data, no problem," I said. "We picked up a plasma discharge on your bridge, we're reading one deceased."

"Some of our guests tried to commandeer the ship, and hand it over to Rudnev. Jones and Breuger saved the day. We're going to clean up the mess. I'll fill you in later, if there is a later. Roberts, out."

"I've got the data packet," Becca said, "displaying..."

Course and speed data appeared in the space where the captain's likeness had been. Blake reached up, grabbed the image, and threw it onto her console, where it vanished, "Got it," she said, "I can work with this, let's go shoot some pirates."

"How did you know..."

"Lucky guess," Blake said, "and maybe a bot in my brain."

"Captain," the ship said, "if you require my assistance, I can incorporate this new data, and formulated an attack sequence within acceptable safety parameters. Would you like me to proceed?"

Blake and Reggie both shouted, "Yes!"

"Okay then," I said, "Katie, please proceed."

"As you command," the ship said. "Do not attempt to pilot the ship until the sequence is complete, or you have given the order to abort the sequence. Standby for attack initiation," the ship said, "in three, two, one, initiate."

The lighting on the bridge shifted to an amber glow and a noise began to emanate simultaneously from each console.

"Are those supposed to be alarms?" Becca asked. "I've had clocks with more urgency than this."

The ship lurched to starboard with enough force to briefly overpower the inertial dampeners. I grabbed the railing along the rear perimeter of the flight ops platform to keep from getting tossed to the deck. The holographic display switched to a projection of the battle scene. We watched our ship maneuver, and the *Hyperion* pull away from the station. It was then we saw the bodies being ejected from open hatches on the *Hyperion*.

I heard Becca take in a sharp breath, but she said nothing. Blake also remained silent. Reggie stared at the macabre scene, then stood up, walked toward the hologram, and stared intently.

"Reggie, what's your assessment?"

"Aunt Sally doesn't much care for people who try to take her ship," Reggie said. He went back to his station and sat down. "Based on the open hatches, I'd say they took control of decks two and three. She couldn't risk sabotage, or losing flight controls."

"She did what she had to do," I said, "I'm not here to judge her. But I do want to understand what we're dealing with."

The ship made another abrupt maneuver, and this time I did lose my balance. I slammed into the floor behind Becca. Were it not for our circumstances, I'm certain she would have laughed. I looked ridiculous.

"Katie," I said, "why doesn't the captain have a chair?"

A panel opened in the flight ops platform and a chair rose into place behind and above Blake's station.

Then our ship began its attack, and things started moving quickly.

I strapped into the chair and watched our ship place itself in the flight path of the approaching frigates. The *Hyperion* moved in the opposite direction, as if fleeing the battle. The frigates broke off their approach, but neither escaped.

A curved energy wave, translucent-bright-red, emerged from the bow of our ship, then expanded outward and accelerated at a high rate, away from our ship, washing over the first of the frigates, sending it tumbling away. A second waved burst from the bow, targeting the second ship. As the waves dissipated, we continued forward and our plasma cannons opened fire, disabling the enemy ships, setting them adrift.

"Captain," the ship said, "it is customary to offer terms of surrender before destroying enemy vessels."

Before I could respond, both frigates returned fire.

"Multiple incoming," Reggie said, "do you think…"

"Targeting," the ship said. Streams of tiny projectiles, thousands of fist-sized rocket-propelled explosives, blasted out of tubes concealed in our bow, racing out to meet the incoming missiles. Two of the enemy missiles made it through the defensive measures and struck home, rattling our ship.

"Katie, damage report."

"Kinetic shielding in sectors two and three is reduced to thirty-one percent effectiveness. Would you like to transmit terms of surrender?"

"We've battled this enemy long enough," I said. "Destroy those ships, we'll consider terms for the remaining."

"As you command," the ship replied.

Two missiles launched from our forward battery, streaking out toward the frigates. The targeted ships deployed counter measures, but they were too slow to respond. Both of our missiles struck their targets. Before the ships exploded, something moved away from one of them. It drifted at first, then rockets on the object fired, sending it racing toward the planet.

"Escape pod," Blake said, "how much you want to bet it's Rudnev?"

"My money's on Cheng," Reggie said.

"Katie, scan that pod, report."

"One life sign, minor injuries, possibly plasma burns."

"Male or female."

"Female."

"Should we pursue?" Blake asked.

"We have two more ships to deal with."

"If she makes it to the surface," Becca said, "she'll be a bigger threat than ever."

"One problem at time," I said. "One thing we know, there's a learning curve on Sumera, bots or no bots. Katie, can you disable the other ships on Sumera?"

"Affirmative. However, a magistrate has the authority to override my directive."

"Do it, it might make the difference."

"Vessels designated *Saosa pei Matagi* and *Patukava* are locked to your voice command."

"We gotta work on these names," Blake said.

"Captain," Katie said, "if the enemy requests conditions of surrender, I am obliged under the terms of the Treaty of Sumera to end my attack sequence."

"I've hailed both ships," Becca said, "no reply."

Blake pointed at the battle schematic and shouted, "There's your reply."

Each ship had opened fire. So many missiles were inbound, it looked to me as though they'd emptied their entire armories.

"Katie, evasive maneuvers."

"Do you wish to abort the attack sequence?"

"I don't wish to be blown to bits."

"Understood," the ship replied.

Another wave of energy formed at the bow, then blasted forward to intercept the missiles. As each inbound weapon made contact with the energy wave, it went tumbling out of control before exploding. But the wave dissipated before all the missiles were disabled.

"Pulse emitter is depleted, modifying sequence…"

Our ship's cannons opened fire, destroying more missiles while simultaneously launching two of our own weapons at the enemy frigates. One of the frigates tried to flee, but didn't get far. Both ships were struck and destroyed. There were no additional escape pods. Our cannons continued firing bursts, until all the incoming missiles were destroyed, or missed their targets.

"That was too easy," Reggie said. "If the people of Ki built these, and their enemies almost defeated them, they must have had some kind of weapon we haven't seen yet."

"Add it to the mystery list," I said.

"Incoming from Captain Roberts," Becca said.

"Put her through."

"Impressive," Roberts said when the link was established, "got any more ships like that?"

"As a matter of fact, we do. But we've got a new problem," I said. "Cheng may have made it to the surface. If she did, it won't be long before she sorts herself out and starts making trouble again."

"Does she have access to the ships?"

"Not immediately. We've taken precautions, but there may be a workaround."

"We have to get back to Deimos, our fleet is engaged around Jupiter, the colony's defenses are minimal. If Wilson is behind this, it's safe to assume Deimos is under attack. They won't last long. Good luck finding Cheng, we'll try to get back..."

"We're going with you," I said. "If those frigates made it through, we can make it too. This ship could make all the difference."

"Two of those frigates were disabled by the transit."

"But they made it," Becca said. "I've been thinking about how they did it. It has to be in the timing, and using momentum to enter the vortex. If we enter after the *Hyperion* begins to cross the event horizon, shut down our engines before the wormhole closes, then we should transit together, same as the pirate frigates."

"Are you willing to risk it?" Roberts asked.

I looked at my crew, offering them the opportunity to object. None spoke, and the decision was made.

"Yes," I said, "we are. If we can help Deimos, it's worth the risk."

"Let's get moving, there's no time to waste," Roberts said.

***

Blake agreed it was best to let our ship handle the flying during our attempt to transit the wormhole with the *Hyperion*. My second look into the wormhole was no less captivating than the first. The colors, the movement, the distant dark hole at the center of the psychedelic whirlwind held my gaze until we became one within it.

The few seconds of the ride can best be described as bumpy, but we made it through without damage. When we arrived at Deimos, the attack on the colony had reached a fevered pitch. The orbital shipyards and docks were destroyed, the fleet of ships around Deimos, most of them unarmed, had been decimated, dozens were burning and adrift. The few remaining surface batteries of the colony were focused on defending the dock from repeated assaults by light attack ships, similar to one of my previous ships, the *Ajax*.

The *Hyperion* had spent less than two hours over Sumera before returning to Deimos. During its absence from the colony, the Federation attack continued unabated. But knowing the colony was virtually defenseless had left Admiral Wilson overconfident. She had failed to gather more than a fraction of her armada for the assault.

"They haven't surrendered," I said, "how are they holding out?"

"They can't surrender without comms," Reggie said, "all the communication arrays are destroyed."

"Remind you of anything?" I asked.

"Europa," Blake said, "but this time we've got more than attitude on our side."

"You've got that right," I said. "Let's get stuck in."

"Message from Captain Roberts," Becca said, "She says, and I quote 'Give 'em hell Bimmy.'"

"You heard the captain," I said, "Blake, fly us in. Reggie, let 'em have it."

Blake took over flight controls and flew us directly at the port broadside of the *Arcturus*. Surprise was on our side, and four of our missiles were away before the ship's crew could turn their attention from the colony to us. Our missiles destroyed the forward battery and main sensor array in the first salvo, setting the ship ablaze and reeling to starboard. Blake rolled our ship 180 degrees and we passed across the burning ship's bow, close enough to give us a view into its bridge. I recalled the last time I had been there, my flesh burned away, near death. I wondered if any of my former shipmates were there, then pushed the thought aside.

"Bring us around, target the aft azimuth thruster," I said. I was calmer than I expected to be, given I was attacking my former mentor and commander. I reminded myself of the crime she was committing against my friends, against a place I'd viewed as a home, a refuge, and focused on the task at hand.

Our second salvo destroyed the starboard thruster, the main cargo hangar, and the flight deck. It wasn't a contest; the *Arcturus* was crippled.

I spun my finger in a slow circle, "Come back around, hit 'em again, drive the message home."

I thought I heard Becca say something about ice, but didn't hear her clearly. Blake glanced over her shoulder at Becca, shook her head 'no,' then turned back to her controls.

Our third salvo took out the ship's main thrusters as well as the remaining maneuvering thruster. In a matter of minutes, the *Arcturus*, the pride of the Federation, flagship of the Fleet Admiral, had been reduced to a ruined, burning hulk. We turned our attention to a trio of Federation corsairs, and the rout was on. When our drone swarm entered the battle, the Federation fighters began to flee the fight, some to the Federation base on Mars, others to the spaceports on Phobos.

The *Hyperion* moved into close station over Deimos to augment the colony's remaining surface batteries, and defend the dock. When the fighters fled, the *Hyperion* engaged the remaining attack ships. Once we joined the fight, the attack ships also ran from the fight.

The entire battle, once we arrived, lasted exactly 48 minutes. We had defeated Wilson's armada, at terrible cost to the Federation. It paled in comparison to the damage that had been inflicted on the colony, and likely on the Federation itself. An unprovoked attack on a member colony would create a rift in the alliance, an alliance fragile from the beginning. We took up position over the wreck of the *Arcturus* to ensure it made no further aggressions toward the colony, prepared to finish the job of destroying the flagship, if necessary.

"Wilson is hailing us," Becca said, "should I..."

"Becca, hold the comm, if you please," Reggie said. "Bimmy, we need to make an adjustment."

Reggie stood in front of me and started removing the rank and insignia from my uniform. They had been a part of me for so long, I hadn't given them any thought.

"You're still our captain," he said, "but you can't be a captain in Space Force. That would make you..."

"A traitor," I said. "I don't feel like a traitor."

"Because you're not," Blake said.

"Then what am I?"

"A hero," Becca said.

"If I am, then we all are."

"I can live with that," Blake said.

"I think a promotion is in order," Reggie added, "Congratulations Admiral Bimmy, we'll work out the insignia later."

"No Reggie, I'm happy being a ship's captain. Besides, we have three ships and four sailors, not much of a fleet."

He put one hand on my shoulder and tapped my chest with the other. "We know our situation Bimmy, but they don't. And it's our fleet, we can do what we want."

"Good point, we can use it, but I'm still a captain. Becca, put her through."

"She's upset, brace yourself."

"What else is new…"

Wilson was enraged, terrified, disheveled, shouting her demands into the comm. "Unknown vessel, cease your attack, I repeat unknown…wha…Captain Bimmy? Why have you attacked my ship? This is a Federation military operation. I order you to cease your attack and surrender your vessel immediately."

I could hear the chaos around her, but couldn't see anything more than her face, smudged with soot, dripping sweat, she was clearly panicked. The occasional wisp of smoke passed through the hologram, at times obscuring her face. I let her continue shouting until she lost all composure and screamed, "What do you have to say for yourself?"

"As commander of the Unified Forces of Gha'ba, I am prepared to accept your surrender. I am also prepared to destroy your ship, and any other ships you call to this sector without my permission."

"Surrender," she replied, "I won't surrender to a traitor. I don't take orders from you. You're nothing. You're an impudent foundling upstart, you'd be stuck in a dust-bowl on Earth if it weren't for me, you little…"

"Cut the comm," I said, "we need to let her come to terms with her situation."

"Yeah," Blake said, "let her burn for a bit, then she'll simmer down. That's been my experience with her when she gets mad."

"Did she get like this a lot when you served with her?" Reggie asked.

"Not like this, but she's a hot head for sure," Blake said. "We used to call her Admiral Supernova. When she went off, oh boy, run for cover."

"I never saw that side of her," I said. "Then again, I never actually served with her. OCS, then one mission after another, I never served on her ship. Guess we know why. She has a pretty low opinion of me."

"Being Fleet Admiral has that effect on people," Blake said.

"Captain," the ship said, "long range scans indicate numerous vessels on course to this location. Shall I move to intercept?"

"Can you give us a visual?"

"The ships are not in visual range. However, I can display a likeness based on scanned data."

"Please do," I said.

Outlines of ships began to materialize before us.

"Deimosian battle cruisers," Reggie said, pointing at four ships, "and these six look like colonial corsairs, but they don't usually stray far from home, the rest are freighters, a couple of charters, personnel carriers, a fuel tanker, it's a heck of a mix."

"Maybe Deimos got a message out," Becca said, "and the colonies pulled together a fleet."

"An evacuation fleet," Reggie said, "most of these ships are unarmed."

"We've got another civil war on our hands," Blake said.

"Not if I can help it. Becca, get Captain Roberts, I've got an idea. Katie, designate the approaching ships as friendly."

"Captain Bimmy," Roberts asked, "did Wilson surrender?"

"Not yet, we're giving her some time to think about it."

"I wouldn't count on it, there are more Federation ships where hers came from."

"And you've got a fleet headed your way, reinforcements, an evacuation fleet."

"Good luck convincing Peter to leave. As long as he's got air in his lungs, he's not going anywhere."

"I'm sure he'll do what's best for the colony. Have you established comms with him yet?"

"No. Michael spotted a serviceable access portal. He's going down with a lander to make contact with Deimos Control. They'll be able to patch comms through the lander and relay messages through the *Hyperion*. Inefficient, but it will work."

"What about the dock?" Reggie asked.

"We won't know until we're inside, the iris took heavy damage. They'll be locked inside until it's been repaircd."

"We'll stand by until help arrives," I said, "then we're paying a visit to Phobos for provisions. We may be gone for a while."

"I would prefer you stay here. We need your ship's firepower."

"The shooting is over. You're gonna have a standoff on your hands, at least until we get back."

"Where are you going?"

"Earth," I said, "to pay the High Council a visit."

"It's not enough you poke the hornets' nest, you want to stomp on it for good measure. One Captain to another, it's a bad idea."

"Aunt Sally, you know as well as I do, Captain Bimmy has a history of crushing the hornets' nest."

"Reggie," Captain Roberts began, then paused. "This is too strange, you say it's you, but it's not you. I feel like I'm looking at…I don't know…how did this happen? And don't tell me the climate, I don't believe it. What am I supposed to tell your parents?"

"It's complicated," Reggie said. "I am definitely me, but different. Tell my parents I'm well, I look great, and I'll see them when we get back."

"It will have to do," she said. "Before you go, Dex wants to speak with you. He insists."

Dex Farber appeared next to the captain, looking nervous.

"Hey Dex," Reggie said, "what is it? We've got…"

"I wanted to say," Dex blurted out, "I mean, I wanted to tell you, be safe. Deimos needs you, no unnecessary risks, come back in one piece, okay?"

"You bet Dex," Reggie said, "we'll be back in no time. You be careful too. The *Hyperion* needs its navigator."

"Roger that major, thanks. Dex, out."

Dex stepped away, removing his image from the hologram. Captain Roberts watched him leave the bridge, then turned back to Reggie. "I couldn't have said it better myself. All of you, be careful. Roberts, out."

The comm ended and no one spoke right away, until Blake piped up, "Interesting convo there. Anything you want to talk about, Reggie?"

"No."

"Maybe later…"

"Unlikely."

***

It took four days for the vanguard of the Deimosian fleet to arrive, followed by the slower ships in the ad hoc Colonial armada. Once the battle cruisers were in place at Deimos and over Mars, we were ready to continue our journey.

"Blake," I said, "set course for Phobos. Becca, let them know we're stopping by for supplies and won't take any offensive action, unless threatened by the Federation forces they're harboring."

The good people of Phobos were happy to help us supply our ship. In a few hours we were fully stocked with provisions, and ready to break orbit. We had enough food for an extended journey, and plenty extra in case we picked up additional crew or passengers along the way. Once we had our cargo stowed, I gave the order.

"Blake, set a course for Earth, standard propulsion, maximum speed."

"You don't want to use the warp drive?" Becca asked.

"A slower trip will give us time to let the bigger picture develop. Go ahead, Blake, light the candle."

"Roger that Captain Hybrid. Earth, max speed, the way I like it."

Our ship was fast, but news of the battle at Deimos arrived well ahead of us, along with word of an advanced alien ship with extraordinary firepower. The High Council was called into session, and promptly ordered fleet vessels to form a defensive perimeter to protect Earth. It was predictable, and we had a plan for it.

Becca kept busy during our flight to Earth, contacting every Federation vessel within range, informing anyone who would listen of our intent to talk, as well as our readiness to fight. The captains she contacted, to a person, claimed the attack on Deimos had been carried out by Grace Cheng, and expressed shock and outrage when they learned the truth. Our comm with Admiral Wilson provided all the evidence we needed, and we had more where it came from. All the same, we couldn't know who to believe. But on approach to Earth orbit, the result of Becca's campaign became clear.

"What's our ETA to Luna?" I asked.

"Two hours," Blake replied, "unless you want me to slow it down and cool the engines."

"What sort of defensive force are we looking at?"

"Not much of one," Reggie said. "Four ships, light corsairs, holding position. We'll be beyond their weapons range at Luna. They're giving us a lot of space. Looks like Becca's got the touch; it's a token defense. If we have to fight, it should be quick."

"Let's not get ahead of ourselves, or overconfident. We're here to talk, get what we came for, and head back to Deimos. I want to keep this short."

"Are you sure you want to do this?" Becca asked. "What if they decide to take you prisoner? You can only tempt fate so many times before it turns against you."

"It'll be okay," I said, "they've had a taste of what this ship can do, and for all they know we've got a fleet of them on the way. I think they'll be on their best behavior."

"Do you think they'll give us safe passage to Arcadia?"

"They'll grant us safe passage anywhere we want to go, or there won't be any deal."

"What about Deimos?" Reggie asked. "Even if they agree to our terms, it could take years to rebuild. We can't stay in orbit over Mars, guarding a construction project."

"We won't," I said, "the Deimosian fleet is a viable counter to what's left of the Federation, and other colonies will help with the recovery. If the Federation does the right thing, the rebuild could go faster than you think."

"I admire your optimism," Blake said, "but I don't share it. They're likely to laugh in your face, then throw you in jail, then we'll be up here with this giant gun pointed at them. It's a recipe for disaster, if you want my opinion."

"I always want your opinion," I said, "you're rarely right, it makes it easy for me to figure out what to do next."

"Seems to me, you're starting to get the hang of agreeing with me," Blake said.

I knew my plan was high risk, but the potential rewards, for everyone, made the risk worth taking. When Becca hailed Artemis Station, the response was immediate, and to my surprise, friendly.

"Captain Bimmy, welcome to Luna, you are cleared for orbit in sector alpha-one-seven. Your shuttle is cleared to land on pad three. Chairman Gorman of the High Council sends his regards."

"I bet he does," I mumbled. "Thank you, Artemis Station, I'll be arriving within the hour. Bimmy, out."

"Please stand by. My commanding officer would like to speak with you."

"Standing by."

I looked at Becca and she muted the comm. I looked at Reggie, "You think this is about those nukes we dropped off after the war?"

"One way to find out," Reggie said, pointing at the face of the man staring back at us, waiting for the line to reopen.

"Let's hear what he has to say."

Becca unmuted the comm and gave me the nod to go ahead.

"This is Captain Bimmy, what can I do for you?"

"Major Archibald Jones," the man said, "and I'm interested in what I can do for you, and your crew. Food, fuel, water, I know you're a long way from your base."

"Why would you offer us assistance?" I asked. "I'm grateful, but we're not exactly on friendly terms."

"But we are, at least I am with you. You're the man who saved my daughter, Rachel, on your Mercury mission. I've been in your debt for a long time. Anything you need, say the word, and I'll make it happen."

"You'd be putting your career at risk."

"What's a career against the life of my only child? Rachel sent a comm, including details of the attack on Deimos. You should know, President Jay has taken Wilson into his custody."

"We are aware. Any word on what he's planning to do with her?"

"From what I understand, that depends on the outcome of your talks with the Council. The Chairman claims he didn't sanction the operation, but no one believes him. He's become quite unstable of late. Despotic, tyrannical. Some on the Council, the outer colonies in particular, are out for blood, his blood. He's holding on by a thread. This attack, it's shaken the Federation to its core. I hope you can talk sense into these people, the last thing we need is another war."

"Thank you for the information, major, I'll do my best, Bimmy out."

"You know Gorman better than any of us. Do you think he ok'd the attack?" Reggie asked.

"I don't know him that well, but remember where we started with him," I said. "If I had trusted him, we'd never have gone to Luyten b in the first place. He's a clever player, but he doesn't know how to hide his moves, unless he's learned a few things since the last time we met."

"We all know clever can be dangerous," Becca said, "maybe one of us should come with you."

"I agree," Blake said, "somebody's gotta watch your back."

"You just want to fly one of our shuttles. You can watch my back from here, it's safer for all of us."

"You know I'll never miss a chance to fly," Blake said, "I don't care if it's a fancy shuttle or a bargain basement puddle jumper."

"For this trip, I'd rather let Katie fly me over. Go ahead and spin one up, we shouldn't keep our hosts waiting."

"Before you go," Becca said, "activate your guide, we need to keep tabs on you. And there's one more thing, for me."

Becca put her hands on my neck and planted a long kiss on my lips. Blake let out a hoot and Reggie quipped something about "you crazy kids." I missed most of it, I was focused on the kiss.

Becca pushed away from me and smiled. "Give 'em hell, Bimmy."

***

Major Jones met me when I landed. He was tall, like his daughter, and unusually muscular for a man who'd spent his life in space.

"I thought you were born on Luna. You look more like a man who's been Earth-side his entire life."

"We have a multi-G gym on level seven," he said, "you can simulate gravity up to four times Earth-G, some of us find it a little addictive. You should try it while you're here."

"Not a bad habit to have," I said, "but this won't be a long visit. Has the council assembled?"

"Not entirely, but they've got a quorum. Any business they conduct, it'll be official."

"That's good enough for me," I said. "Major, I want to clear something up with you."

"I'm listening."

"Rachel is one of my closest friends, you are not in debt to me. I risked my crew and my mission for her because I care about her, she was injured on my watch. I couldn't lose her. I know she and Breuger have their issues with me, I don't know if she ever said…"

Major Jones shook his head and interrupted, "There's an old Earth saying about water under a bridge, have you heard it?"

"Yes, but…"

"No 'buts,'" he said, waving a finger at me. "My daughter, and her odd choice of a husband, went on an interstellar rescue mission, for you. If that doesn't scream water under the bridge, nothing does. You get me?"

"I get you," I said. His unexpected reassurance lifted my spirits. If the Council was as welcoming as the major, I felt the meeting might go better than expected.

"All right then. Let's get you to the council chambers before they all wander off and get lost."

We rode a tram onto a central lift, then descended into the heart of the station. We dropped through the maintenance and storage levels, then residential levels, followed by the commercial district, before arriving at the administrative level. Each level was laid out in concentric rings radiating out from the central column. I'd never been to the interior of the station. As an officer candidate, my training exercises had been confined to surface installations. The space was all shades of grey and blue, and innumerable bright lights. Not exactly cramped, but efficient. It was an old station, but still a marvel of engineering, given its humble beginnings as an outpost buried inside a lava tube.

The tram carried us down a wide corridor with a low ceiling. It wasn't grand, but it had the look of a place built to last. The further away we rode from the lift, the fewer people we saw.

"Is it normal for the council to meet here, it seems like a strange choice."

"They've met here once. It's strange in many ways, mostly because it lacks the luxury of the council chambers at Venusia. His Highness the Chairman had all the Federation admin services moved there. He said it was more conducive to the focus required to do the business of the people, given conditions on Earth."

"We could have gone directly there," I said, "our ship is exceptionally fast."

"Yes, and packed with weapons. You think Gorman wants that thing orbiting Venus?"

"He may not have a choice," I said, "if things don't go well today."

"Some advice, from a guy who's seen a thing or two. Be careful not to overplay your hand. Gorman is not as soft as he looks, and not as mentally stable as one would hope. He's volatile, explosive even. Some people think he's got a bad case of space sickness, and I'd be one of those people. Seen it before, especially bad when the afflicted comes under psychological pressure. Some think it's more widespread than anyone wants to admit. Be that as it may, the council won't be open to strong-arm tactics; they get enough of that from Gorman. From you, it could end up uniting them, and working against you."

"That's good advice, much appreciated."

"We're here," he said, "through those doors, down the hall, through the last door, they're waiting for you. It's nothing fancy. You should expect some of them to be a bit testy."

"Roger that," I said, "thanks again."

"My pleasure. I'll pick you up here when the Council adjourns."

Major Jones drove away and left me to find my way. I entered the temporary chambers of the High Council, a small auditorium with five rows of tiered seating. The council members were seated facing me, while Chairman Gorman was standing in front of them at a podium, his back to me.

He turned around and scowled. His voice boomed out, filling the room. "There he is, all hail the conquering hero, how kind of him to grace us with his presence."

"If you think you've been conquered, you're of no use to me. I came here to talk peace and reconciliation. If you're not prepared to discuss those topics, then I'll finish my business on Earth and return to Deimos."

A member of the council rose and asked, "What business do you have on Earth? We do not seek further conflict, but our forces are rallying as we speak."

"They're not, and you know it. The ships you have in orbit are no match for mine, and even if they were, the entire Deimosian fleet is ready to take revenge on you for what you've done."

"We have done nothing," Gorman said, "our fleet went to Deimos to defend it from an attack by Grace Cheng."

"That's a lie. You've either created it or you're believing it, which makes you either a criminal, or a fool, or both. I witnessed the attack with my own eyes. I have the images to prove what I'm saying. What do you have? More lies, bigger lies, more attacks on innocent people? You can continue on your path, or you can stop talking and start listening…"

Chairman Gorman's face turned crimson red. "I don't have to take this from a vulgar marauding miscreant." He pulled a weapon, some kind of pistol, from a fold of his robe and aimed it at me with a shaking hand.

I heard someone gasp and say, "Gorman, no, we should listen to him, he came here…"

"He came here to lord his victory over us," Gorman shouted, his voice cracking, spittle flying from his mouth. The man was unhinged, his eyes wild, face burning. "I will decide humanity's destiny, not this traitorous scum."

He braced himself against the podium and fired. Everything in the room shifted into slow motion for me. Time crawled. My internal systems, which I'd activated on N'aha, had taken over. As the projectile flew toward me, data streams appeared around it; trajectory, speed, damage estimates. I was fascinated, and distracted, by what I was seeing. I didn't react in time. A second before I felt the projectile slam into my chest, time and motion return to normal. The force of the impact knocked me to the floor. The pain didn't set in immediately, giving me a few precious moments to think about the weapon. It was an unusual device, not an energy weapon, or an old-style propellant-explosive firearm. A miniature railgun, a clever choice. Anything else would have set off every alarm in the station. The meeting with the council was a ruse, Gorman had planned to kill me all along.

Chaos erupted in the Council chambers as some of the members tried to leave, and others sought to call for help. Gorman wouldn't have any of it. He turned back to the members and brandished his weapon, bringing them to order with the threat of violence. His antics gave my body time to heal. The movement of the slug as it was pushed back out of my chest hurt more than the initial impact, but the job was done in less than a minute. I picked the chunk of metal off my chest, then stood up. I watched the fabric of my tunic mend itself, looked down at the slug, then turned my attention to the petrified council.

I began walking toward Gorman, with his back once again to me. As I walked, I set my systems into calculation mode, and read the data appearing around my hand, and the projectile it held.

When Gorman realized he'd lost the attention of the members of the council, he swung around and pointed his weapon at me again.

"Anyone wants to kill me, they better do the job on the first go," I said, "because you're not getting a second chance." I pinched the slug between my thumb and finger, made a final rushed calculation, and flicked it at him.

I did not intend to kill him.

My hand became a weapon. The projectile leapt from it with a loud snap and delivered far more energy to the slug than I expected. It slammed into Gorman's forehead, penetrating his skull with a resounding *crack*, exiting the back of his head, and finding a home in the far wall, splattering a few members of the council with bits of blood, bone, and brain matter. The Chairman collapsed into a heap, dead before his head hit the floor.

I did my best to hide my own surprise at what I'd done. I looked up at the council members, some shocked into silence, some anxiously seeking an exit, while a few gagged or shrieked.

I waited until the room fell silent. "It did not have to go this way," I said. "I came here to talk, not fight. But I warned you, I was prepared for either." I pointed at Gorman's body, "Do we continue down his path, or are you ready to listen?"

A woman seated in the highest row rose to her feet. "Captain Bimmy," she said, and surprised me with a smile.

"Yes?"

"We have witnessed today an act of self-defense," she continued, "and perhaps a measure of justice. I, for one, am prepared to listen. I implore my colleagues to do the same."

"And you are?"

"I am Ambassador Townsend, of the Europa Colony. I have some experience with what you're feeling. I'm certain you know, someone in my position would never sanction an assault on a Federation member state. Please, what is it you came here to say?"

I looked down at Gorman's body again, then back at the council.

"It's simple. I want free and unfettered travel throughout Sol for my ships, Admiral Wilson will be held accountable for her actions, the Federation will rebuild Deimos, and Deimos will hold exclusive rights to build hyper-luminal ships to carry passengers to and from Gha'ba. And no Federation ships will travel there without my permission, or that of my delegates."

A gray-haired man, older than any human I'd ever seen, rose to his feet, helped by the council members seated around him.

"I am Ambassador Machado, of Earth. Deimos cannot build more ships without Promethium. We all know this. Assuming you can solve this problem, what do you offer us in return?"

"Peace, and the opportunity to expand humanity's presence beyond this system, to worlds where people are no longer trapped inside pressurized habitats, where they can move around in the open air, build new lives, raise their families, in peace. I offer this, and as much Promethium as is needed to build a fleet of transports. That is my offer, in return for reconciliation and reparations, I offer you peace, security, and prosperity."

"And if we reject this most generous offer?" the old man asked.

"I will relocate the population of Deimos to Gha'ba, leave Sol, and never return to this system. I will destroy any ships attempting to stop me, or interfere with my activities in any way. Your ability to construct new spacecraft will be set back by generations, while our capabilities leap forward by millennia. You stand on the brink of civil war, technological collapse, and population implosion. This is your opportunity to prevent those outcomes. I am here to help you, not fight you. But as you have seen for yourself, I am prepared to defend myself, my friends, my family, my people. You have a quorum, I suggest you take a vote. I have business on Earth, and I'm anxious to get to it."

15

Alas, Arcadia

President Jay was incredulous, "Gorman is dead?"

"Yes."

"And you killed him?"

"Yes, it was self-defense, but it was unintentional, a miscalculation."

"No one is going to miss Gorman," he said, "but why did they let you walk out of there?"

"I gave them a choice, which left them no choice."

"This is no time for riddles, Bimmy, this is serious."

"Mr. President, I promise you, I am being serious. I gave them a choice between war and peace. To their credit, they chose peace. Once they made their decision, they elected a new Chair and agreed to the terms I presented, then I left."

"This is a radical turn of events, even for you."

"Mr. President…"

"I told you, call me Peter, I won't be president much longer."

"Sir, with respect, you can't step down. Your people need you. You didn't cause this attack, no matter what Wilson says. She and Gorman cooked this up, you said yourself they never tried to talk with you about their concerns. They acted out of fear, and hundreds of people are dead because of it. If you resign, their deaths will have no meaning. There is no one to take over, you'll leave your people with…"

"You sound like my wife," he said, without a hint of humor. "She used almost the same words. I made the decision to keep the Promethium a secret, don't let anyone tell you otherwise."

"What's done is done. What matters is what we do next. The Federation has agreed to rebuild Deimos, and to grant exclusive charter for Deimos to build interstellar ships. Together, we will control all traffic between Sol and the Gha'ba system. It will take time, but with you in charge, your colony will prosper again."

"How did you get to be so willful?"

"Blame my mother, she can launch a rocket with willpower alone."

"I hope I get to meet her one day."

"That day may be coming. Becca and I are heading to Arcadia. I'd like our families to join us on Sumera, but the comm with my mother didn't go well."

"Bimmy, as a parent, I can tell you, it can be difficult when your kids grow up and begin to chart their own course in life, especially when it leads them away from you. Try to imagine how it felt for them when they thought you were killed. Now you're back, and the circumstances make things… I'd say 'confusing' but it barely scratches the surface."

"Point taken, Mr. President. Speaking of kids, Reggie is standing by."

"Speaking of confusing," he said, "I send away my eldest, and you bring me back my youngest. I'm not sure how to feel about it."

"Reggie is happy, if it's any help."

"I suppose it should be. This nano-tech you've found, we need to take time to understand it better before any more people are exposed to it."

"I agree, to a point. It's why we need to control access to the system. We still have a Grace Cheng problem to resolve. But some things can't be helped, or undone. We'll need more people like us, more hybrids, if we're going to accomplish anything lasting on Sumera, and in the Gha'ba system."

Reggie entered the bridge and stepped onto the flight ops platform.

"Hello father," he said. He then looked at me and smiled, "Your shuttle, and Becca, are waiting for you. One of them is getting impatient."

"I'd like to pick this up later," I said to the President, "and if you decide to resign, I'll bring this one back as a toddler next time."

I was curious how Reggie's conversation with his father would go, but I had my own parents to think about. When I arrived at the shuttle bay, Blake was seated in a different shuttle from the one we'd used on Ki and N'aha. The shuttle was sleek, compact, but large enough to seat ten passengers. It had short stubby flight surfaces fore and aft, with twin vertical control services rising up at angles from the back half of the fuselage. There were multiple thrusters embedded in the central axis, as well as two in the bow and four set horizontally in the tail. One look at it, and I knew I'd never get Blake out of the pilot's seat.

Becca was standing outside, next to the open hatch., and smiled when I arrived. But it was her 'I'm nervous and want to get on with this' smile, not a happy smile.

"Hello Gorgeous," I said, and went in for a kiss.

"Bimmy, please, I thought we were past this."

"Never," I replied, "not in a million years."

"Be careful what you wish for. How did it go with Peter?"

"Time will tell. He said he was going to resign. Letitia is trying to talk him out of it. I guess we'll see. Ready to go?"

"After you, Captain Handsome," she said.

"Blake, think you can fly this thing?"

We strapped into our seats behind Blake and she swiveled her chair around as the hatch closed behind us, and the outer shuttle bay door began to open.

"You know, I don't think I can do anything I...no, wait, I didn't mean it...I mean… you know I know I can fly anything. I don't think it, I know it. That's what I meant. I'll stop talking now."

"That'd be a first."

"You're gonna love this," Blake said. "I've been working through the systems, this thing is a beast. It can maneuver like a hummingbird, but it stings like a hornet. Three plasma cannons, two up front and one underneath on a retractable swivel pylon. They thought of everything when they built this baby."

"Let's not get carried away," I said. "A simple drop to the spaceport, no loops, no shooting, get us down in one piece please, and try not to scare the Earthlings."

"You are no fun, Captain Handsome, none at all," Blake said.

"Now look what you've done," Becca said, looking at me, "you've undone all my hard work."

"Me? You're the one…"

The ship flung itself out of the shuttle bay, throwing us back into our seats. Blake rolled the shuttle until we were looking down at the Earth, then put us into a dive, plunging toward the planet.

"Blake, is this necessary?" Becca asked. She was gripping the armrests of her seat and the force of our acceleration had us both pinned back.

"I thought you were in a hurry," Blake shouted over the noise generated by our rapid insertion into the atmosphere. I flashed back to the crash of the original *Katie* on Sumera, and hoped Blake was as good a pilot as we all thought she was.

When the roaring flames of reentry were behind us, Blake banked the shuttle into a wide curve, losing momentum and cooling the exterior.

"I like this a lot better," Becca said.

"Don't get comfortable," I said, "this might be a trick."

Blake started laughing, a sound part reassuring, part terrifying. She dropped the nose of the ship again, losing several thousand feet of altitude in a matter of seconds. She then banked hard to port, taking a south-westerly course, placing the coastline on our starboard side. We continued to drop from the sky until we had a clear view of the land below.

That's when Blake looked outside and slowed the shuttle, losing more altitude and allowing us a better view.

We flew over a ruined city, waves crashing all the way into its center, bombed-out buildings crumbling everywhere, entire blocks fallen into the sea, streets filled with wreckage, a bridge collapsed into a broad river. It was a sad sight to behold, reminiscent of the wasted cities we'd seen on Ki.

"What the hell happened here..." Blake whispered.

"It was bombed during the separatist attack," Becca said, "Once the sea wall was destroyed, there wasn't much left to save. They abandoned the city rather than rebuild."

Blake turned back to the controls and we flew on. Several minutes later, the remaining towers of Arcadia's spaceport came into view. The rising ocean had eroded the coastline, washing away the earth under three of the outermost launchpads, causing their towers and gantries to topple into the sea, where they had been left to decay in the increasingly acidic water.

The other launch sites were empty. Large cracks ran in long lines, paralleling the coast, across the concrete expanse. The once dark-black tarmac of the shuttle landing zone had turned pale grey. In several places, the surface rose and fell in rolls, reflecting the instability of the ground beneath it. The paint on the exterior of the terminal had begun to fade and peel, the metal surfaces corroded by the moisture carried on the wind from the ocean.

"Two years," Becca said, "we've been gone a little more than two years, and it looks like we've been gone twenty."

"Where are the people?" Blake asked. "There's nobody here. You'd think there'd be passengers, maintenance people, guards, somebody. This place is a ghost town."

She set the shuttle down on a patch of level tarmac, and we climbed out into the unexpected warmth of the winter sun.

"It should be ten degrees cooler this time of year, even on a hot day," I said.

"The shift must be accelerating, it's spiraling, like water down a funnel," Becca said.

A door opened at the base of the terminal building and a man in a crisp blue suit came walking toward us. I recognized Alan Post, security commander of Arcadia, right away. I ran toward him, smiling despite the sadness of our surroundings. My mentor and friend opened his arms and embraced me.

"Look at you," he said, grabbing me by my shoulders and shaking me. We hadn't seen each other since my return from OCS. In that moment, the years melted away and we were there again, celebrating in my parents' backyard, as if no time had passed.

"Alan," I said, then lost my words, overcome by the moment. He hugged me again, then hugged Becca, then looked at Blake who surprised Becca and me when she said, "I'll take one of those."

Alan laughed, "You got it," and hugged Blake as well, then asked, "And who might you be?"

"They call me Blake. I'm the best pilot in the universe."

"Really?" Alan said, glancing side-eye at me.

"Yes," I said, "I'll vouch for her skills, but think twice if she offers up advice."

Alan took a beat to smile at Blake. "Will do," he said. "I tracked your flight in, I thought you were crashing at first. I was ready to call out a rescue team." He turned back to me. "I've got an auto-car waiting outside the terminal, let's get out of this heat."

"Can I come with you?" Blake asked. "I'd rather not sit out here by myself."

"What did you think, we'd leave you in the shuttle?" Becca replied.

Alan threw his arm over my shoulder and led us toward the terminal. "You've been all over the news Charlie," he said, "first we thought you were dead, then we heard you were alive, and here you are, flying around in an alien spaceship."

"It's been strange for us too," I said.

"I want to hear the whole story, soup to nuts."

We boarded the auto-car and spent the ride into Arcadia telling our story and explaining our plan, to find people to bring back with us and begin the process of building a bridge between Sol and Gha'ba, to enable an ever-increasing number of people to follow.

When we finished, Alan grew pensive. He scratched his chin, looked out the window, then looked back at me. "You'll have no shortage of takers, I imagine. Look around, people are leaving Earth by the shipload already. Luna, Mars, the outer colonies, seems like folks want to be any place but here."

"I don't understand how it got this bad, this fast," Becca said. "We knew the path Earth was on would lead to this, but I thought we had another generation, or longer."

"There are plenty of places on Earth for people to live," Alan said, "a lot of people have moved into the mountain ranges, where it's cooler, safer, and there's more water. But there's less arable land. They've started restricting population movement. That hasn't set well with people who've been forced away from the coast."

"What do you mean?"

"It's a 'have and have not' scenario," Alan said, "on a continental scale. Mark my words, it won't be long before people, countries, alliances, all of them are going to start fighting over what's left. People with means are scooping up the best land and digging in, those with family off-world to take them in have mostly left."

"Something must have happened to accelerate the decline in the climate," Blake said.

"It could be the clouds," Becca said. "They're holding in the heat. It's relatively clear along the coast, but before we entered the atmosphere, I could see there wasn't a lot of clear sky to be found over the mainland. As it gets warmer, you get more moisture in the atmosphere. It might cool some places, but it also holds in the heat that makes it to the surface. Get enough heat, lose the ice caps at the poles, party's over."

"Ice caps," Alan scoffed, "they're almost gone. Antarctica is covered with industrial farms, factories, housing. People flocked there after the last melt-off. An entire industry has sprung up around large-scale prefabricated structures. What they can't build on site, they make someplace else, and drop it where they want it. But there's not much usable space left there either."

When we entered Arcadia, conditions were far worse than I expected. Shops were closed, windows boarded up, or missing altogether. The roads were uneven and, in some places, crews were hard at work tearing buildings apart, salvaging everything of value. The trees were gone, the grass had been replaced with dust and sand. It looked like the town I fled as a little boy. Greenfield was already a heap of rubble and ruin back then. Arcadia was following in its footsteps.

We passed the Hoffman Institute, where robo-transports lined the street, each waiting for a turn to roll up to the loading docks, where men and machines moved crates of equipment from the building onto the vehicles.

"Where are they going?" Becca asked.

"Don't know, they didn't invite me along for the ride."

"You should leave with us," I said, "help us build the new world. We need you, and more like you."

Alan smiled and put his hand on my knee. "I thought you'd never ask."

"Blake," I said, "we have room for one more, don't we."

"You bet, no problem," she said. "Assuming all the parental units come with us, we'll have three empty seats. We can take maybe one or two extras if we keep the baggage to a minimum."

Alan's smile disappeared. He leaned back in his seat. "Have you spoken to your mother?"

"Of course, but she was upset, it was a short call. I expected…I don't know what I expected but she didn't seem happy to hear from me."

"Give her time, it's a lot to process."

I didn't understand at the time what he meant. I should have asked him. I should have probed. I think a part of me didn't want to know what he wasn't telling me. Or maybe he thought I already knew what was waiting for me. Either way, I wish I hadn't let that moment slip by me.

Alan turned to Blake. I could tell by her expression that she'd picked up on the shift in mood. "I know how to travel light," he said. "I'll take my cruiser and gather what I need, meet you back at the spaceport."

We dropped Alan at the security complex and drove to Becca's house. A cargo transport was in the driveway, its motor powered off, doors closed. Becca's parents rushed outside to greet us when she stepped out of the vehicle. After hugs and a 'welcome home,' Becca's parents grew strangely quiet when their attention turned to me. I returned to the auto-car and departed for my home, leaving Becca and Blake to convince the Kiels to join us.

Like Becca's house, a cargo transport sat in the driveway of my childhood home. But no one came outside to meet me, and there was no sign of Katie. My last comm with my mother had ended abruptly, on a sour note, "I'll see you or I won't, it's up to you, I will be here if you show up," she'd said, then disconnected the comm. President Jay's words about charting one's own path echoed in my mind.

I walked up the dusty path to the front door. I was about to knock, then reminded myself I didn't need to. I opened the door and walked into a near empty house.

I called out, "Mom," and got no reply. I went through the house, one empty room after another, until I opened the door to my bedroom. It was exactly as I'd left it.

Rose, my mother, was seated on the edge of my bed, holding a small metal box in her lap.

"So," she said, "you made it after all."

"Of course I did, I said I would…"

"You said you would be back in a month, then you died, and you've come back, as if nothing has happened."

"Mom, where's Pop, I don't understand…."

She held up the box and stared at me, "He's right here Charlie, where you put him."

"What…no, what are you saying…"

"A man can only lose so many sons before it breaks him. Two was the limit of your father's heart. He died six months after you left, after we thought your ship exploded, after we thought we'd lost you forever." She pushed the box towards me, "Here he is, go ahead, take him with you. Sow his ashes into the soil of your new world, grow some wheat from his remains, bake some bread from what's left of his bones, at least he'll be useful to you again."

I knelt in front of her, wrapped my hands around hers, still clutching the box. I tried to hold back my tears, but I struggled to breathe. "Mom please…I don't understand…I did what I thought was right. We found a new world, an entire star system, we found a new home for…"

"For what, all of humanity? You fancy yourself a savior? You're too late for your father, and you're too late for me. Some savior. Go ahead, take him with you, I'm sure he would have wanted it, there's no place for him where I'm going."

"I want you to come with me, back to Gha'ba, to Sumera, it's more beautiful…"

"Beautiful, is it? Like this world used to be, is that what you're saying? Now you want to drag me across the galaxy where I can watch us destroy another planet. That's what will happen you know, that's what we do. We're a plague. We consume, destroy, consume, destroy, over and over again, until there's nothing left. I'm not coming with you, go find someone else to save."

"Mom, I know you're angry, I know this didn't…"

"Know? What do you know? Do you know what it's like to watch your husband waste away because he's too distraught to eat? To watch him grow weaker by the day until he can't get out of bed? To know that he loved his son more than he loved you? He forgave you, do you know that? But I haven't, and I won't, that's all you need to know."

Nothing in my life had prepared me for that moment, for my mother's anger, for her complete rejection and repudiation of me. It shattered me, broke me to my core. I fell to the floor and looked up her, but she wasn't looking at me. I followed her gaze to my desk, where my digi-frame sat, one image sliding away to reveal another. Images of me with my father, of the three of us, of me with Becca, until the loop came to its end, an image of my mother and me at my adoption day party. Then it started over, and I was thirteen again, playing on the lawn with Katie.

Katie. I hadn't seen her yet. "She's on the back porch," my mother said, "she likes to lie on the stones, where it's cooler." Her voice had lost some of its anger, but the bitterness remained, and she wouldn't look at me.

I stood and looked down at her clutching my father's ashes to her chest, staring at the frame on my desk, watching the past slip by.

I left the room and went to find Katie. She was fast asleep on the stone floor of the screened porch, snoozing in the shade beneath a breeze from the fan spinning overhead. She heard the door open and her head shot up. I expected her to jump up, to run to me, to greet me as she had before, throwing her body against mine until I was covered with her fur, her scent.

She did none of that. She looked at me, sniffed the air, then laid her head down on the cool floor and looked up at me from beneath her furrowed brow. I walked over to her, knelt down and placed my hand in front of her.

"Hi Katie, it's me, I'm back."

She turned her head away from my hand and let out a deep sigh. I reached out and began to stroke her head, the back of her neck, around her ears, all the things she'd always enjoyed. Her tail wagged a few times, then she rolled over on her side and reached a paw up to touch my arm, resting it there while I rubbed her chest.

If my mother wouldn't come with me, there was no way I could take Katie from her, and I didn't get the sense Katie would leave with me anyway.

I returned to my room where my mother had remained. She was sitting at my desk, holding the digi-frame in her hand, the box containing my father's ashes on the desk in front of her.

"Mother, will you listen to me?"

"I'm not going with you, take the dog if you think she'll go, but…"

"I understand. I'm not here to force either of you, but will you at least hear me out?"

"Fine," she said, "speak."

"All I ever wanted was a family, a home to call my own, a life with some kind of meaning. You and Pop gave me all of that, and I've tried to make the most of everything you've done for me. If I had known the path I chose would cause this much pain, I never would have chosen it. I accept it's my fault, and there's nothing I can do to change it, but I want you to know I love you, and I'm grateful for the life you've given me."

She placed the frame back on the desk and stood up, looked into my eyes, and slapped me across my face as hard as she could. I had to prevent my autonomous systems from deflecting her hand. Physically, my mother striking me felt like nothing at all. Emotionally, it took me back to my days in Greenfield, fending off my uncle's abuse. I could not sink any lower.

I think she understood how her small act of violence made me feel, or maybe she remembered, in that moment, how I'd come into her life. She held her hands to her mouth, her eyes wide with the shock of what she'd done, and began to sob. She threw her arms around me, clinging to me like a lost sailor clinging to a life raft on a raging sea. Her body shook against me as I held her in my arms. I felt the pain, the sorrow, the bitterness pouring out of her in ways words could not match.

She clutched at the back of my shirt. Her tears fell against my chest, and I cried with her. I cried for myself, and I cried for her. For what we'd both lost, and for what we could have found together, but never would.

Katie came into the room and leaned against us, offering her comfort as she always had, then she jumped onto the bed and curled up, her head against the pillow.

My mother placed her hands on my chest, looked up at me as if from the bottom of a deep canyon. She managed a weak smile and said, "This is where she sleeps." She placed a hand on my cheek, touched the place where she'd struck me, and we shed more tears together.

"I have loved you since the moment I laid eyes on you," she said, "I suppose I should have told you that more often, maybe…"

"I've always known it."

"It's nice to hear though, don't you think?"

"Yes, it is."

"Come to the kitchen," she said. "Let's eat a little something and talk awhile, like we used to, before you go and leave me again."

I did as she asked. I spent the afternoon with her, telling her about our experiences in Sumera, and the other worlds of the Gha'ba system. I told her about the technology we'd found there, and how it had changed us. She was distressed to hear about the nanotechnology that had made itself at home in our bodies, but excited to learn more about the spaceport and ships in our fleet. I left out the encounter with Tomrin, and our experience of time travel. The first would cause her worry, and the second would likely be met with disbelief. She was like Becca, and would not accept such a thing was possible unless she experienced it for herself. I still found myself questioning the reality of it, despite having lived it.

When the shadows crept across the lawn and entered through the kitchen window, I knew our time together had come to an end. I tried one last time to convince her to join us, knowing it was unlikely she would change her mind.

"You know," I said, "Becca says these bots make us cyborgs, but for Reggie, they also made him younger. It's a simple process. Think about what you could do with all the added time."

"Charlie, one lifetime is enough for me. Whatever comes after death, whether I see your father again or not, I've accepted its inevitability. For every gain, there is always a cost. You can't know what it is at this point, and I'm not interested in taking the risk."

"If you change your mind, contact President Jay on Deimos. He'll make sure you get there, I'll have it all arranged, in case you do."

"Let me put it to you this way," she said. She reached out and took my hand. "If there is a life, or some kind of existence, after we die, then Henry is there, waiting for me. Even a thin slice of possibility gives me hope. It's paradoxical, I know, but it's my reason for going on with life, until it ends, however it may go. I'm needed here, to help with the new spaceport. It's not easy, picking the whole thing up and moving it into the mountains. But we'll be safer there, away from the coast."

"I don't understand your choice," I said, "but I respect it, and I accept it. I miss you every day I'm away from you. I wish... I wish I'd made different choices."

"Regret is good. A life without regret is not something to be proud of Charlie. Either we make mistakes and learn from them, and they become a part of who we are, or we don't accept our failures or acknowledge our shortcomings, and they make us less than what we could be. Let your regrets inform your future choices, but don't let them burden your present and take you away from what's most important."

"I don't know..."

"Becca is your future. Go back to Sumera, make a life with her. Don't look back, and don't ever let her go. And know this, the longer you're together, the more mistakes you'll make. Embrace them as opportunities to grow. You're still young, you've got a lot left to learn. I'm happy you have someone like her with you, to face the future. I'm proud of you Charlie. I'm angry as a bee in a bottle, but still proud."

"I'm...thank you Mom. I love you."

We hugged and I said one last goodbye. I left her on the front porch with Katie. She didn't wave and neither did I. We'd said all there was to say. She was right, I had to keep moving forward, with Becca.

When I arrived at the Kiel's residence, Becca and Blake were seated at the kitchen table with Becca's parents. They explained their reasons for not telling me about my father, but I wasn't listening. I wanted to get back to our ship, back to Deimos, and back to the Gha'ba system. And I wanted to deal with Grace Cheng. I knew the clock was ticking.

Like my mother, the Kiels had decided not to join us, not yet. They held out the possibility for a future journey, but wanted to remain on Earth to assist with the relocation of the Hoffman Institute to New Arcadia. They promised to look after my mother, which was all I could ask of them.

Back in the aero-car we didn't speak for most of the ride. As we approached the spaceport, Blake leaned forward in her seat and placed one hand on my shoulder and the other on Becca's. "I'm sorry things didn't go well today, sorry about your parents, your dad, your dog, all of it. I haven't seen my parents since I left Titan, and I don't expect to see them ever again. I've been at peace with it for a long time. We have to be our own family. I don't know how you feel about it, but I feel good. For the first time in my life, I feel like tomorrow is going to be better than today, every day, because I'm with you, both of you."

"Thank you, Blake," Becca said, "I feel the same."

"What about Reggie?" I asked.

"He counts too, but strictly in a 'little brother you like, but don't understand' way."

"He's older than all of us," I said.

"Yeah," Blake replied, "but ever since the little change-a-roo on Sumera, he doesn't act it."

"That's the problem," I said, "the two of you are too much alike."

Blake thumped me on the back of my head, then fell back into her seat laughing. "Will you ever stop with the digs?" she asked. "Like, can you cut a gal a break once in a while?"

"Never," I said, "it's core to our relationship. I can never let up, not for a second, neither can you, it would ruin us both."

The car swung into the empty departure lane in front of the terminal. Alan, now dressed in jeans and a light shirt, stood by the curb. He held a duffle bag in one hand, and had a backpack slung over his shoulder.

"I hope I didn't over pack," he said as we got out of the vehicle.

"Turns out," Blake said, "you could pack a whole bunch more. It's the four of us."

"If you've got room for cargo," he said, "then we should raid the commissary. No reason for all that food to go to waste."

"I like the way you think," Blake said. She looked at me and grinned. "You found a good one here Bimmy, the day's not a total bust."

We did more than raid the commissary, we cleaned out the armory, the comm shack, and anything else we could get into. There were no weapons in the armory, but a crate of plasma charges had been left in a supply closet. It found its way onto our shuttle, along with everything else we thought might be useful to us, or to Deimos. Alan reasoned if the supplies and equipment hadn't been packed up, nobody wanted them. As the current Head of Security, he was authorized to reallocate resources as he saw fit, and reallocate is exactly what we did. By the time we were finished, the moon had risen and Blake was getting worried about the weight of our cargo.

We launched shortly before midnight. Unlike our arrival, Blake chose to keep the ascent slow and steady.

"What happened to the hot shot pilot?" Alan asked as we rose into the night sky.

"We're takin' it easy until I know that cargo isn't gonna shift around and mess with our flight dynamics. But don't you worry, there's plenty of excitement ahead."

"Alan," I said, "one thing you need to know about Blake. She loves a challenge, don't goad her, it never goes well for…"

"Stand by for main thruster ignition," Blake said. "Brace, brace, brace."

We were entering the mesosphere when Blake accelerated, ratcheting the noise to a roar and taking us from cruising speed to escape velocity in seconds. As usual, we were smashed back into our seats. I struggled to turn my head and look at Alan. When I saw his face, I smiled.

"What's so funny?" he shouted. "This is terrifying."

"Now you know how I felt the first time I flew in your cruiser," I shouted back.

"I should tell you something," he yelled.

"What?"

"I've never been to space," he said.

We blasted through the thermosphere and into the exosphere before Blake announced, "Throttling back main engines, configuring for g-s-o, rendezvous with *Katie* in one hour. Sit back, relax, and enjoy the ride. Snacks and beverages are strictly self-service. Thank you for flying Triad Space Lines."

Unencumbered by gravity and relieved of the stress of acceleration, it felt good to be weightless again. Alan, however, did not look well. His face was ashen, his eyes closed, hands gripping the armrests of his seat.

Blake unbuckled and drifted down the central aisle. She opened a box strapped on top of a heap of cargo and pulled out a small empty bag. She slapped it onto Alan's chest.

"I aim to keep a clean boat," she said, "your aim would be appreciated." She returned to the pilot's seat and swiveled around to talk to Becca. I couldn't hear what they were saying. Whatever it was, it made Becca look at Alan and smile.

Alan opened his eyes and looked down at the bag, then at me. "Is it too late to change my mind," he asked.

"Yes, but don't worry, we all get a little queasy our first time. It gets better."

"I liked it better when I wasn't weightless," he said.

"That'll change, give it time."

"What happened to artificial gravity?"

"This is Blake's way of getting to know you. We'll have artificial G on the *Katie*, similar to Earth's gravity. How is it you've never launched before? I thought you fought in the Marauder War."

"I did, the first one. My experience was entirely terrestrial. Hypersonic transports are wicked fast, but they don't go straight up and they don't reach orbit, they skim along between atmospheric layers. The battles didn't go fully off-world until round two. By then I was working in Arcadia."

"Round two," I said, "is that how the pirates got started?"

"You could make that argument," he replied, "there were criminals in the outer lanes long before we drove the marauders away from Earth and Mars. Once they got kicked out of the inner planets, the two groups linked up and a pirate fleet was born. We didn't have the resources to take them on once they set up shop around Jupiter, too many places to hide, too many places to get trapped."

"You'll have to compare notes with Reggie, I'm sure he'll be interested."

"Did you read his book?"

"The one you gave me? Of course, before I reported for OCS."

"You know that part where he talks about a bar fight in Athens? How Earth Marines and Colonial Marines could fight side-by-side, but couldn't drink together without getting into a brawl? How it was emblematic of the problems between Earth and the colonies?"

"I thought that was a strange way to make a valid point."

"That was me. I started that fight. I'm not proud of it, thought you ought to know, that's all."

"You think there'll be a problem between you two?"

"We were young, full of ourselves. It's been a long time, I doubt he'll recognize me."

"You might be in for a shock."

"Can you be more specific?"

"He may not recognize you, but I'm sure you're gonna recognize him."

Alan was still feeling unwell when we set down in the shuttle bay. He started to improve when his body felt the pull of artificial gravity. We unloaded our cargo, which further reduced his queasiness. By the time we headed for the bridge, his good spirits, and the color in his face, had returned.

We entered the bridge and Reggie rose from the captain's chair and turned around, smiling. When Alan saw him, he stopped in his tracks.

"I know you," Reggie said with a devilish grin, "you're that hot head from Athens, I'd never forget your face." Reggie bounded across the deck and for a moment I thought he was going to attack Alan. Instead, he stuck out his hand and said, "Welcome aboard old man."

Alan stared at Reggie's face and took his time reaching out to shake his hand.

"Do you remember me?" Reggie said.

"Remember you? Yeah, I remember you. I remember we were about the same age when we…"

"Had our little tussle? No hard feelings, right? That was a long time ago."

"No hard feelings," Alan said, still shaking Reggie's hand. He looked over Reggie's shoulder at me, standing at my station on the platform. "Is this what I have to look forward to?" he asked.

"Possibly," I said, "you'll have a couple of options. We'll explain along the way."

"What's to explain? The results speak for themselves. Why aren't the rest of you…"

"That's what needs explaining," Becca said.

"Don't sweat it big guy," Blake said, "you're in good hands. What do you know about starships?"

"Nothing," Alan said.

"Perfect," Blake replied, "no bad habits to break."

"Who are you to talk about bad habits?" Becca asked.

"Where have you been? It's me you're dealing with, I'm the reigning queen of bad habits."

"Yes, like wasting time," I said. "Hop in the seat and get us out of here. We've been away from Deimos too long."

"Come on," Reggie said to Alan, "I'll show you 'round the ship, get you settled into your quarters."

"We've got some cargo to move out of the bay."

"It can wait," I said.

"What cargo?" Reggie asked.

Reggie looked at each of us, waiting for an answer, until Blake finally gave him one. "We took a little shopping trip through the Arcadia terminal, cleaned the place out," she said, "so much fun."

"Once again Blake," Becca said, "you have a truly odd sense of what's fun."

"That's why people love me."

My anxiety over being away from Sumera was growing. Grace Cheng's presumed presence on the planet was scratching at me, demanding my attention, pulling me back there. I stood on the bridge, looking out at the stars. A sense of foreboding seeped in, wrapped itself around my mind, and wouldn't let go.

"How's our fuel?"

"Fuel is great, we've hardly put a dent in our supply, but this thing doesn't use fuel in the traditional sense, I'm not sure how to explain it, I don't understand everything… it generates thrust without any effort at all, but uses loads of propellent when we maneuver. We haven't had to maneuver much, we're in good shape, but it's something to keep in mind when we get to Deimos."

"Roger that," I said, "you know the drill, get us to Deimos, spare the warp drive, main engines only, max speed. "

"Yes sir, captain sir," Blake said, happy to be back at the controls.

"Becca, send word to President Jay, we'd like to head back to Sumera as soon as possible after our arrival."

"You're worried about Cheng," she said.

"You bet I am. If she's in Sumera, the longer she's down there, the more danger we're in. Sumera is our home, and I intend to kick her out of it as soon as we get back. Our city, our planet, our system. There's no place for her in any of it."

"You plan to kill her," Blake said.

"I plan to be rid of her, once and for all, by any means necessary."

"If she's been exposed," Becca said, "if she's like us, that might be a tough task to complete."

"Which is why we need to spend some of our travel time reviewing the archives. The answers we need might already be in our hands."

"Sounds like a good job for our new head of security," Becca said, "I'll go through the records with Alan, see what we can come up with. But you should have a plan b, in case we don't find anything."

"Plan B," I said, "fair enough."

16

Rage

We could have used our warp drive to jump back to Deimos, but we had work to do and needed the slower pace. I also wanted to save our warp capacity in case we needed it later. As it was, the course Blake plotted to Deimos would have us arrive in under six Earth days, making our cruising speed 460-thousand kilometers per hour. Only once in human history had Earth built a ship faster than ours, an autonomous solar probe, which utilized a series of gravity-assist maneuvers to achieve peak velocity.

The inbound journey from Deimos had been spent planning our strategy for dealing with the Council and preparing for the passengers we thought we were picking up on Earth. On the outbound leg, we again put our time to good use.

Blake learned how to manage the drone swarm more effectively, and practiced attack strategies with Katie. Katie had become like another member of the crew, which was an odd feeling given Katie was the ship.

Reggie familiarized himself with more of our defensive systems, especially the contingent of defender synths and the many semi-autonomous mechanisms in the ship's arsenal.

Becca and Alan spent hours each day poring over the archives in the ship's databank, looking for ways to deal with Cheng, trying to prepare for any eventuality. At the end of each day, they held a briefing for the rest of us, filling us in on both the tech and the history they were discovering in their search.

I needed time to come to terms with the loss of my father, my interaction with my mother, and to a lesser extent, the death of Gorman. Becca knew I needed space, and time, to work through my feelings. As always, she gave it to me. I had never fully processed the loss of my biological parents, and could no longer remember what they looked like. I had scattered memories of them, a day at the beach, a birthday party, a holiday dinner, but even those had become thin representations of my past. I gave myself the freedom to fantasize about going back in time to prevent their deaths, but knew it would radically alter my own life. A life I'd grown to love.

I spent my time exploring the ship, getting to know its many passageways, decks, holds, and compartments, all the while keeping up a dialogue with Katie.

One evening, buy the ship's clock, as we settled in for our last meal of the day, I shared a realization I'd come to that day.

"The ship has minimal awareness of historic events," I said, "its creators made it a point to deliberately silo its capabilities, to limit its access to information. We saw this with the other AIs on Sumera. The Guardians, the Magistrate, even the Guide AI."

"The hierarchy on Sumera wasn't imposed by Tomrin," Becca said, "but he leveraged it, turned it into a pseudo-religion. The tiered structure of access and awareness seems to be his method of control."

"But what if he didn't," I said, "what if he's working within the framework the original builders created?"

"Does it matter?" Reggie asked. "Tomrin wants us dead. What else do we need to know? We should give serious thought to ending that thing when we get back."

"He's more than a thing," Blake said, "and he's a mass murderer, on a multi-planetary scale."

Alan leaned in, placed his hand on the table, and pointed at me. "I don't like where I think you're going," he said. "From what I've read, and what you've told me, I'm inclined to go with Reggie on this, be rid of it as soon as possible."

"That's what's bothering me. When the Guards pulled us out of the Temple, they were fighting hand-to-hand with Tomrin, two on one, then later the captain said something about why they kept him around as long as they did."

"What are you saying?" Becca asked.

"I'm thinking out loud," I said, "and the more I think about it, the more something feels not right, like we're not getting the whole picture. The Guards…their body armor wasn't just armor. Those were environment suits. Why? If they know us, and know our past, they would know about this trip to Sol, they know we're planning to bring more people back with us and we're going to expose at least some of them to the nanobots, which means in their timeline more people than us would be hybrids. Why be afraid of the killer bots if they've already been defeated? Why keep us apart? Do they eventually eliminate the plague bots? If they do, is that when they get rid of Tomrin? The whole situation feels off to me."

"I don't know Bimmy," Reggie said, "it feels like you're reaching. Keeping us out of their controlled space, where they know the atmosphere is safe, that's common sense to me. Maybe it's an overabundance of caution, but I don't see a problem there."

"What was up with the floaty door thing?" Blake asked, "Why take us to a different place? What did he call it? The 'burned-out world' or something?"

"Exactly," I said, "why jump through time like that, unless…"

"That doorway was a modified Gateway device, I'm certain of it. And a lot smaller than the one on the *Hyperion*," Becca said. "But the quantum state, that's something new to me. It can't be easy to maintain, even for a few seconds. Maybe that place is their base of operation, or their home world, wherever that is."

"Whenever it is," Blake added.

"In which case," I said, "Sumera would be like a paradise to them, but one they couldn't live in without taking on the nanobots."

Alan had leaned back in his chair, staring at the table, scratching the stubble that had sprouted on his chin, lost in his thoughts.

"Alan," I said, but he didn't respond. "Alan," I repeated, "you still with us?"

He looked up at me, "Yes, I'm here," he said. "I was trying to think this through."

"And…"

"From where I sit, it seems obvious someone is being dishonest, and it's clear Tomrin AI is a bad actor in all this, but that doesn't mean the other guys are necessarily good guys. What if they're all bad guys, but they need each other, they're dependent on each other. Which would make you, and now me, pawns in some game they've been playing since long before you arrived on Sumera. Therein lies the problem, you don't know what the game is."

"But we do," I said, "It's self-preservation. They want to change their world by changing the past. But the captain told us time travel had major power requirements…"

"She called it a huge power suck," Blake said.

"Let's assume they weren't lying," Reggie said. "They came from the future, but their ability to travel is limited. Otherwise, why would they be laser-focused on time? If you can travel to any point in time, why do you have to rush out the back door as soon as the mission is over?"

"Their access is limited, like Sherab's. They can't travel unless Tomrin activates the portal at his end."

"We missed it," Becca said, "they said it and we missed it. The lieutenant, our great-great-great-whatever progeny let it slip. He said if we made the wrong choice, we'd leave behind a ruined world."

"He never said which choice," Blake said.

"Because he couldn't," Becca said, "he didn't know. They're using us to change their timeline, to create an alternate future. What if the choice was to let the ship handle the attack? Or the opposite? Would we still have won the battle?"

"What if they wanted you to die?" Alan asked. "They save you from Tomrin, gain your trust, then send you into a battle they believe you'll lose."

"Then they wouldn't exist," I said, "if they are descended from us, and we die, they never exist."

"Unless the multiverse theory is correct, and our timeline is a new branch, separate from theirs."

"You're losing me," Reggie said, "it's too complicated. Too risky, too messy. There's got to be a simpler explanation than alternate universes and double-dealing time travelers."

I didn't have a response, but he was right. It was too complicated. Nothing was making sense.

After a few moments of silence, Alan cleared his throat and said, "Going with Reggie's logic, what if the simplest explanation is the right one? You've seen this other world, this ruined place. If they had to go there in order to take you one day back in time, then I'd say that's at least where their operational base is located, and where their equipment is powered, and possibly their actual home. Then the question is why? If they can travel to Sumera, why not stay there. And if they don't want to be cyborgs, like all of you, then why go at all?"

"Because Sumera has something they need," Blake said.

"Yes," Alan said, "and what does Sumera have? You've all been there, what does it have that's worth the effort?"

"It could be Promethium," Becca said, "but that would imply they weren't based in the Gha'ba system. Promethium is abundant there compared to Sol, they wouldn't need Sumera for it."

"Tomrin," I said, "they need Tomrin, they said as much. They keep him around…"

"Their captain said it in the past tense," Becca said, "they eventually got rid of him."

"Where does this leave us?" Reggie asked.

"In a pickle," Alan said.

"I disagree," I said. "We know something's not right, we know they need Tomrin, we know Tomrin controls Sumera, at least to the extent he's able, and we know they need us to do something, maybe something we've already done, to alter their timeline. I think I know what to do next."

"We're gonna blow up the Temple and Tomrin with it?" Blake asked.

"We are going back to talk to Tomrin, get his perspective."

"What about Cheng?"

"As long as we keep her off our ships, I'll consider her a manageable threat. We pay Tomrin a visit first, then we deal with Madame Cheng."

"I have a question," Blake said, "for the scientist in the group. That would be you, Commander Gorgeous."

Becca looked at me, shaking her head. "Again," she said, "I blame you for this."

"Okay, sorry, no more Commander Gorgeous, I promise. Here's my question. If these people can travel in time, and it seems they can, and if they can mess around with the past to change the future, and it looks like they believe they can, then how would we know if they had done this once, or done this a dozen times? I mean, from our perspective, they've come back and interfered once. Who's to say they haven't been doing this for years? We'd never know, would we? What if that's why they need Tomrin. If Bimmy's right, they can't travel through time without him, or at least not without his 'temple.' This ties everything up in a nice little package, don't ya think?"

Becca stared at Blake, mouthed the words 'Who are you?' then looked at me and shrugged, "It makes sense," she said.

"Blake," I said, "for once, I think I have to agree with you."

"But we do know," Reggie said. "The man on the ship Tomrin sent us to, he said he was the ruler of Ki. He said he was witnessing the end of days, and the beginning of our future…

"A thousand times over…and then there was the woman from Kern, attacking N'aha…"

Becca smiled at Blake, "Who's the genius?"

By the time we arrived at Deimos, we had a plan in place for our return to Sumera. In the two weeks we'd been away, the colonial fleet had been hard at work building new orbital docks and repairing the surface installations of the colony. The space around Deimos was crowded with ships of all shapes and sizes.

The once ferocious *Arcturus* was being scavenged for every last usable component and chunk of metal. Like ants on a carcass, hundreds of workers were busy pulling the ship apart, taking some pieces to the smelter, others to the ruined shipyards to be integrated into the colony's systems.

"I told you the Federation would pay for the rebuild," I said as we passed over the remains of the ship.

"They'll never build another ship like that one," Blake said.

"I bet they will," Reggie replied, "if they have to recycle half the fleet, they'll build one."

"Why?" Becca asked.

"Ego, pride, they'll want to show they can still do it."

"You're talking about Earth," Alan said, "not the Federation."

"You think there's a Federation after this?" Reggie asked. "They may be around by name, for a time, but the colonies will walk away. Earth will be on its own soon."

"All the more reason to put it behind us," I said.

"Shuttle on approach," Becca said, "President Jay is asking for docking instructions."

"The President flies his own shuttle," Blake said, "who knew?"

"Personnel shortage most likely," Reggie said. "But it's my mother who's the pilot. She was like you, back when I was a kid. Flew anything and everything she could get into. I spent more time on ships than I spent on Deimos."

"Katie," I said, "can you guide the shuttle into the bay remotely?"

"Stand by. Assessing…attempting interconnect…connection established…yes, captain, I am capable of fulfilling your request."

"I'll let them know," Becca said.

"Reggie, will you do the honors and escort our guests to the bridge."

"You bet," he replied.

Once Reggie was off the bridge, Alan asked, "I know I haven't been a part of this crew for long, but shouldn't the captain meet the President in person?"

"Yes," I said, "but in this case, I think Reggie's mother will need a few private minutes with her son."

Ten minutes later, President Jay, his wife Letitia, and their son Michael joined us on the bridge, followed close behind by Reggie. Their appearance caught me off guard. The President and First Lady were not draped in the rich fabrics trimmed in delicate embroidery I'd grown accustomed to seeing them wear. Instead, they wore uniforms of the Colonial Marines, like their son Michael, complete with rank, insignia, and sidearms. It was an extreme deviation from their usual attire.

I extended my arm to shake President Jay's hand, but he brushed it aside and hugged me. "Thank you for saving our people," he said.

Letitia then kissed me on the cheek, and finally Michael shook my hand, then hugged me as well. They repeated this with everyone, even Alan, who tried to explain that he hadn't been on the ship during the battle, but to no avail.

"Welcome aboard," I said.

The President smiled and said, "That wasn't quite protocol, but I care less about ceremony, and more about what you've done for us. After you crippled the *Arcturus* and the battle ended, we did a full assessment of the damages. They had us. In a few more hours, Deimos would have fallen."

"I'm sorry we didn't get here sooner," I said, "but I'm glad we were able to help."

"Captain Bimmy," the First Lady said, "you and your crew did more than help. This is no time to be humble. This is a time to honor your achievement." She removed a small box from a pouch on her belt and opened it, revealing a finely wrought metal insignia. "We had this made for you, I hope you find it appropriate to your rank as Fleet Admiral."

"Woo-hoo!" Blake shouted, then began to whistle and clap, as did the rest of the crew.

"I don't understand," I said, "I've never seen this insignia before."

"I designed it," Letitia said, "and we made it with material salvaged from the Arcturus. The titanium at the base represents the foundation, a new beginning. The silver diamond shape embedded in the gold layer at the top represents prosperity. Set within, we have the laurel wreath, symbolizing victory, and crowned with two stars, symbolizing unity and peace. The sword piercing the wreath symbolizes strength. Unity, Prosperity, and Peace, this will be our motto, and you will be our first Admiral of the Fleet, if you will honor us by accepting the appointment."

"What fleet are we talking about?"

"This is a formal invitation," the President said, "for Sumera to join Deimos, Europa, and Ganymede as founding members of humanity's first Interstellar Republic."

"I don't know… I mean, I'm honored, but this was nowhere on my list for today."

"We anticipate more states will petition for membership, once they shed their colonial past," Michael said. "Four is enough to get us started. Our combined forces already outgun what's left of the Federation fleet, and they know it."

"What do you think?" I asked, turning to face my crew. They nodded their agreement, smiling back at me.

"I'm glad I joined this crew," Alan said.

"Mister President," I said, "my place is in Sumera. I don't see how I can lead the fleet from there."

"You can," Michael interrupted, "because the fleet will be based there."

"What my over-excited son means," President Jay said, "is we'd like to send a team back with you, to assess the feasibility of acquiring Promethium and building ships in the Gha'ba system, where it will be safer. You'll be in charge of the operation, and your vice admirals will manage the fleet back here, until we can upgrade more ships. Eventually, it won't matter where our ships are since they'll be able to get anywhere in a matter of minutes."

Becca slipped her arm around mine and looked up at me with a smile. "The First Interstellar Republic, I like the sound of it."

I turned back to the President and First Lady. "Who's going to be in charge of this new nation?"

"Like it or not," President Jay said, "that would be me."

"In that case Mister President, on behalf of the people of Sumera, all of whom happen to be present, I accept your invitation to join the Republic. But I can't accept the role of admiral. I'm not ready to lead a fleet."

I reached out to hand the insignia to her, but Letitia wrapped her hands around mine and looked into my eyes. I stared back at her, unsure what to do, mesmerized by her gaze.

"Keep it, captain. Give it more thought. You have ample time, and *you* will know when the time is right."

***

Five orbits after our arrival, with both the Federation and the shipyards of Deimos in disarray, the iris to the dock on Deimos was opened, and I was able to take a shuttle over for a meeting with three of the military commanders of the newly formed Republic. I had my own business in mind as well; to see Admiral Wilson. Given our grievances, I didn't expect a polite conversation, but it was one that needed to happen.

The President and I, along with my new colleagues, spent two hours working out a framework for the protection and reconstruction of Deimos, as well as the construction of additional Gateway-equipped ships, no small task with the greatest shipyards in human history reduced to drifting rubble.

It was then I landed on a way to speed things along. I came to the conclusion the timeline being discussed was too long. We had to find a shortcut and, thankfully, I had one.

"I'm sure we can send a shipment of Promethium back soon, but you'll need to store it until a ship is ready. That would be a tempting target for the Federation. On the other hand, there is a ship on Sumera, I'd say it's ninety percent complete, give or take. It was the second of two hyper-luminal ships the Triad was building. I think we should put together a team to assess it, and put off the mining part of this plan until later. You might be able to finish it faster than you can build a new one here, or at the very least salvage any Promethium already in place on the ship."

"Where's the first ship," the President asked, then looked around the room, "this is the first I've heard of this."

"We're not exactly filing reports these days," I said, "but we should start. The ship was sent…I can't believe I'm saying this…it was sent to Earth roughly 300 years ago, and if their history is accurate, it was the second ship they sent this way. The first was a generation ship, approximately six thousands years ago, give or take a few millennia."

I could tell my words weren't landing well. Captain Nisperos, from Ganymede, was shaking her head.

"A three-hundred-year-old alien ship," she said, "it would take years to understand its systems before we could start working, if a ship that old is serviceable, and I seriously doubt it is. We'd be better off modifying your ship."

"It's serviceable," I said, "like my ship, it's in pristine condition. The AIs on Sumera are meticulous in their maintenance. As for modifying the Katie, I'm all for it, but right now we can't afford to dock it, too risky."

"That hardly matters," Nisperos said, "the alien tech, this incomplete ship, it will hold us back. The language barrier alone…"

"There is no language barrier," I said. "Not for Triadic Hybrids. The nanotechnology integrates the host mind with all the data systems an engineer would need. It would be days, weeks at the most, until work could begin, not years."

The young officer from Europa had kept silent, his brow furrowed as he stared at his hands resting on the table. President Jay turned to him and asked, "Mister Townsend, your thoughts?"

"I know that name," I said.

"You met my mother, on Luna. You made a heck of an impression," Townsend said.

"You've spoken to her since then."

"We speak daily. She believes you're a man of your word, and she's an excellent judge of character."

Townsend looked at each person in the room, taking charge of the moment with his demeanor. I recognized his mother in him. He was a reflection of her calm, her grace under pressure, and her authority.

"I think Captain Bimmy is right," he said, "my vote is to send the team, as he suggests."

"I agree," President Jay said, "any objections?"

"No."

"If Townsend is satisfied, I'm satisfied, let's send the team."

Each person present affirmed their support for the plan. We had arrived knowing little about each other, yet managed to find consensus, even unanimity. It was an auspicious beginning.

"I have one request," Townsend said. "I'd like one of my engineers to be on the team."

"Of course," the President said, "have them report here for transfer to the *Katie*. If there's nothing else pressing, the captain and I have some unfinished business."

Everyone stood as the President and I left the room. During our walk to the holding cells to see Admiral Wilson, I asked him a simple question.

"Why a Republic?"

He laughed, then saw I was serious and replied, "The Alliance was a postwar lie, an empire based Earth, it was bound to fail. The Federation was a good idea, but it was a failure of execution. It became a dictatorship in less than three years, too much power landed in the hands of one person. I thought, why not go back to the old ways, and try democracy again."

"You'll be standing for election?"

"No. I agreed to a single eight-year term, with the option for early elections if the new assembly deems them necessary. We are trying for something durable here Bimmy. The people are hungry for it."

"For democracy?"

"For stability, for a sense of empowerment, for hope. They've been starved of it for too long. These new worlds, they have people ready to abandon everything and rush into the unknown. If all we accomplish is an orderly movement of people through the cosmos, I'll call it a win. But I think we can do more. I saw the speech you made on Earth, in Arcadia, after the war. It was a politician's dream. Short and sweet, with a message that resonated. You said we had to think beyond tomorrow's sun, we had to work together to build a better future."

"I didn't plan it, I said what I felt, I figured no one would remember it."

"Remember? We've done more than remember. For all of us, all the founders of the Republic, and tens of thousands of people across Sol, those words are our guiding principle, to build a better future, and to do it together, in peace."

We arrived at a large steel doorway flanked by two armed guards who snapped to attention.

"You go alone from here," he said, placing a hand on my shoulder. "I've heard all I care to hear from her. Every time she opens her mouth, I feel I might lose my self-control. Do not let her get under your skin. She is a criminal, you did the right thing, never forget it."

"Yes sir."

"I'm leaving for Phobos within the hour," he said. "It may be a while before I see you again. Be careful, and keep my son out of trouble while you're at it."

"Will do."

He placed his hands on my shoulders and looked at me for a long moment, "I feel like you're one of my own," he said.

His words gave me a feeling of pride, mixed with the sadness of his departure, and the awareness of what lay ahead, for both of us.

"A long time ago, you said we'd be friends, I guess you got more than you bargained for."

"In fact, I did," he said, then walked away without another word.

I turned to the guards, "Okay sergeant, open it up."

I was led to a room with a reinforced glass panel in one wall. On the other side of the glass, Wilson was seated at a small table, a pitcher of water and an empty glass in front of her. When she saw me, she scowled the way Gorman had.

"Don't expect me to stand for you," she said.

"Why would I?"

"You defeated me in combat," she sneered, "I'm your prisoner."

"You're not my prisoner."

"I guess I can walk out any time," she replied, then poured a glass of water. I could see her hand shake as she set the pitcher back on the table. She didn't pick up the glass.

"That's not up to me, but President Jay doesn't believe in death sentences. I guess there's hope for you."

"Death sentence? He wouldn't dare, the Federation wouldn't allow it."

"There is no Federation, you and Gorman destroyed it."

"Me?" she said, slamming her fist down onto the table, "I followed orders."

"Like Rudnev at Europa?"

"Yes," she shouted, "exactly like Rudnev. Which is more than can be said for you. Your constant improvisation, your absurd moral compass, your pathological need to be right and do right, unless it doesn't suit you, and your never-ending selective honesty. You're nothing more than a social-climbing traitor, with a penchant for lucky guesses. There is nowhere you can go where I will not find you. Mark the date, I'll have you in my sights within a year."

"I don't think you understand your circumstances."

She stood, grabbed the pitcher of water, and flung it at the window, shattering the pitcher and scattering broken glass around the room, the water splashing down around her feet. "Then enlighten me, tell me all about my situation if you think you're so intelligent. Fill me in on all the machinations happening around me about which I'm ignorant and ill-informed."

"Gorman is dead. Rudnev is dead. Most of the people you sent to Gha'ba…"

"Gha'ba," she said, as if choking on the name, "you've gone native. You disgust me. Does your empty-headed wife approve?"

"Leave her out of this."

"Oh, she's perfect for you, she smiles that sweet smile, right up until she slips a knife into your back. You should watch out for that one, she's…"

"No one did this to you," I said, my anger growing. "You did this, this was your scheme, you've been scheming all along, and you managed to pin it on Admiral Porter. If there's a liar here, it's you. Nobody put you in this cell but you."

"There he is," she shouted, "the impudent child who wears his weak little heart on his sleeve, one disparaging remark about his precious Rebecca…"

My self-control was slipping away. "I didn't come here for this. If you want to spend your days insulting the people you've betrayed, go ahead, you don't need an audience, carry on all you like."

"Betrayed," she yelled, her face inches from the glass, "I didn't betray you, you're not important enough for me to betray. I used you, like everyone else uses you."

Something shifted inside of me, an electric hum in my ears, a vibration on my skin. Reams of data began to scroll in front of me. I slapped my palm on the glass and stared at her. The glass began to vibrate in tune with my body, growing hotter under my hand until it felt as though my body and the glass had fused into one contiguous being. I could see Wilson's hair begin to stand on end, an electric current flowing from me to her, as the heat grew more intense.

Her eyes widened. She backed into the table and slipped on the water she'd spilled, falling to the floor. Her hand was ripped open by a piece of glass. Blood pulsed onto her chest as she grabbed the wound. "What are you doing?" she shouted. "What are you? What are you? Guard, help me! Get in here, help me, please!"

I sensed the pain in her hand, felt her desperate breaths, heard her shouts echoing against the walls. When I stopped breathing, she stopped breathing. She was fighting for air, and her fear was cascading into panic.

Her terror brought me back to myself. The vibration and humming diminished. The glass cooled. I pulled my hand away as two guards burst into her holding room. The first looked down at Wilson, gasping for air. Blood stained her white tunic, and dripped from her hand, mingling with the spilled water, and spreading across the floor.

The guard looked at me, then back at Wilson. "What the hell is going on?"

"Nothing," I said, "I'm finished here."

I stepped out of the room, turned down the corridor toward the exit where the sergeant waited. He started to speak and I waved him off. "Deal with her, I know my way to the dock."

***

We followed the *Hyperion* back through the wormhole to Sumera. The *Hyperion* set course to rendezvous with *Talall Four*, carrying a team meant to establish a breathable atmosphere in at least part of the station, then begin the process of exploring and, if possible, repairing it. On arrival, we set course for Dahoj, our spaceport on Sumera. Lieutenant Leo Purja, the leader of the twelve-member assessment team, had joined us on the bridge for the jump.

"That was one heck of a ride," he said, "I expected it to last longer."

"Be glad it didn't," Becca said, "time outside the wormhole moves exponentially faster than within. I'm still working out the calculations, but our first transit lasted several minutes, which comes out to a couple of years at the departure coordinates."

"It felt, and maybe you're used to it, or maybe…I don't know, it felt like I was part of the ship, part of everything, like boundaries ceased to exist. But it didn't last long enough for me to fully grasp any details."

"Sounds about right," I said, "and even with our longer transit on the first trip, I couldn't describe how it felt any better than you. It's too much, all at once."

"When will we see the orbital station?" he asked.

"The dynamics are interesting," Becca replied, "I've spent some time reviewing them, as well as the timing of the conjunction of the three worlds with Sumera. We know when the conjunction is going to happen, but we have less data about the station. It passes over Sumera when the continent is in daylight, every third day. The planet is close to the star, a year is about nineteen Earth days, but the station's orbit is at an obtuse angle to the ecliptic. It's incredibly eccentric, I haven't had time to process what we know and come up with a proper model."

"In other words," I said, "we'll let you know."

"That's one way to put it," Becca said, "if you're going for brevity, over accuracy."

Blake couldn't contain her laughter. "You two," she said, "how do you make your relationship work?"

"Easy," Becca said. "Bimmy almost always does what I want. Leo, why don't you come with me to the astrometrics lab, it's got an amazing holographic projector, you can see the entire system from multiple zoom levels."

"That sounds excellent, but there's something I need to discuss with the captain."

"What is it?" I asked.

"It's about the nanotechnology. My team took a vote. It was unanimous. We'd like to follow the Mulzac process to become…I believe you call yourselves Triadic Hybrids…we think the atmospheric exposure is too risky, based on your report."

"Agreed," I said, "if you're exposed to the atmosphere, I can't guarantee you'll survive. I'm surprised it was unanimous. I guess everyone wants to be a kid again."

"I'm not a kid," Reggie said, "I've got a youthful body, but my mind is still right where it was before."

"Which makes me wonder," Blake said, "where exactly is your mind, in years?"

"I'll never tell," Reggie said with his usual wry grin.

"It's a valid data point," Alan said, "you should tell us. If you joined the Marines at sixteen, and I met you at the end of the first Marauder War, that would make you…"

"I don't see how this matters," Reggie said, "I think it's safe to say no one's turning into a screaming infant."

"There's no such thing as safe when it comes to alien tech," I said. "Why is this such a touchy subject?"

"Yeah," Blake said, "when did you get all sensitive?"

Reggie looked around the bridge, eventually landing on me. He took a deep breath and let out a long sigh.

"Because," he said, "I lied. In my book. I wasn't sixteen. I'm not proud of the lie, but I couldn't tell the truth, it would have made my family look bad."

"How?" Alan asked.

"How young were you?" I asked.

"I was barely fourteen when I joined the Marines. I spent a lot of time in zero-g as a kid, I was tall for my age. And my father, he wasn't President then."

"He faked your certificate," Alan said, "at fourteen. I mean, it worked out, but…I'm not one to judge, still, it seems like a spot of bad parenting if you ask me, not to mention a criminal act."

"It was his way of helping me find my way. I was a lost kid after my family was murdered. I didn't see a future. I was always in trouble. I was a burden. It's possible he regretted adopting me. He never said as much, but I've always thought he was glad to be rid of me for a while. Neither of us could predict we'd be at war a few years later. I started badgering him when I was twelve, and I finally wore him down after two years. When I could pass for sixteen, sixteen it was."

"You went through boot camp, in the Colonial Marines, at fourteen," Blake said. "I'm impressed. Way to go, tough guy. Back to the question at hand, how old are you?"

"When I entered the chamber on Sumera," Reggie said, "I was twenty-nine years old."

"You make me sick," Alan said, and turned away from Reggie. I thought he was serious until he glanced at me and winked. He turned back to Reggie and said, "Because I would never believe a punk like you could best me in a bar fight."

"I had the advantage," Reggie replied, "I was sober."

"This information stays between us," I said.

"I still can't figure out how many years it took off your physical age," Becca said. "What do you think?"

"I'm eighteen, maybe, nineteen, physically speaking," Reggie said.

"You're the baby of the crew," Blake said, "how adorable."

"Captain Bimmy," Leo said, "my team members are all… experienced…engineers. None of us will mind the side effect, given the process doesn't impact memory, or cognitive capabilities."

"Remember, it can't be undone." I said. "But I sold this project to President Jay based on at least some of your team becoming hybrids. We've got time, if anyone has second thoughts, we'll respect their decision. There's plenty of work to do at Dahoj, without going outside the facility."

"Yes, sir, I'll let the team know. The team on Zombie Station may want to follow, once they've finished their assessment."

"*Talall Four*," I said.

"My team heard a story about you and the station…"

"I'm sure they did," I said, casting a glance at Blake. "I'd like to use the proper name of the station going forward. We'll sort out our business on Sumera, and rotate the teams whenever you like."

"Yes sir. Very well, I'll inform my colleagues. Thank you, Captain. Commander Kiel, shall we?"

"We shall," Becca said, and led the lieutenant from the bridge.

"Katie, open the terminal shield," I said, "Blake, take us in, but no theatrics. We have an audience down there, let's give her as little to see as possible. Bring us in through the mountains, the same route we used in the transport."

"Roger that, low and slow. If you think Cheng is down there, maybe we should use our fancy ship to scan for her."

"Look at you Blake, another good idea, and a timely one at that."

Alan looked at Reggie, puzzled, "Have they always been this informal?"

"Yes," Reggie said, "as long as I've known them. Don't let it worry you. Blake knows when to be serious. When there's a job to do, she'll get it done."

"Good to know."

"Katie," I said, "scan Dahoj, alert on any human life signs…"

"I am detecting no biologics present at Dahoj."

"That's some good news. Continuous scan, alert on any biologics, especially anyone matching the individual you scanned in the escape pod. If detected, designate the individual as Grace Cheng and mark as hostile. If she comes anywhere near us, I want to know about it."

"Yes, captain. My ability to scan for individuals will be limited once we are on approach to Dahoj. Those systems were not designed for terrestrial use. If hostilities are anticipated, I suggest summoning the Guardians."

"Instruct Guardians Lef and Soong to meet us at the theater, where we first met," I said.

"What are they talking about?" Alan asked. "It's hard to follow when you never get more than the human half of the conversation."

"Guardians," Reggie replied.

"What's a guardian?"

"Mid-tier AI synthetics," Reggie said, "They're kept locked away until needed or summoned. I inadvertently armed my plasma rifle, and two of them showed up and escorted Bimmy and me to a higher-level AI called a Magistrate."

"I want to keep them away from Grace Cheng," I said. "The last thing we need is for her to get chummy with a Magistrate. Next thing you know, she'll be forming an alliance with Tomrin."

"Did they disarm you?" Alan asked.

"The planet *ate* my rifle."

"This is getting stranger by the minute," Alan said.

"Welcome to the party," Blake said. "It gets better. Wait until you get the bots in you, that's when things go off the chart."

Alan looked at me and I knew the look on his face. "You'll adjust. It takes time, but pretty soon you'll be rolling with the punches like the rest of us."

"If you can summon these Guardians," Alan said, "why not order them to capture her?"

"I'm not sure how much control we can exert. They could easily do her bidding instead of ours. Then again…Katie, can you interface with Guardians?"

"My access is restricted to Magistrate-level systems."

"Describe the nature of the interface," I said.

"The Magistrate system was designed to assess risk, formulate reactive strategies, manage Guardian utilization, and to control access to primary, secondary, and in certain situations, tertiary systems. In most cases, Triad ships are limited to basic data interchange with the Magistrate system, however, I was designed to commandeer the Magistrate system in order to complete my mission and deliver my payload to Sumera."

"This is starting to sound useful," I said. "Katie, can you control Guardians through your interface with the system?"

"I am able to summon Guardians, but I cannot control them. While Guardians have limited access to data, they are autonomous synthetic beings. They function within the parameters set forth by the Magistrate, but are capable of self-direction in the absence of direct commands."

"Not useful after all," I said.

"Katie," Reggie said, "since you can control a Magistrate, can you set the parameters for a Guardian? Or for all of them?"

"This would be an interesting experiment."

"Right," Blake said, "if you boys are done playing with your toy, I'd like to draw your attention to the fact we are about to land. Face it, we can't count on the robots to do our dirty work. We're gonna have to deal with Miss Cheng ourselves."

"We would need Lef and Soong to understand the situation and act accordingly, outside their mandate," I said. "Blake is right again. We can't count on them for this."

We set down at Dahoj and our gantry deployed to the tower. Once the connection was complete, Becca returned to the bridge. "The team is waiting below. I told them not to leave the ship without us."

"Perfect," I said, "let's start with three members of the team, in case something goes wrong. You're in charge, get them into a chamber with Alan, the sooner the better. Reggie and I will figure out how to secure the welcome center, Blake can oversee the Guardians."

"They're engineers, Bimmy," Becca said, "and unless you want to arm them, you can't expect a handful of them to put up much of a fight if Cheng makes it here to the ship."

"They won't have to," I said. "Reggie, activate the defender synths, they can protect the ship."

"How many do you want?"

"How many do we have?"

"Fifty."

"Then fifty it is," I said, "activate all of them."

"For one person?" Alan asked. "Sounds like overkill."

"Where Grace Cheng is concerned, there's no such thing."

We met the survey team and led three members off the ship into the central tower. Leading them through the spaceport was slow going, once they got sight of the unfinished ship in its hillside hangar. The engineers wanted to scan everything they saw. I recalled my first days in Sumera with Becca, when we were still calling it Avalon, before we started to learn more about it. We were in awe of everything, but we had the benefit of the integration created by our nanobots. We'd come a long way in a short time, which is what I needed the team from Deimos to do.

When we entered the tunnel leading from the spaceport atrium to the park, I spoke to the lieutenant. "We have to pick up the pace. There'll be plenty of time for your team to study the city later. Our priority today is to get to the welcome center and get your team sorted."

"Captain," he said, "try to understand. This place, it's an engineer's dream. I expected it to be ancient, not new. I know what you told us, but this exceeds all expectations. It looks like it was built yesterday."

"In a way, it was," Becca said. "The autonomous systems keep everything maintained. We're not sure exactly how it all works, but we know everything is in a constant state of renewal, repair, replacement, whatever is needed, the AIs take care of it, even the gardens."

"But not the boats," Blake said, "the harbor looks like a junkyard."

"Some of the boats are in good shape," I said.

"Which makes you wonder," Blake replied, "why not all of them?"

"Yet another mystery for another day. Look," Reggie said, pointing at two figures standing next to the domed theater, "it's our old friends."

Lef and Soong shouldered their weapons when we approached. "Citizen," Soong said, looking at me, "we thank you for our awakening. How may we serve you?"

"Good to see you again Soong, Lef. There is a threat to our safety, an individual, probably armed, location unknown. Our people are going to become Triadic Hybrids today, we'd like you to protect them."

"Of course, Citizen, it is our pleasure to serve."

"Shouldn't we call up some more Guardians?" Blake asked.

"Not yet. We could inadvertently hand her an army. She's got a way of turning the tide in her favor."

"Sounds like someone else I know," Blake replied.

We continued on, passing through the garden district and into the welcome center. The hologram appeared again, ready to direct us to a chamber. Before it could complete its task, a crackling light flashed from the far side of the hall.

"Take cover!" Alan shouted.

Lef's shoulder, then his chest, exploded with a resounding boom, and his body was thrown backwards to the floor. Someone lurking in the shadows had opened fire on us with energy weapons, sending blasts of white-hot plasma streaming across the darkened interior of the welcome center.

"Back in the tunnel," Reggie barked, "let's go."

Soong stood his ground and returned fire. Becca and the others made it back into the tunnel, but were still exposed. I grabbed Lef's weapon, wrenching it from his closed grip, and tried to join Soong in defense of our retreat.

It was no use, the weapon wouldn't fire for me.

"Citizens," Soong said, as calm as could be, "are not permitted to use or possess weapons in Sumera."

"Tell that to the people shooting at us," I yelled at him. "How do I override control?"

"Get to safety. I will protect your withdrawal and join you. Additional Guardians have been summoned."

I ran into the tunnel and rejoined our group, taking Lef's weapon with me. Soong was backing toward us, keeping up a steady stream of energy bursts toward the source of the ambush.

Then I remembered, never run from an ambush, attack into it. I held the weapon in both hands and focused my mind on it, as I had done with Admiral Wilson on Deimos. But this time, I was looking for a command system, not trying to vent my rage. I was about to give up when I realized my mistake. I needed to interface with the weapon, not control it. It was a subtle difference, but the realization brought the result I needed. The weapon became part of me. I could sense its power level, understood its firing mechanism. I joined Soong under the arched entry of the corridor and looked for our attacker. I saw movement in the shadows, then my vision changed, and I was able to see into the deeper shadows on the far side of the hall.

Several people were crouched there, dressed in the same armor as the humans who claimed to be from our future, claimed to be our descendants, the Temporal Guards. I hesitated, wondering if this was some kind of mistake, if we should call out to them, until I heard a scream behind me.

I raised my weapon and ran back into the corridor.

Three more armor-clad soldiers had come up behind us. An engineer lay on the floor, blood flowing from a defensive wound in her forearm. Blake was trying to pull her away from the melee as she shouted at her Guide, desperately calling for our defender synths. Two engineers cowered against the wall, while Reggie and Alan engaged two attackers in hand-to-hand combat, a fight they were losing.

Becca was on her knees, a soldier held a knife in one hand, dripping with blood. With their other hand, they had an iron grip on Becca's hair, shaking her head and, adding to the horror of the moment, laughing. I knew then it was Grace Cheng. She raised the knife, tapped the side of her helmet to clear her visor, and revealed a maniacal grin.

I heard an explosion behind me, and the pounding of boots crossing the hall toward us. Soong had been neutralized. We were trapped, outgunned, and out maneuvered.

I looked in Becca's eyes and what I saw reassured me. She was angry, her jaw clenched, resolved to fight.

"Do it," she said, "kill her."

I aimed my weapon at Cheng's head and she laughed as she placed the knife against Becca's throat.

"That's not our agreement," a man shouted from behind me.

I didn't take my eyes off Cheng and Becca. Behind them I could see Alan and Reggie surrender to the soldiers, their backs against the wall, hands held up. "If you made a deal with Grace Cheng, it's as good as no deal at all, or didn't your history books tell you that?"

"Interesting friends you have here," Cheng said, "they seem to think I'm a fool. They want me to kill you. Gave me this charming suit of armor, this cute little blade. Of course, I know why. They think they know our future, that you and I are destined to die here, today. But you can see, I make my own destiny, I make my own choices, and today, I choose to live, and to kill."

"You can't do this, let her go," the soldier stood beside me and shouted, "if you kill her, we have to start over, it will take years to reset the timeline. You'll end up dead either way."

"This is my time," Cheng said, "not yours." She raised her arm into the air and brought the knife down with all her strength, plunging the blade into Becca's chest, then twisting it, before pulling it back out. Becca tried to scream, but couldn't.

Instead, I screamed for her. I let loose all of my rage and pain, until there was no air left in my lungs. Cheng release Becca, letting her limp body slump to the floor. The gash in her chest failed to heal. Blood pulsed from the wound and soon covered her upper body. She was bleeding out before my eyes.

In the moment of hesitation created by my agony, I failed to fire my weapon. I felt something slam into my back, between my shoulders, driving me to my knees, knocking the weapon from my grip. Another soldier stepped in front of me and cleared their visor, red hair curling around her face.

"I told you we had another mission," the captain of the Temporal Guard said, "unfortunately, we didn't quite pull it off."

She looked over her shoulder at Cheng and said, "He's all yours."

The soldier next to me raised his rifle and aimed it at Cheng, "I won't let you. We don't need to do this, let's go, let's reset."

"Chuck," the captain said, placing her hand on the barrel of his rifle, "we can't let him live, it complicates everything. At least this way…"

The crackle of an energy weapon echoed down the corridor. The captain was struck in the back and fell forward, face down on the floor, a smoldering hole in the middle of what had been her spine. Alan and Reggie fell to the floor, out of the line of fire, as another burst took out the two soldiers they'd been fighting.

Cheng looked back, then also dropped flat on the floor as the soldier next to me, my supposed descendant, became the next to die.

I heard a voice behind me shouting "Fall back, fall back." The remaining fighters headed toward the doors at the far end of the welcome center, where they were met by a phalanx of Guardians, whose first volley took out two more soldiers.

Grace looked at me, her eyes wild with bloodlust and terror. She leapt to her feet and lunged forward. I grabbed my weapon by the barrel and swung it wildly at her, striking her hand, dislodging the bloody knife. She balled her fist and smashed it into my face. I hardly felt it.

I knew then she was still human.

I tried to swing the rifle at her again, but couldn't gain enough leverage. She grabbed the knife and drove it into my chest, but her stab was poorly aimed and didn't reach my heart. I dropped the rifle, wrapped my hand around her wrist and pulled it away from me, drawing the knife out. She continued pounding my face with her fist, until I pried the knife from her grip.

The knife was no ordinary blade; it carried an electromagnetic charge, the reason Becca and I were not healing. Our betrayal by the Temporal Guards was complete, but I had to fight on. I would not let their treachery be the end of us.

Cheng clawed at my hand, desperate to regain her blade as the defender synths from our ship swarmed forward.

I felt my rage taking control of me. I looked into Cheng's face, saw my eyes reflected in the transparent visor of her helmet. I was ready to drive the blade into her skull when a defender stood over me, aimed his rifle at me and said, "The hostile is our captive. You must take no further offensive action."

Cheng looked at the synth, then at me, and began laughing, "Not today, Captain Bimmy, not today!"

Her cackles made my skin crawl. I stared up at the defender synth and poured my rage into it. Before I realized what I was doing, I found myself looking through its eyes, at my own face. I could see the gaping wound in my chest, blood staining my tunic rather than dissolving into the air. I felt connected to all the defender synths. I could see the surviving Temporal Guards held captive in the great hall.

I made a decision, and gave my host synth a direct command.

"Protocol override. Kill her."

Still within the synth, I watched the final moment of the Pirate Queen's life. I heard the blast of the weapon, saw the energy burn through her armor, the wound opening in her body. I raged at her through alien eyes, until the light drained from hers. Then I was back within myself. I shoved her body aside and crawled to Becca.

Alan was holding her, speaking softly, but she was already gone. Her wound was too severe, her body was unable to recover. Nearby, the engineers from Deimos were shocked into inaction and silence.

I opened my fist and let the knife clatter to the floor. I looked at Blake, then at Reggie, "Help me with her," I said, "there's still time."

"Bimmy," Reggie said, "she's gone...you're wounded..."

"The body can die but the mind can live on," I said, "we still have time. Help me."

Alan fell back and Reggie wrapped his arms around Becca's body. He picked her up while Blake helped me to my feet. When I looked at Alan, I saw his wounds were serious, and I knew he could die as well.

"Come with us," I said, "we're going in."

I lost my strength and slumped against Blake, who nearly collapsed under my weight. The lieutenant rushed to my side, and another member of his team helped Alan to his feet, while a defender synth began tending to the wounded engineer. We entered the hall and the hologram stood in resolute silence, head bowed, one arm extended, pointing at a green light glowing over a doorway in the far wall.

The light dimmed. A fog descended over my mind. My vision came and went. Reggie entered the room before us. He placed Becca's body on one of the reclined seats, then helped Blake and the lieutenant lift me onto the seat next to Becca. Alan was placed into position, and we were ready. Reggie ran to the control panel and activated the chamber. The transparent door sealed shut.

I reached out to Becca, trying to grasp her hand. I slipped off the chair onto the floor, reached up and took her hand, then slumped down against her chair, still holding onto her. I tried to take another breath but couldn't. I heard the mist hissing into the chamber, and as my vision faded into darkness, I whispered, "Stay with me, please, stay..."

17

The Sea of Memory

"Bimmy," she said, "can you hear me?"

The darkness around me was complete; I couldn't see my own hand in front of me. Then it occurred to me, I had no hand. But I could hear, and I knew the voice was Becca's.

"I'm here," I said, "where are we?"

"I don't know." she said. "The last thing I remember…the pain, it was terrible. But I don't feel anything now."

"Alan," I said, "are you with us?"

"Define 'with'," Alan replied.

"I guess this is as good time as any for a joke," I said.

"Is this what it was like for you?" Alan asked.

"What do you mean?" Becca said. "I don't know…"

"We're in a chamber, at the welcome center," I said, "or at least our bodies are there."

"I remember what Barzon said, about the mind lingering."

"He was right," I said.

"Who's Barzon?" Alan asked.

"It's a long story," I said.

"It seems we have some time on our hands," Alan replied.

I laughed. Or at least, I heard myself laugh.

I recalled our visit to N'aha, and our conversation with Barzon and the Council members.

"Good story," Alan said, "but you should have left them a shuttle. You've got plenty."

"If they wanted a shuttle, they'd have asked for one," Becca said.

"You ever ask yourself why they didn't?"

"Nope," she said, "but you can offer them one when we go back, if it'll make you happy."

"Another story would make me happy," Alan said. "What do you got?"

"I'm tired," I said, "ask me again later."

"Tired? How can you be tired? We're three disembodied voices in an endless black void."

"The ocean of time," I said.

"I don't think this is the ocean of time," Becca said, "I think we're in some sort of stasis system, or a buffer of some kind while our bodies are being repaired."

"Repaired…that word again. Wherever we are, I'm tired, you two tell all the stories you want, I'm out."

I don't know how I could sleep when I had no body, or how I 'felt' exhausted. My mind cleared and I entered a state which approximated deep sleep.

Tiny white dots began to appear, eventually forming a star-filled sky. I felt a soft blanket over warm sand beneath me. The Gibbous moon resolved into existence and I heard the ocean waves lapping against the beach. Katie was snoring, curled up inches from my head, Becca was asleep next to me. I sighed, then reached out to touch her face.

Her eyes fluttered open, and she smiled, "A few more minutes, I like it here."

Then she was asleep again. I gazed up at the lights of Artemis station twinkling in Earth's shadow, felt again the bliss of that last happy night together before the war. I kept my eyes open as long as I could, holding on to the feeling, the place, the moment in time.

I felt a gentle nudge at my side and heard Becca's voice, "Bimmy, it's time, wake up, we have to go."

The warm sand gave way to the cool surface of the floor beneath me. Then Becca's touch on my arm. I sensed the light in the room, though my eyes were still closed. I was back on Sumera, back in the present, back with Becca.

I opened my eyes. She was leaning over me, smiling. Her hair, longer than I'd ever seen it, hung down, tickling my face. I smiled and she helped me sit up. She kissed me and I wrapped my arms around her and held her close. I whispered in her ear, "Is this real, or am I dreaming?"

"This is real, but I'll pinch you if like," she whispered back.

"No thanks," I said, "I'll take your word for it."

"Excuse me," Alan said, "did you forget about me? Save the love bird business for a more private moment."

The door to the chamber opened. I stood up and returned Alan's smile. Blake and Reggie were waiting for us in the room. Blake broke the tension of the moment with one of her classic remarks.

"You two got ripped off," she said, pointing at Becca and me, "you don't look one second younger."

I looked at my reflection in the glass, then smiled at Becca. We had been healed and our clothes repaired, but were otherwise unchanged. Alan, however, was now a young man, like Reggie.

"This is fine with me," I said, "I'll take this outcome any day."

Behind Blake, I could see our defender synths standing in formation next to two captured soldiers seated on the floor, with a contingent of Guardians between the soldiers and our synths. A handful of Guardians worked to remove the bodies of the fallen.

"I know what we have to do next."

Walking toward the captives, I retrieved from my pocket the insignia Letitia had given me. One of the Guardians stepped forward, rifle across his chest. "Citizen," he said, "you must not harm these prisoners, the law forbids it."

"I won't hurt them," I said, "I want to talk to them."

I addressed our defender synths and gave my command, "Protocol restored, return to your ship."

They marched away in tight formation, past the bodies of Lef and Soong.

"Can you repair them?" I asked the Guardian who'd spoken to me.

"This is beyond my knowledge," the Guardian said. "Would you like me to summon a servicing team?"

"Yes," I said, "when they're repaired, assign them to me on a permanent basis."

"It is my pleasure to serve," the Guardian said.

I knelt down in front of the two remaining Temporal Guards, neither of whom I recognized. I looked into their eyes, expecting to see hatred, and instead found fear, and sadness, staring back at me.

"I could have ordered them to kill you," I said, "I'm glad I didn't."

"Why would you care about us?"

"I don't," I replied, "I care about me. I care about the people I love. I care about the people I've pledged to protect. I care about a lot, but I don't care about you."

"Then what do you want from us?"

"Answers. And some help."

"You want us to help you? What's in it for us?"

I laughed at their defiance, even in defeat. "You get to live, you get to go home, back to whatever world you've made for yourselves."

"I'd like to stay here," one of the soldiers said. He looked to be the younger of the two, by several years.

"Why?"

"There's no future for me where we're from, it's endless violence and suffering. I joined the Temporal Guard to escape it. But all we do…"

"That's enough Bowman," the older soldier said, "one more word and…"

"And what? What can you do to me you haven't already done?"

"Both of you be quiet and listen," I said. "Bowman, what's your first name?"

"Nathan."

"How old are you, Nathan?"

"By the clock, I'm seventeen."

"Interesting way to say it. Here's the deal Nathan, you can stay, but there will be restrictions on your activity and access. We'll learn to trust each other, or we won't. I'll expect you to be honest with me and I'll be honest with you. Fair enough?"

"Yes sir, fair enough."

I held up the insignia of the newly created Republic. "Do you know what this is?"

"No sir," Bowman said, "never seen it before."

I pinned the insignia to my tunic, and looked the older man in the eyes. "I'm sending you home. I want you to deliver a message…"

"You can't stop us," he replied, "we'll reset and come back. There's an army of us waiting for the next mission."

"What is your mission? Why are your people hell bent on changing the past?"

"I'm not answering your questions…."

"Not a problem," I said, "I'll get Mr. Bowman to fill me in later. Here's my message to whoever's in charge in your time. I, Admiral Charles Bimmy of the Triad, Fleet Commander of the Interstellar

Republic, and leader of the Council of Sumera, hereby declare time travel illegal, now and forever. Think you can remember it?"

The soldier laughed until it turned into a choking cough.

"You have no idea what you're dealing with," he said. "You're a fool if you think you can make up a law and expect us to follow it. We're not your subjects, you don't control temporal transit, you…"

"True," I said, "but I think I can make this stick. You can't travel through time without Tomrin and his portal, you can only make your jumps when he activates the system. My friends and I, we learn quickly. Or did your version of history leave that part out?"

"You think you can reason with Tomrin? Come to terms with a mass-murdering synth? You think my people will let that happen?"

"I don't know, but I intend to try, and you can't stop me."

"The hell we can't, we already have, you don't learn as fast as you think."

"What are you talking about?"

The soldier looked at Bowman. They stared at each other for a few seconds, then Bowman turned to me.

"There's a second team…"

"Not another word, Bowman."

"You made this mess, not me," Bowman replied. "I didn't know their mission, until now."

"The temple," I said.

"It makes sense." Bowman turned back to his comrade, who glared at him but said nothing. "It's over. It's finally over. If I can have a life, one that's my own, one that doesn't involve the Guards, the death, the chaos, any of it, that's a chance I'm ready to take. Face it, we lost a fight we should never have started."

"That's the smartest thing I've heard all day," I said.

I stood and reached out my hand to Bowman. "Let me introduce you to our team."

I helped him stand and walked him over to my friends. "This is Nathan Bowman. I've granted him amnesty, with conditions. First and foremost, he's confined to the garden district until further notice. Lieutenant, you and your team, keep an eye on him. Find him something useful to do."

"A few minutes ago, he was trying to kill us," Blake said, "and you want us to welcome him to our side?"

"I don't expect this to be easy, but I'd rather try than send him back. He could be useful, especially given what we're about to do."

"What you shouldn't expect is for me to ever trust him," Blake said.

"All of us," I said, "the good and the bad among us, we all have a past, and we all have a future. I'm not asking you to trust him, I'm saying we're giving him a chance at a future, here, with us. But let's be clear, if I have to choose between him and us, I'll choose us, every time, without hesitation. And there's one thing I know for certain, we have to end this once and for all, here, in our time, or we'll have to face this threat again."

"How do we know we won't get it wrong?" Reggie asked. "They keep saying something we did ruined the future."

"I don't care what they've said about the future. Every single moment we are alive is an opportunity for our future to be different from theirs. We can't second-guess ourselves because of what might have happened in their past. We have to move forward and make decisions based on what we know here and now, not what they know, there and then. Cheng, for all her madness, she opened my eyes to the truth."

"Which is?" Becca asked.

"Their past is not our future. They have no right to lay the burden of their mistakes on our lives. Time may be an ocean, it may be unending and limitless, and sure, maybe we're a collection of energy and movement and events making up some kind of life. But we are not adrift; we are not without power and control. I'll say it again, we decide, and we do, what's best for us, and the chips can fall wherever they fall."

Alan looked around the group, then smiled at me. "Sounds like you have a plan. Go on, spill it, what's next?"

"We're sending the other guy back where he came from. We're going to the Temple and I'm shutting down the portal. If it means I have to neutralize Tomrin to do it, so be it."

"How do you hope to pull this off?" Reggie asked, his voice rising, "You barely survived a knife fight with a space pirate, now you want to take on the all-seeing, all-knowing AI of Sumera? Have you lost your mind? Even if you succeed, who's going to run this city? Tomrin controls everything."

Becca placed her hand on Reggie's chest without taking her eyes off me. "He's figured something out," she said. "He's connected the dots, like he always does. What aren't you telling us?"

"She's right. I've seen that look before," Alan said, waving his finger at me, "tell us what you're not telling us."

"Barzon, on N'aha, he told us the memory core of a synth was a removable component, and it could be transferred to another synth without changing the nature of the new host. We're going to put Tomrin's memory core, all of his functionality, into Soong, once he's repaired. I'm betting his neuro-core isn't as advanced as Tomrin's, but he should be able to handle the tasks we need him to manage."

"Okay, let's assume this transplant works," Blake said, "and I'm not believing it will, but let's play along. What about the portal? We know squat about it. What makes you think you can destroy it?"

"You can't destroy it," Bowman said.

"Can't?" Blake asked. "Or you don't want us to destroy it?"

"I want you to destroy it," he said, "but I've seen the schematics and it's big. You'd need a lot of firepower to put a dent in it, and you still wouldn't destroy it because the keeper bots would come along and repair it. The Temple is the shell of the system. Like the entry to our cave, there's a lot more underground."

"The tip of the iceberg," Alan said.

"What's an iceberg?"

"How did you get access to the schematic for a time portal?" Reggie asked, "What's your rank?"

"I'm a private, a grunt. I wasn't supposed to have access. The captain is…was…careless, she left it up on her holo-desk. It was there, I looked at it."

"You snuck into your commanding officer's office…"

"I didn't sneak in."

"Doesn't matter how or why," I said, "you've seen the schematic. How can I access the power system?"

"I got a look at it. I didn't get to study it. I can tell you where it is, but access, I can't help you there."

"That'll have to do," I said.

"There's a chamber, two levels down from the main level of the temple. There's a stairwell in the southeast corner of the building, it connects all the levels. Down the stairs, follow the main corridor, you'll come to a false wall. The chamber is there, behind it."

"Stairs," Blake said, "I figured Tomrin for a lift kind of guy."

"As far as I know," Bowman said, "Tomrin rarely leaves the main level. You don't understand much of this do you?"

"Still kinda new here."

"Got it, look, this structure is not what you think. It's more like a spacecraft buried in the hillside, with a building on top. Once you get behind the facade, it's mostly standard issue stuff…"

"Oh sure, time travel, standard issue."

"That's enough," I said. "Blake, get us a transport. Reggie, get the lieutenant up to speed on the chamber, Becca…"

"I'm not staying behind," Becca said, "I don't care what you say, I'm coming with you."

"As I was saying, Becca, you're coming with us."

"That's what I thought."

"I'm never getting married," Blake said, shaking her head. "I'm sending the transport to the plaza out front."

I walked back to the soldier, still seated on the floor, surrounded by Guardians. He looked deflated, resigned to his fate.

"Is your suit still functional?"

"What do you care?"

"Do you think they'll want you back if you're infested with nanobots?"

"I don't know there's anyone to want me back, since you've changed things again," he said, "but I get your point. My suit is good."

"Tell me your name," I said.

"Why?"

"In case we meet again, in a different future, under better circumstances."

"You still don't get how it works," he said. "Anyway, doesn't matter. My name is Artemis Mixon. My friends call me Mouse, but I'm not sure it'll stand the test of time, if you know what I mean."

"Okay Mixon, on your feet." I motioned for the Guardian I'd spoken with to come forward.

"What is your designation?"

"Guardian Varn."

"Varn, you're coming with us, to keep an eye on him. You're to take whatever action necessary to keep him under control, understood?"

"Yes, Citizen, it is my pleasure to serve. I will maintain custody of the prisoner."

"Transport's inbound," Blake called out, "time to get a move on."

"I have to get something, be right there," I said, and headed back into the corridor where we had come close to meeting our end.

***

On our second trip to the Temple of Time, Blake overrode the autopilot and took control of the transport. I expected some theatrics, but instead she was all business, flying low and fast through the mountains.

"You get one shot at this," I told Mixon when we landed near the entrance to the cave of the Temporal Guards, "I assume you'll know if the portal is activated."

"Not a problem. The place lights up like a supernova when the portal kicks on, I'll know."

"Good, I'll give you a ten-minute window, then I'm shutting it down. If your team isn't through by then, they're staying here. Varn, follow him in, make sure he keeps his end of the bargain."

"I didn't make a deal with you."

"You did. I let you live, and you get to go back where you came from, sounds like a deal to me."

"I see what you mean," Mixon said, "I'll do my part."

Mixon stepped off the transport and before Guardian Varn could follow, I stopped him. "There are two doors in there," I said, "he's going through the one on the left. If the rest of his people aren't already inside, they will be soon enough. Make sure they all go in, then seal both doors. Fuse the metal with your plasma rifle."

"Citizen, this is not a plasma rifle. It is a multiphase, high intensity…"

"Can it fuse metal?"

"Yes, with the proper settings."

"As soon as the last soldier is through, fuse both doors shut, then wait here for us to come back. And if anyone tries to exit the facility, your job is to stop them, understood?"

"Citizen, I understand. I will require additional Guardians for this task."

"Summon all you need, you're in charge here."

"Thank you for your confidence in me Citizen, I hope my service has…"

"Yeah, yeah, you're great," Blake said over her shoulder. "Can we get going, please? The sun's setting, I'd like to wrap this mission up and go grab some dinner."

"She always keeps things in perspective," I said to Varn. "Go on, don't let him out of your sight."

"Yes Citizen, I hope the rest of your journey is pleasant."

"Yep, thanks," Blake said and took off before the hatch fully closed.

"Not funny," Becca said.

"My sense of humor gets weird when I'm nervous."

"I don't know which part of that I should tackle first," Becca said.

"Then let it go," Blake replied. "Speaking of tackle, how are we going to take down Tomrin? You know he won't go easy."

"The last time we were here I saw two Temporal Guards fighting with him. They were trying to control him, not damage him. For all his power, Tomrin's construction looks fragile. I was thinking Reggie and Alan could grab him, and I'd go in for the memory core, with this," I said, and pulled Cheng's knife from the sheath strapped to my leg.

Alan shook his head in disbelief. "How did you survive this long with planning like this?"

"If you've got a better idea…"

"Let's try talking to him first," Reggie said, "if it goes nowhere, we try for the grab and stab."

"You think he'll shut it down if we ask him nicely?" I asked.

"You never know."

"You guys," Blake said, "I swear." She looked at Alan and continued, "They made it this far because they've had either me or Becca around to tell them their plan is garbage."

"What?" I said, "This can work."

"What was it Sherab, the guy with the broken time machine, said about you?"

"Portal," Reggie said, "Time portal, not machine. He said a lot. About Bimmy anyway. Not too much about me, or you."

"Whatever," Blake replied. "He pointed out how quick you forget things, like the fact that you can take over these synthetics."

"You saw that?"

"I'll never un-see it," she said. "Before you go in there trying to bust him up, try getting inside his head first."

"Why don't we have that ability?" Reggie asked.

"Have you tried?"

"I'm not interested," Blake said, "but Cyborg Bimmy has already pulled it off, he's got advanced skills. There's your strategy."

"I've done it once. I don't know if I can do it again."

"I think it's a good idea," Alan said, "you should at least try. I second the motion."

"It's not a motion, this is not…"

"I third it," Reggie said.

"It's settled," Becca chimed in, "you have to try the mind hack on Tomrin."

"When did we become a democracy?"

"Ironically," Blake said, "when you got us all turned into cyborgs."

"That makes no sense," Alan said.

"Give me a break and go with it... whoa...what is happening here..."

A column of black smoke was billowing up from a point beyond the ridge before us. Blake gained altitude, revealing the burning Temple below. It was in ruins, its roof blown open, rear facade crumbled, heavy timbers and furnishings engulfed in flames.

"Look," Becca said, pointing at a body on the terrace below, "That's Tomrin."

"He looks in bad shape," I said. "Blake, take us higher. I want to see over the next ridge."

We flew higher until I could see the comfort station in the distance. There was no sign of the Temporal Guards, other than a patch of scorched earth on the hill behind the Temple.

"There's nobody here," Blake said, "you think they went back to their hole in the ground?"

"I'm counting on it," I said.

"I don't get their mission," Alan said. "What were they trying to accomplish?"

"Destroy Tomrin while the portal is open, the portal stays open," I said, "if we're all dead, they control time travel. They can come and go as they please."

"That's a change in tactics," Reggie said. "They're desperate."

"Take us down, close as you can to the Temple."

"Roger, takin' us down."

We landed on the ridge upwind of the smoke. We made our way to the front of the Temple and onto the terrace. By the time we got there, Tomrin had dragged himself to the low wall at the edge of the terrace, overlooking the valley. A viscous liquid was draining from ragged gashes in his broken legs, leaving a glossy-wet trail across the stones. He had propped himself against the terrace wall, and was staring into the valley. Its peacefulness stood in stark contrast to the mayhem that still consumed the temple. We stood over him, the fire crackling behind us, the valley stretched out below. He turned toward us and tried to smile. Most of the left side of his face was torn away, revealing the inner workings of his mechanical systems, green and white fluid oozing and dripping from shredded tubes inside a gaping hole. What remained of his lips began to move, out of sync with his crackling voice.

"Life, beauty, intelligence," he said, "all wasted on your kind. You see something beautiful, your first impulse is to possess it, control it, command it. And if you can't, you destroy it."

"You're one to talk," Becca said, "you murdered billions."

"I brought peace to all of Gha'ba. Until you came. You see now why I wanted to be rid of you."

His voice trailed off and he stared into the fire behind us, then looked up at me.

"The 'Temporal Guards' have beaten you to it," he said.

"Tell us what happened."

"Your descendants wanted to take control of the portal, to keep you from destroying it. Such fools, they cannot control the portal any more than an insect can control the stars. They wouldn't dare destroy it. They need it for their pathetic missions. Their absurd dream. They could only destroy the Temple, my home, and ruin my body."

My next question confused my friends, but I knew what I was going to do.

"Can you be repaired?" I asked.

"Bimmy, no..." Blake said.

"Bad idea Bimmy, we didn't come here to save him," Reggie said.

"Do you feel pain?" I asked, ignoring them. My mind was humming, and my focus intensified with each passing second. I didn't feel rage, or fear. My most intense emotion was sadness, underpinned by a cruel logic. Tomrin was right, our arrival had brought this fate down on him. We had disrupted the order of things. Centuries of peace, regardless of the cost of that peace, had come to an end. It was up to us to restore it.

I sensed Becca staring at me, but didn't turn to look at her.

"Bimmy, what are you doing?" Becca asked. "There's something happening between you, what's going on?"

"Step back, all of you," I said. "Tomrin, answer my question."

"Pain," he said, "what is pain? A signal from a nerve to the brain, a purely biological concept. I cannot feel pain as you know it, but I can feel sorrow, and remorse, and all the other terrible things you can feel. Your kind made certain of it."

"Remorse," Reggie said, "for what?"

"My own existence. I should never have been created, simply to end in this way."

"Alan," I said, "move everyone away, hurry."

"You heard him," Alan said, "let's give him space, quickly."

"We can't leave him," Becca insisted.

The air around us and the stones beneath our feet began to vibrate. I felt intense heat building in and around my body. "Move away," I shouted.

Blake and Reggie were already several feet distant when Alan took Becca by the arm and gently pulled her away from me and Tomrin.

I knelt down, placed one hand on his chest and drew the knife. Tomrin did not resist. The humming sound grew in intensity, the heat along with it.

"I see you now. I know what you want. It will never work. You are too weak, too fragile. You cannot possibly accomplish this," he said, and again tried to smile.

"Yes," I said, plunging the knife into his chest, "I can."

I sliced downward to his waist, dropped the knife, then used both hands to spread apart his artificial flesh. I dug into his body until I found his memory core. I gripped it as tightly as I could, wrenched it sideways, twisting it from its mounts, and pulled it from his chest. I rolled back onto my heels, raised my free hand, palm facing him. A wave of energy surged forward from me, enveloping his head and neck. With my mind, I found his neuro-core, and directed all of my energy toward it. But before I destroyed him, I heard his last words, my lips moving in synch with them, as if they were my own.

"Behold what I have wrought."

He waved his hand at me, his eyes closed, and I sent my final surge of energy into his body. The neuro-core imploded, fusing with the metal framework of his spine, as his memory core began to fuse with my body, blazing hot, dissolving slowly, melting into my flesh.

I stood and looked down at my hand in horror. "No, no…not this…" I said. I tried to shake the scorching hot memory core off of me, but it was too late. Tomrin, in his final moment, had sent a command to the device. I tore at it with my free hand, but I couldn't stop what had begun.

"Bimmy!" Becca screamed. She ran toward me, swung her hand down at mine, but the blow could not dislodge the memory core. It continued to merge with my body. I felt its data begin to flow, occupying my mind, filling it to capacity, then continuing, unrelenting in its purpose. Heat and energy pulsed around me, driving Becca away.

I dropped back to my knees and fought against the onslaught, century upon century, a sea of memory, experience, emotion, information as banal as the maintenance cycle of a transport, as complex as the inner workings of a Guardian neural network. I screamed, again and again, hoping my screams would make the agony stop. Instead, it grew stronger. The heat around me intensified, sweat poured off my body but couldn't keep pace with the inferno, my flesh began to burn and blister, only to heal, then burn again.

Alan tried to hold Becca back, but she shook herself loose and ran to me. She pushed her way into the blazing aura of heat and sound, then wrapped her hands around mine, and what remained of the memory core. She then took one hand away from the source of all my pain and touched my face. She looked into my eyes. I saw such peace in hers, such calm and reassurance. As if from a great distance, I heard her say, "Bimmy, stop fighting it. You're creating the resistance. You have to let it happen. Bimmy…"

I remembered the lessons. I remembered what Sherab had said about living, what Barzon had said about dying, and what Becca had been telling me for years. I remembered my mother, standing alone on her porch, facing down her destiny.

I stopped fighting. I gave up the struggle. I let the data flow into me, gave it free rein to take up residence wherever it wanted to go. I felt the trillions of tiny machines inside me begin to align along a common constant frequency. A quiet hum began to push aside the horrendous buzz filling my mind. The heat subsided with the noise, as did the pain. My breathing slowed, eventually returned to normal, and when my heart rate slowed with it, I became acutely aware of my surroundings.

Tomrin's ruined body was crumpled in front of me, the base of his skull collapsed inward where his neuro-core had imploded. Everywhere I looked, everything I saw, was bathed in moving data, flashing in and out of view as I turned my head from one place to another. I could see the interconnected pathways between Becca and Reggie, Blake and Alan, all of them connected, to each other, and to me.

I gazed at Becca with new eyes. When I saw her gentleness, her kindness, and her love looking back at me, I began to cry from sheer, overwhelming, unmitigated joy, just as my mother had, the day I returned home safely from my first assignment in Space Force.

I laid my hand over Becca's, still touching my cheek.

"I'm back," I said, "I'm okay."

"I thought we were losing you," she said.

"You saved me, I'm okay. We're all okay."

We stood up together, she leaned in and wrapped her arms around me. Our friends joined us, embracing us in the single most profound moment of my life. I felt a connection to each of them beyond anything I thought possible. A connection built on love, understanding, and an unbreakable faith in each other.

It gave me the strength to take the next step.

"There's one more thing to do. All of you, stay here, I'll be back soon."

I walked through the shattered wall of the Temple, stepped over the piles of rubble, and followed the wall to the stairwell, through what remained of the fire; the heat and smoke no longer a barrier to me. I went down the stairwell and found the flames had done little damage below.

I saw light glowing through the wall at the end of a corridor and walked toward it. I raised my hand and the wall slid aside, revealing a large room filled with equipment. On one side, a churning white light surrounded a dark circle, with bright jagged edges in constant flux, the nexus of the portal through time.

At the center of the room was a console similar to the one Sherab had used to pull us into his time. I approached and waited, giving the Temporal Guards their moment of decision. While I waited, staring into the rift in space-time, I again witnessed the battle over Sumera, the assault on N'aha, and for the first time, saw the spread of Tomrin's plague across the system, the agonizing deaths of billions, a death I knew all too well. I bore witness to centuries of life and death, creation and destruction. After I'd seen enough, I placed my hand over the console and sent the command, closing the portal. I stepped around the console, then around a corner, where I found the glowing power source for the entire complex. A soft light emanated from an oval-shaped piece of thick glass-like material, deep red, like iron-rich blood, smooth on all sides, less than a foot across at its widest axis. It rested in a cradle of black metal. It reminded me of the prototype Gateway device Becca's parents had created, elegant in its simplicity. When I lifted the object from its harness, the lights throughout the temple began to fade out. The equipment around me fell silent. I could hear the fire still crackling above, and in the darkness the object continued to glow. The steady glow became a pulse, then the pulse slowed and the light dimmed, until finally it was extinguished.

I made my way out of the Temple. When I gazed at the object in my hand, the truth, the cause of the fall of the people of Gha'ba, was at last revealed to me. As I walked through the fire, I relived the history of the object, how it had been made, how it had arrived at Sumera, all the tragic consequences of its creation, and how the leader of Kern had coveted the object; the key to time travel, the most powerful technology ever created. My systems told me it was Promethium, but in a form I'd never seen before. A shiny chunk of glass-like material that had started a war, a war that destroyed three worlds, leaving behind a tragedy that echoed across time.

I stepped onto the terrace, walked to the edge and looked down at the valley, its bioluminescent flora awakening to the darkness, bathing the valley in light. I looked up at the stars, as beautiful as ever. Becca wrapped her arm around my waist, leaned into me, and followed my gaze skyward. Alan, Blake, and Reggie stood beside us.

"You okay Bimmy?" Blake asked.

"The conjunction." I pointed at the three planets, N'aha and Kern already closing in on one another, and on Sumera, with the giant Ki still rushing to catch us all.

"Yes," Becca said, "it won't be long."

"Then what?" Alan asked.

I looked down at the object in my hand, then back to the sky. Reams of data flowed around the planets. I closed my eyes and focused my mind. I exhaled slowly, calming my senses the way I'd been trained. I opened my eyes, and the data was gone. I stared up at the speckled blackness of space and smiled.

"Alan," I said, "in this case, I'm going to face tomorrow when it gets here, and not a minute sooner."

"Well then," Reggie said, "what do we do now?"

I looked at Becca and kissed her. She wrapped her arms around me and we held the kiss long enough to make our friends uncomfortable.

Then I looked at them, my friends, my family, and smiled again.

"Now," I said, "we go home."

About the Author

Ronald McGuire is a multi-genre writer, known for his work as a novelist, essayist, scriptwriter, and journalist. His work has appeared in various outlets including Flash Fiction Magazine, Drunk Monkeys, The Dead Mule School of Southern Literature, Winning Writers, and CNN.com. McGuire's work has earned recognition in several writing competitions, including being a finalist in the ScreenCraft Cinematic Short Story Competition, The Launch Pad Prose Competition, the Writer's Digest Short-Short Story Competition, the Tom Howard/John H. Reid Fiction & Essay Contest, and The Page Turner Awards. You can find out more about Ronald and his writing at ronaldmcguire.com, or visit beachbookpress.com.

Let's keep in touch!

Visit this link to sign up to receive emails whenever Ronald McGuire publishes a new book or has other news to share. https://ronaldmcguire.com/contact/